Blame It On Paris

A Suspenseful Romantic Comedy

Helen B. Aitken

Blame It On Paris is dedicated to the amazing Down East community and all the teachers who love adventures, especially Marsha Sirkin, my fearless travel buddy. Paris wouldn't have been half as fun or chaotic without her.

Chapter 1

"LET'S GO, SAM. I've been waiting to go to Paris all my life, and you're keeping me from it." Chloe Davis stood by the back door, her purse hanging on her shoulder, tapping her foot. Her gaze shifted between her watch and the hallway as her best friend and roommate, Samantha Williston, appeared and disappeared.

"Don't throw a hissy." Sam moaned. Dresser drawers slammed in rapid succession. A door banged against the wall, followed by a string of profane words. "I can't find it." Her voice became frantic. A chair overturned, a book fell, and a metal trash can skittered across the floor.

"I don't know what you're looking for, but it can wait. Come on, it's time to go." With no response, Chloe knew Sam hadn't heard her. She tucked her blonde hair behind her ear, breathed deeply, and let it out slowly. *Relax. We're ten minutes ahead of schedule.* She spotted two framed photographs on the countertop and studied each. One was of them on Sam's first sailboat as college students; the other was Sam dressed in a Captain's uniform the summer after college graduation—the youngest female ferry boat captain in the area, still captaining cruises in the summer. So much has happened since college. Chloe sighed. *I owe her for supporting me through college, and as my art career took off. So, whatever she needs...*

Sam's running from room to room brought Chloe back to the present. Sam stopped in the hallway, twisting her red curly hair between her fingers. "Fer the life of me, I checked... not there.... I can't go ta Paris without a passport." Her voice quivered in helplessness as her voice rose an octave, her Down East accent growing thicker. "Everythin's gone!"

Chloe had seen Sam fret like this two other times: four years ago, before she took the state teacher exams with a hangover, and three days ago, after receiving a large envelope from a publishing company. Chloe placed her hands on Sam's shoulders. "I have the hotel information, our itinerary, and the French phrase book in my backpack. Your passport and tickets are in your purse."

Sam's eyes were squeezed tight. "What about my laptop and charger?"

"They're in your backpack with the snacks, sleep masks, earplugs, neck pillows, and refillable water bottles."

Sam opened one eye. "How about the first-aid kit, medications, hand sanitizer, hand wipes, sewing kit, toilet seat covers, bedbug spray, flashlight, washcloths, lotion, and sunscreen? I need those, too."

"I threw those out. They expired." Chloe mentally counted to five. Sam's green eyes opened wide. Chloe grinned. "Gotcha."

Sam swooned. "Gaud amity. I'll get you for that when you least expect it."

Finally, some of the stress was gone. Chloe giggled. It was rare to pull something over on Sam. "They're in your backpack. I packed it last night, including everything on your exhaustive list." She pointed to the luggage by the door. "It's not like you to wait 'til the last minute. Is something wrong?" Sam shrugged. "Suit yourself. When you're ready to tell me, I'll listen. Come on, we have a two-hour drive to the New Bern airport."

Sam frowned. "I may have overpacked, and you'll need to help me lift my suitcase." Her face turned serious. "Don't get your panties in a wad, but I forgot to fill the car with gas."

"Bless yer heart. My car's gas tank is full, and I'll drive."

Sam stuck her tongue out at Chloe, mimicking the high school freshmen she taught at East Carteret High School in Beaufort, North Carolina. She and Chloe taught at the same high school and grew up together on Harkers Island, about ten nautical miles from the Outer Banks. As the most easterly part of Carteret County, Down East was a tight-knit community with a unique language and, to people 'from off,' had unusual sayings and idioms sometimes hard to translate.

Chloe handed Sam one of her homemade double chocolate brownies. "Why don't you take a chill pill and relax?"

"I thought of that, too. Dr. Martin gave me some pills to help us sleep on the plane; you know how I hate to fly. We'll take one before we board in Newark and be ready to take Paris by storm when we arrive." Sam's eyes twinkled. Chloe knew Sam was back to normal.

"Every time you get that look, I regret it, and there's no room in my luggage for Kevlar underwear." Chloe touched her purse. She had the American Embassy's address and phone number in her wallet and cell phone. Overkill? Hardly. Over the years, she had added three top North Carolina attorneys to her speed dial, and so far, she had managed to keep them out of jail. And thanks to Clinique, still wrinkle-free. A win/win.

Chloe set the cruise control and sped to the airport. She exhaled, trying to keep her left leg from bouncing up and down. They were going to Paris, France—her dream destination. They needed to complete the requirements for the travel contest they had won, but more importantly, she and Sam agreed to experience everything Parisienne. *Ooh, la la.*

As she sipped her coffee, Sam almost relaxed in the passenger seat while eating her brownie and drinking a Coke, *her* addiction. Sam snuck a side glance at Chloe. "Thanks for looking after me. I've been discombobulated lately."

"Uh-huh. You're welcome. This trip is a team effort." She patted Sam's hand in reassurance. "We're going to have a wonderful time. What would *I* do without you?" *Bored stiff, I'm sure.*

Sam sat up taller in the seat. "Just think, we beat out forty-eight female teachers, and we're going to P-a-r-i-s!" She danced in her seat, hands over her head, swaying with internal music. "Don't let me forget the daily journaling and sending captioned photos to the cloud. If we do an amazing job, we might even become supervising teachers next summer."

"Let's get through this trip before you plan us out of our teaching jobs. But on another note, I hope we get along with our male counterparts. What if they're unbearable dit dots?"

"Surely the travel agency vetted them. They can either go along with us or get out of our way, but if they act out, we'll have a "come to Jesus party," and they won't be walking straight for quite some time." Sam winked at Chloe. "No one messes with Down East women."

Chloe folded her hands in prayer on the steering wheel. "Forgive us, Father, for the sins we are about to commit."

"Amen, sister!"

FLIGHT 5349 FROM Charlotte to New Bern landed ten minutes late. Thirty-one people exited the propjet, leaving the last passenger hiding in the shadows by the exit door. An olive-skinned man with shoulder-length brown hair, wearing dark sunglasses and a floral silk shirt hanging over khaki shorts, scoured the building's waiting area for anyone watching the plane. No one. Good. Felix lifted his duffel bag and stepped slowly down the plane's stairs onto the tarmac.

Felix scrutinized the area and the people as he strolled through the airport. His contact came into view—a man in blue coveralls wearing a New England Patriots ball cap mopping the floor in front of the men's bathroom. The janitor looked up and nodded slightly. All clear. Felix hefted the duffel bag on his shoulder and entered the bathroom. The janitor moved his cart to block the entrance. He placed a yellow plastic "wet floor" triangle on the floor, hung a "Closed for Cleaning" sign on the door, and followed Felix inside.

"Simon, secure the door."

The janitor wedged a rubber shim between the door and floor and pushed a heavy-duty trash can under the handle before removing his coveralls and stuffing them in the trash. When Simon turned around, Felix had removed his wig.

"Woah, what happened to you?" asked Simon.

Felix rubbed his bald head and rolled his eyes. "Bubblegum… while I slept."

Simon snickered. "Your two-year-old got you good."

"It had to be cut out, so it was easier to shave it all off." Felix rubbed his head again. "There'll be no gum in the house for the next ten years."

"With a ring in your ear, you'd look like Mr. Clean."

"Enough!"

Simon straightened. "How was the trip?"

"Dicey. In Miami, an agent met me inside the airport with a change of clothes, a wig, and a makeup kit. I barely made the flight to Charlotte and was here without incident. It's a good thing you were here fishing offshore. The Spaniard may have had people looking for you in Boston." He reached into his pants pocket, retrieved a tube of lip balm, and handed it to Simon.

"Burt's Bees." Simon pulled off the top and sniffed. "Strawberry. Thanks."

Felix sighed in exasperation. "Twist the bottom to the right. When it clicks, pull out the thumb drive. *These* are the only photos of the drug lord's new face. Don't lose it."

Simon sobered. "Got it." He pocketed the tube and waited for further instructions.

"Your tickets to Paris are in an envelope at the ticket counter. Remember, the agency thinks you're going on vacation. Screw up, and you may find yourself without a job, in jail, or both. This time… leave Paris in one piece."

"Minimum destruction. Understood."

"Watch your back and don't get killed… the paperwork is a nightmare."

Simon dropped his hat on the counter and retreated with a two-finger salute.

A few minutes later, a different-looking, fair-skinned Felix strolled out of the bathroom wearing jeans, a t-shirt, sunglasses, and a Patriots' ball cap.

Chapter 2

B EAU JACKSON SHELVED a bag of soccer balls and then stacked orange cones on the floor of Croatan High School's athletic storage room. Croatan was one of three high schools in Carteret County, a top-ranked academic school in North Carolina, and had an up-and-coming athletic program.

Matt Richards, his best friend and co-teacher, entered the room singing, "Frère Jacques, Frère Jacques, dormez-vous, dormez-vous?"

"Give it a rest," said Beau.

Matt continued to sing the same song softly.

"Now, you're just doing it to irritate me." Beau grabbed the first thing he could find and hit Matt in the face with a dirty jock strap.

"Gross." Matt batted it away so that it landed in the trash can.

"You deserved it. That stupid song will be on my mind for the next hour."

Matt grinned. "Hurry up. I inventoried books and completed my student-teacher evaluation last week."

"I'm finished. There's nothing like being last-minute contest replacements, but we're going to Paris." Beau headed to the door and motioned for Matt to follow. "Where's your stuff?"

"In the back of your new car, Mr. Athletic Director."

"F-you. I loved my old car. Sadly, it was silver only because of all the duct tape holding it together. But Annie is a gorgeous ride. Admit it, I look good in the driver's seat, and she'll be with me a long time."

"Annie, huh? Do I know this Annie or Anne? Hmmm…. I'm glad you used the money from selling our tech stocks to buy her. I may design and build another racing bike."

"Pfft. Another bicycle? Your priorities are misplaced." Beau headed to the highway and cranked up the radio. "Check out this sound system." The windows vibrated as Beau yelled to be heard. "I love the reclining leather seats and the moon roof…I can't wait to pull up on the beach, dial up some cool jazz, open a good bottle of wine, and share the moonlight with some fine ladies." Beau wiggled his eyebrows. "Who knows, I might let you borrow Annie if you find someone who tolerates your nerdiness." Matt's fingers plugged his ears while looking out the window. "Besides, you can't date on a nine-thousand-dollar carbon fiber all-terrain touring bike unless you redesign it to be a tandem."

Matt gave him the finger and then reinserted it in his ear. He refused to talk until they stopped in long-term parking. Beau snickered.

The New Bern airport was big enough to manage propjets from two airlines with limited schedules. What it lacked in flight options, it made up for in a cheery atmosphere: bright county flags hanging from the ceiling, posters of beach scenes, photos of historic New Bern, friendly employees, and a snack bar that sold excellent breakfast sandwiches and coffee. Passengers could sit in generic plastic seats or, as in other North Carolina airports, in white rocking chairs near New Bern's mascot, a four-and-a-half-foot decorated bear. Like other bears in the city that honored businesses or organizations, this bear commemorated the Marine Corps wearing a USMC dress blues, white gloves, a corporal's rank, and an expert shooting badge with a good conduct medal. This bear was dedicated to the Marines who bravely serve our nation.

Beau and Matt arrived an hour earlier than necessary, ready to meet the two female teachers traveling to Paris. Wheeling their suitcases to the sidewalk, they noticed a man pull off a New England Patriots ball cap and toss it in a trash can before getting into a taxi.

"With their last season, I'd throw it in the trash, too," said Beau.

"You know, the Carolina Panthers had a worse season."

"Blasphemy. Where's your loyalty, man? The Panthers will come back. Just wait."

They passed through the entrance and proceeded to the ticket counter.

"Hello, I'm Matt Richards, and this is Beau Jackson. The Miller Travel Agency was supposed to leave our tickets to Paris here."

"Yes. A courier left your tickets, these envelopes, and a note."

Beau picked up the tickets, and Matt read the note aloud:

On behalf of Mr. Miller and all of us at the agency, we congratulate you on winning the trip to Paris. Your itineraries are included in the envelopes, and we especially hope you enjoy your visit to the Museum D'Orsay. Bon Voyage.

Matt's face scrunched up. "That's Strange. Of all the museums to comment on, they picked that one. Maybe something special is on exhibit."

"You and museums. It's probably something weird like you. Forget it."

Matt shrugged. They checked in their large bag but held on to their carry-on and backpack. He pointed toward the snack bar. "We have at least two hours before we board. Might as well eat and charge our phones." He wiped sweaty palms down his jeans and watched Beau do the same thing. The waiting and anticipation were as bad as going on a blind date.

Fifteen minutes later, the twenty-eight-year-old men carried their coffees and food to the rocking chairs. Even though both were six feet tall, Beau barely squeezed between the armrests, having maintained his old college quarterback physique while working out with his student-athletes. His thick blond hair hadn't been cut in months, so he habitually pushed it out of his face when he looked down. Sipping his coffee, his light brown eyes lit up as women walked by. He couldn't help it; he flirted with ladies of all ages, shapes, and sizes. He glanced at his best friend.

Matt polished an apple until it shone. On the first bite, his eyes closed, and the juice ran down his chin. He hurried to wipe it off before it stained his starched white button-down shirt, and in the process, he knocked over his coffee. With lightning speed, he righted the cup without spilling anything.

"You may be a geek, but you're still The Flash," Beau laughed at the nickname he had given Matt in middle school on Harkers Island because he could process information quickly, and like the comic book character, he was one of the fastest long-distance runners he'd ever seen, even in college.

Matt flashed Beau a lopsided grin and ran his hand through his black hair, causing it to spike out in several directions, then pushed his black rectangular glasses back into place. His arm flexed, showing sculpted muscles honed from frequent kayaking, biking, and training with the high school soccer team as Beau's assistant coach. Matt stretched his long, muscular legs in front of him; his toned body generously filled his jeans, and he used his heels to rock the chair as he finished his apple, lost in thought. Soft hazel eyes and a scruffy beard gave him a sexy professor vibe, and women looked at him more than once.

Beside them, a lengthy line formed at TSA, and Beau watched it fill with a crowd of college women wearing Sigma Sigma Sigma sorority t-shirts. They didn't give him the time of day. Instead, they ogled Matt.

"Amazing," Beau mumbled under his breath. "He's so oblivious to women."

Beau swatted Matt on the arm, which broke the apple fixation. "I was thinking about all the *French things* we could try in Paris."

Matt grinned. "French pastries, French champagne, French press coffee, and 'oh, pardon my French.'"

"No. I'm thinking about French women, French kissing, and French letters... you know, condoms." Beau fist-bumped Matt. "I also brought several boxes of 'letters' in case you forgot; the things I do for you. You can thank me later."

"F-you. I'm prepared."

Beau jabbed a finger into Matt's chest. "Yeah, but what's their expiration date? Six years ago? You need to get back out there."

"You're a jerk. Keep it up, and I'll tell every French woman you meet, *Il a le clap*."

"And that means?"

"You have an STD."

Beau laughed heartily, "That's a Good one. Hurry up and eat. Our Paris ladies should be coming through the entrance any minute now."

CHLOE AND SAM tried their best to maneuver their overseas bags, carry-ons, a camera bag, raincoats, backpacks, hats, and purses through the circular revolving door. Something dropped, and, like dominoes, everything fell. Bags turned over, purses emptied, and things stuck in the door, wedging it open. It was a train wreck. Sam cursed at the top of her voice. Through the thick glass, travelers nearby gasped.

Hearing the commotion, Matt and Beau got up from the rockers. Matt sucked in breath and grabbed Beau's arm. "Samantha Williston and Chloe Davis just showed up."

They both moved behind the New Bern bear

with lightning speed to watch and wait.

Beau broke out in a cold sweat. His mouth hung open. Eventually, he had to wipe the drool from his chin. "She's beautiful."

"Yeah... she is." Matt shoved Beau. "Stop looking at Chloe that way."

"Chloe? I'm not looking... at her." Beau's words slowed. "Could they possibly be the other teachers going to Paris?" He blinked several times. "Of all the gin joints in all the airports in all the world, she walks into mine." The corner of Beau's mouth tilted up, dread turning into delight. "She hasn't changed a bit. This could be fun. We should help them."

Matt grabbed his heart, reaching to pull out an imaginary knife. "This isn't happening.... They're going with us? *Merde alors!*" He sucked in a large breath. "Sam's in a bad mood, and I haven't seen Chloe since we broke up six years ago. Let's wait until they go up to the counter." Beau snorted and then punched Matt in the arm.

Matt sighed. "Okay, let's do this." He rose to his full height, shoulders back and head high. He stepped around the bear with Beau and casually strolled toward the girls.

Sam and Chloe had commanded the attention of everyone in the area, which in turn became fodder for Down East gossip.

Sam got her luggage out the door, dropped her raincoat, and ran over it with the overseas bag. As she pulled on the coat, a wheel broke off and rolled away, causing Sam to lose control of everything again, including her mouth.

While Chloe tried to pull her luggage out of the revolving door, she stepped on Sam's broken wheel, lost her balance, fell sideways, and collided with Sam's luggage. She screamed, and in an instant, her right ankle twisted, trapped between all their stuff and unable to dislodge her foot. Chloe's face contorted, and she wailed as tears streamed down.

"Chloe! Oh my God." Sam turned to help, but her hands shook, and paralysis set in.

Matt and Beau reached Chloe first. Matt lifted Chloe from the floor and carried her to a chair. "Careful now. Chloe, tell me where it hurts."

"Beau? Matt?" asked Sam.

Chloe lifted her head from resting against Matt's strong arms. "No. It can't be." She strained to open her eyes and whispered, "You. What are you doing here?" It had been six years, three months, twenty-seven days, and four hours. She didn't know what hurt worse, her ankle or the remnants of a heart Matt had broken but hadn't healed. He shouldn't be here. He had been out of her life for a long time and was the last person she expected to see.

"I...I'm going to Paris, and I suspect you're going too, right?"

Chloe moaned in pain, sniffled again, and then nodded.

"First things first, okay? Let's check your ankle." Matt grabbed his carry-on and gently eased Chloe's leg on top to rest. Her crying became loud whimpers.

Beau knelt to check her ankle. "It's already swelling, Clo, and you have a nasty bruise halfway up your leg. It may be broken. Can you wiggle your toes?"

She shrieked, "It can't be broken! I'm going to

Paris. Whether it's swollen or broken, it doesn't matter." She sniffled between gasps of air and winced as she barely wiggled her toes, then turned inconsolable as her tears fell once more.

"Sam. Hey, Sam. Uh… would you find some ice for Chloe's ankle?" asked Matt.

Sam couldn't speak or move—she only nodded. Beau glanced up at her and tilted his chin toward the snack bar.

"Ice. Find ice. Got it," said Sam.

Within a minute or two, Sam returned with a double-zipped baggie of ice. She dropped the bag on Chloe's ankle and watched her wince. "Sorry." Sam dug through her purse to find a small pack of tissues, pulling out several to hand her. *It's all my fault. She tripped over that stupid wheel.*

Chloe blew her nose several times, and Sam handed her more tissues. Using two fingers, Sam picked up the used ones by the corners and tossed them in the trash with a "Yuck."

This wasn't happening.

Sam eyed Beau openly, her heart pounding and a knot forming in her stomach. *Them, him, us, here, why?* There were too many questions that had to wait for later. She focused on Chloe and twisted her hair between her fingers. This had to be the world's worst prank…a black cat had crossed her path, or she had broken a mirror… or perhaps it was a full moon on Friday the thirteenth.

THE AIRPORT EXPLODED with deplaned passengers moving from the tarmac toward the luggage turnstile. Dr. Martin and his wife from Down East exited last from the flight. They recognized Sam and Chloe and moved towards them. "What happened?" asked Dr. Martin.

"The wheel on my luggage broke, and Chloe tripped on it. She hurt her ankle," said Sam.

He tenderly examined the whole leg. "You need to go to the hospital for X-rays, Chloe."

"No," everyone said at once.

"Sam and I are on our way to Paris," said Chloe, drying her eyes. "I can have it looked at there." She hiccupped twice.

"I-I can push her in a wheelchair or find some crutches, but she has to go," said Sam. "She may be able to go to Paris anytime, but I'm counting on going now. Otherwise, I don't know when I'll ever go."

Dr. Martin eyed each person before placing his hands on his hips, the signal for an explanation.

Matt cleared his throat. "I'll take responsibility for getting Chloe around Paris. After all, I might have prevented the fall if I had helped her get her luggage through the door." *Where did that come from?* He should have been the last person to volunteer to help her.

Chloe looked up at Matt, her face splotchy and eyebrows scrunched together. "You'd do that for me?"

"Sure. If this happened to me, I hope someone would help." He was resigned to being the bigger person. "Unless you'd rather I not." He searched her face, trying to detect her true feelings, his mind working frantically. Was he just being polite? No,

Chloe didn't handle pain well, and he could help. Did he want to spend time with her? Did she want that with him? Then again, it was only for seven days. He could endure seven days but would need to be on his guard. She wouldn't break his heart this time because he was wiser now.

Sam spoke up. "Chloe, I'll help you, but it would be better to have at least one other person helping you get around."

Beau moved away from Chloe to sit in a seat opposite her. He looked from Matt to Chloe. He studied their interaction. Matt rubbed Chloe's back, and she allowed it. *Fascinating.* He eyed Sam from his periphery, recognizing a familiar expression—Chloe was being set up. *Okay, Sam, I'll play.* "I agree with Sam. Chloe could use extra help. I'm in." *This trip will be very interesting and test us in every way possible.*

Chloe tried to sit up straighter but winced as her leg scraped the carry-on. Matt reached out to help her. *I don't understand.* Then she looked at Sam's face—it scrunched up and relaxed. Curious. What did she have to lose? "Sam, I suppose you're right. We have our assignments to finish; I'll be taking lots of photographs and with all the walking...." She and Matt weren't a couple, nor were they friends. "Matt... I appreciate your offer, and I accept. Thank you."

She looked back at Sam. *Really? You look like the cat that swallowed the canary.* Chloe sighed behind her tissue. *Eff'n great.* Sam was plotting. Paris was her chance to experience the culture, to take in all the art and the sights, and to feed her soul. All right. She would deal with Sam's scheming and ignore Matt. It was only for seven days.

Then again, seven days were long enough to rename Paris the city of endurance. *Whatever, bring it on.*

DR. MARTIN TURNED to his wife. "Marilee, run down to the drugstore for some crutches, several packages of ace bandages, and a woman's small-size boot. She will need those if she wants to go to Paris." Then he turned to Chloe while the others strained to hear what he had to say.

"A bad sprain can be as bad as a break, and this looks bad. Keep your weight off the foot for at least five days, but seven is better. After five days, see if you can put any weight on it. If it hurts, stay off it. When you come back home, make an appointment to see me.

"Sam, give her eight hundred milligrams of Tylenol now and four hundred milligrams every six hours today, and then as she needs it. This plane trip won't be fun. Reaching high altitudes for extended periods will make it swell even more, so do your best to keep it iced and elevated. If it gets worse, get it x-rayed in Paris." Chloe nodded. Matt nodded. Sam and Beau eyed each other and then nodded, too. Dr. Martin shook his head and mumbled, "The four tornadoes are on their way to Paris. Heaven help the French."

"Dr. Martin, please don't tell anyone Down East about this," pleaded Chloe.

"I'm sorry, Chloe, but Marilee has probably told ten people by now."

The quartet groaned with good reason. They had grown up down the street from each other on Harkers Island, with about eleven hundred residents in an area three miles long and one mile wide, everyone knew everything about everybody. Since gossip had long been Down East's manna from heaven, the antics and mayhem these friends got into made for great entertainment, and now, after a six-year hiatus, the gossip would fly once more.

AN HOUR LATER, in separate parts of the plane, the contest winners were in the air and on the way to Newark Airport for the next leg of their trip. Sam took the window seat, allowing Chloe to stick her foot in the aisle with ice.

Chloe shut her eyes, hoping the medication would help. A lifetime of flashbacks flooded her mind. The neighborhood adults dubbed her and Sam Lucy and Ethel, ancient TV sitcom characters, for childhood shenanigans that often ended with them grounded as punishment. Later, there were college road trips. Thankfully, their parents never heard about those capers—most were fun, some adventurous, and a few were borderline insane. They'd even pulled some stunts in recent months. *Why do I listen to her? Crap, I forgot my lucky rabbit's foot.*

They were twenty-nine years old and had been best friends since diaper hood. Later, despite the trouble they got into as college roommates, they graduated with honors. In a twist of fate, they became housemates after being hired as educators at East Carteret High School, five miles from home. Remarkably, they became role models for the teenagers they taught.

Chloe shook her head, thinking about what

their students could learn from them: picking locks, choosing the right frog for leaving in someone's locker, and how to put a small car on the school's cafeteria roof, to name a few, none of which would help their students' academic endeavors. *Look at me now. I've gone from prankster to respectable art teacher and even a successful artist and photographer.*

Chloe thought about how different she and Sam were. Whereas she was soft-spoken, very messy, didn't like to hurt people's feelings, and was a fabulous cook, Sam was the opposite. Sam spent her time ghostwriting or working on her novel ideas, determined to become a famous novelist by age thirty-five. Besides scheming, Sam's forte was organization and cleanliness to the point of being OCD. They balanced each other perfectly. *I hope the beginning of this trip isn't an indicator of things to come.*

She opened her eyes, realizing Sam had shaken her awake.

"Can you believe Matt and Beau are the other teachers going to Paris?" There was that sparkle in Sam's eyes again.

"Whoa there. I hope you're not delusional enough to think Matt and I could get back together."

"Of course not. But he's good-looking, intelligent, a legal-aged male, and you'd have a good time with him while he's taking care of you."

"You're nuts. Remember college?"

"That was a long time ago, and people can change. Besides, you're strong and smart enough to handle any man, especially Richards."

Chloe rolled her eyes and sighed loudly. "This

conversation is ridiculous. He feels sorry for me, that's all. He's projecting his inner Boy Scout like he used to. Besides, I've sworn off men. I seem to attract clingy men who want to get married and have lots of babies. Like I don't have enough kids at school to oversee. I'm also tired of the drama from men who are jealous, overprotective, and try to dominate me. I need to focus on my work, and you're not helping."

Sam crossed her arms over her chest.

Chloe continued. "If I were looking for a man, which I'm not, I would want a man who's mature, likes me for who I am, doesn't want to change or control me, and isn't threatened by my success."

"What about Rafe, Max, or Steve? They're mature men."

"If you combine all their good qualities, they make the perfect man, but separately, they are severely lacking."

"Bob Miller is mature—"

"*He* can't take no for an answer. Besides, I'd never date a student's parent," insisted Chloe. "Face it, the man for me isn't out there, and I refuse to start looking in Paris."

"You know what they say, once you stop looking for something, that's when you find it."

"Not looking, not gonna find it... Why don't we talk about you and Beau? You want something to happen between you two, don't you?

"I'm not interested in a relationship, and Beau has a reputation for a love'em and leave'em attitude—he's not boyfriend material. I want to have some fun, and Beau's personality fits mine. Besides, Paris is the city of love."

"No, it's the city of light."

"Well, it could be the city of love. Beau's mamma told my aunt that Matt doesn't have a girlfriend. The two of you should... explore your options—"

"Stop it. You're not listening. I'm done with men, and I'm not interested in exploring anything with Matt."

Sam snorted. "We'll see. The guys will be perfect travel partners. We used to be thick as thieves through high school, and it'll be fun to get thick again." Sam wiggled her eyebrows.

"Paris is an artist's dream, my dream. Please don't ruin this for me, Sam."

"No sweat. The bombshell Mae West said it best: "*A dame that knows the ropes isn't likely to get tied up.*"

AT THE OTHER end of the plane, the guys deliberated on their situations as vigorously as Sam and Chloe did. Beau thumped him on the back of his head whenever Matt's voice got louder.

"This will be disastrous," said Matt. "One of us will lose it, and the trip will be ruined."

"I'm not the one who volunteered to care for Chloe, which makes me wonder why you did. Will you kill her with kindness? Make her sorry for the past? Or are you still the big softie, wanting to care for Chloe like you used to?"

Matt covered his face with his hands.

"Maybe I have this all wrong," said Beau. "Do you have a self-destruct button I'm not aware of? Still, I must give you credit for extending the white flag, although I'm more surprised that Chloe accepted it."

"Frankly, I'm not sure why I offered, but what do you have to lose? Nothing. Sam shot daggers at me, and Chloe looked at me like I was scum. I'll be swimming with the sharks, and you'll have a grand old time with Sam."

"Hope and *prey* you don't get eaten," quipped Beau. "Get it? Prey? Never mind…. You're thinking too hard, your head will explode, and you'll be *chum*." He chuckled. Matt stared at him. "Fine, I'll stop. It's time for you to start living again. This could be an opportunity to get Chloe out of your system, to move on, and to find a woman who won't skewer your balls to the wall. Look… how about you take it a day at a time… an hour at a time, and if she gives you shit, hang out with me, and let Sam take over. I'm saying there are options. I'll even step in and help if you're over your head. Give me the signal." Beau ran his index finger across his throat as he cut it. "Or…" He tilted his head and pretended to hang himself.

"What are you—ten? I don't know. You're probably right. I got into this mess and now need to take care of it. How bad could it be? It's not like she can dump me again. What could go wrong? What am I thinking? A lot can go wrong. Holy shit!" Matt reached for an airsick bag and started to breathe into it.

"I don't know what she ever saw in you. When you're not geeking out, you're spazzing out. Calm down before you develop hives…. You get hives again, and I refuse to put Calamine lotion on you down there—you're on your own, pal. It's me I'm worried about."

"You? Why? You're not scared of Sam, are you?"

Beau's face turned beet red.

"No… it can't be. You and Sam, as in you like, *like* Sam?" Matt's continuous laughter earned another smack on his head when the realization hit. Beau had feelings for Sam. "Holy cow. Did you and Sam ever—"

"Watch your mouth. We never went out. Period. End of story."

"I don't get it," said Matt.

"You might as well know. I've always had a thing for Sam. When I saw her in the airport, it hit me like a Mack truck. I've missed her… really, really missed her."

"With your history, she's going to eat you alive. What kind of sign will you give me when you realize you're in over your head?"

Beau's two middle fingers shot up.

"Well, here's another nice mess you've gotten me into," said Matt.

Beau sighed from the depths of his soul. "I'll watch your back if you watch mine."

"Deal." They fist-bumped. Matt looked away to contemplate the what-ifs.

MATT AND BEAU exited the aircraft and waited for the ladies at a nearby kiosk so that they could go through security together. While Matt drank from a water bottle, he had time to think about the past, growing up with Beau, Chloe, and Sam. The four had been best friends, inseparable from kindergarten through sophomore year in college. Chloe and

Sam went to the same university and had always been roommates. At the same time, he and Beau attended different universities but remained close, eventually teaching at the same school, about twenty miles away from home.

Home. Many families had been there for two to three hundred years and used a dialect similar to Elizabethan English, adding sayings that, even today, needed translation. Although they spoke with a heavy brogue, they lost most of it when they went to college, but on occasion, it crept back into their conversations. Since there was no place like home, just like Dorothy in *The Wizard of Oz*, Chloe, Sam, Matt, and Beau moved back to the area to teach and, heaven forbid, to influence their students.

From his periphery, he noticed Beau winking at a pretty brunette about their age who walked by. Less than thirty seconds later, Beau winked at a fashionably dressed grandmother, reassuring a nervous five-year-old boy that flying would be a great adventure. The boy dropped his teddy bear, and Beau rushed to return it.

"Hey, don't leave without your friend." Beau handed the bear to the boy. "You're lucky to have this with you. On my first flight, I needed the flight attendant to hold my hand, and she even got the pilot to give me wings to wear. Maybe you can get some too." His words attracted some travelers to watch Beau interact with the boy. Before the boy walked away, Beau ruffled his hair. "Have a good flight." Beau's mischievous brown eyes crinkled at the corners.

Beau loved being with women and never had to worry about being alone unless he wanted to be.

He had a habit of dating multiple women at once but never kept it a secret. He avoided relationships like the plague and dumped any woman who wanted to tie him down.

Matt was the opposite of Beau. He didn't date unless Beau set a double date for them. He had given up looking for the "right woman." Chloe had broken his heart in college, and recently was burned again by a lying, cheating, party animal girlfriend. Now Chloe was here, and he needed to process the ramifications of being near her again.

"You can't fool me like you did that kid," said Matt. "You were sixteen when you suckered that flight attendant into holding your hand, and she still keeps up with you, right?"

"Maria? Yea. She's a sweetheart. She just had her second child. She wanted me to be the godfather, but I talked her out of it, so she named her son after me."

"What, Beauregard?"

"Of course not. She named him Jackson. It's a manly name, and her hockey-playing husband liked it. What can I say?"

"You're so full of it."

WHEN A WHEELCHAIR attendant appeared for Chloe, there was enough time to pass through TSA toward their international gate. The attendant helped her through efficiently, so she waited for the others. Matt had coins in his pockets that set off the alarm. Beau forgot to take off his watch and left his car keys in his pants—they set off the alarm, and Sam laughed at the guys.

Sam sobered when she found that her boarding

pass had been marked for random searching. She straightened up, her expression serious. Everyone watched tentatively. There was no telling what Sam had packed. Chloe reached into her purse and grabbed her phone, ready to call a lawyer.

Sam's face was ashen. No one had ever gone through her things in public like this. She shifted sideways to block the guys from seeing inside her luggage and smiled uncomfortably over her shoulder at the trio. The agent opened a zippered pouch to find a tube of KY Jelly and a small vibrator. He zipped it up and put it aside. Then he looked in another bag filled with tampons. He replaced it in the luggage and held up an unopened jar of peanut butter before putting that back.

"You may go now."

Sam breathed heavily and reached for the carry-on, thinking the TSA agent had zipped it shut. She picked it up and turned, flinging several lacy bras and matching panties to the floor.

Beau whistled. "Will you model those black thongs for me?"

The TSA agent pointed his finger at Beau in a warning.

Sam punched Beau in the arm. Hard.

Beau smiled, slowly picking up each piece of lingerie and examining them before Sam could grab them back.

The agent rounded the luggage roller belt and stood with one hand on his walkie-talkie.

Sam hurried to finish, zipped the carry-on, and rolled it out of the area.

Beau caught up with her. "Peanut butter?" He snickered.

"I like peanut butter. It's nutritious."

"You mean you'll eat it if French food is disgusting."

Sam checked to see if anyone was watching, and she punched him again. Harder this time.

THE GROUP ARRIVED at the appropriate international gate, and the attendant left Chloe sitting in the wheelchair with her foot propped up on another chair. Sam placed their boarding passes away and cracked her knuckles. This was the perfect time to clear the air and take charge like she used to. Showtime.

Sam stood in front of Beau and Matt. "Well, well, well. You both remind me of something the cat dragged in." She struck a pose, hip jutted out, her hand propped on top, and grinning from ear to ear. "Beauregard Vincent Jackson. You haven't changed much since I last saw you in college."

Beau regarded her with a lopsided grin and a sparkle in his eye. "Samantha Anne Williston. Are you still wreaking havoc like you used to?"

Sam lifted her chin. "I'm a respected English teacher and have no time for juvenile shenanigans."

A snort escaped from Chloe before she giggled, "Sam, your ears turn red when you lie. They're a lovely shade of pink right now." She caught Matt grinning at her, and Chloe's smile faded as she tilted her head downward to concentrate on her ankle covered in ice.

"Matthew Justin Richards. You look better than I thought you would after that ho of a girlfriend dumped you," said Sam.

Chloe gasped, Matt's face paled, and Beau bent

forward laughing. "Sam, you haven't changed one bit."

"Listen up, boys, because this is how it's gonna go. We have contest requirements to finish, which come first, so if you want, we can finish them together. However, Chloe and I intend to have the best time in Paris, including things that aren't on the itinerary. If you behave, you are welcome to hang out with us, but you are not obligated to do so."

Both women watched Matt quietly tell Beau, "I say we stick with them. We're responsible adults. I only hope Paris can handle the four of us."

Beau whispered back, "Paris is the least of my worries." He faced Sam. "You had us at 'Listen up, boys.' We want to spend time with you two in Paris and get to know each other again. I'm positive we can work together and hang out like old times. What do you two say?"

Sam squatted beside Chloe and whispered, "We can wrap them around our little finger." Chloe nodded. Both women held out their hands, and Matt and Beau shook them.

A handshake meant serious business. It set the parameters and the stakes of a bet or a deal that no one could back out of. Handshakes as children were mandatory before attempting each hare-brained idea, despite its consequences. As adults, the results could be severe, with jail time as a real possibility given the type of antics they used to get into, but they were about to cross into international waters—a new frontier. The trip suddenly had more weight as the handshake created a pact as important as a blood oath.

Sam studied each person and grinned. *Oh, how*

I've missed us. Their contest duties would be easy. Returning to how things were years ago would take some finagling, manipulation, and prayer, yet she was confident. Scheming was her forte; she knew what buttons to push to keep everyone moving forward, and she'd need to tap into Chloe's superpowers to prevent an international incident or prevent them from being deported. *Piece of cake. Paris, bring it on.*

Chapter 3

OVER THE LOUDSPEAKER, a female voice announced, "Attention passengers, Norwegian Airlines Flight 5452 to Paris has been canceled. Please go to the main ticket counter to reschedule your flight."

"That's crap. We should have boarded the plane an hour ago," said Beau. "Let's go."

Sam pulled hers and Chloe's things together. Beau also took care of his and Matt's stuff as Matt took charge of the wheelchair. Chloe held her purse and camera bag in her lap while her crutches stood straight up like a flagpole.

"Blessit all," snapped Sam. "First, Chloe sprained her ankle. Then Matt and Beau appeared... no offense, Matt—"

"None taken."

"I'm offended," said Beau.

"Pfft." Sam continued, "We had difficulties with security, and now our flight's canceled. If I didn't know better, maybe the big guy upstairs doesn't want us to go to Paris."

"You think our trip is jinxed?" asked Chloe.

"Mom says things happen in threes, and we've already had four unexpected events. So, if I had to make a prediction, more problems will come."

"Glitches are expected on trips—that makes them memorable," urged Chloe. "Think positive, Sam. This is the last of our troubles." Chloe crossed herself. The others mimicked her.

THE LINES WERE impossibly long, with at least two hundred people waiting to speak to someone at the ticket counter. An agent noticed Chloe in the wheelchair. He motioned for the group to move to his area and asked for their passports and plane tickets.

"I'm sorry, this flight has been canceled until tomorrow," said the agent. Stealthily, he waved Beau closer and spoke to him in a whisper. "But since you're traveling together, four seats opened up on the next flight out. Please don't say any-thing."

Beau made the sign of locking his lips and throwing away the key.

The flight should board at about eleven o'clock tonight. Please don't wander far from the assigned gate. If you're not there, your seats could be given to anyone on standby." The agent issued new tickets. "Check the information board since the concourse and gate numbers might change. You have a four-hour wait until boarding."

The four moved down the correct concourse looking for food. "The choices are sandwiches, pitas, burgers, and pizza close to our gate. Pick your poison," said Beau.

Sam and Chloe headed to the bathroom to freshen up, then met the guys back at the gate with their pizza and salad. Unfortunately, Chloe's baggie had turned into ice water.

Beau nudged Sam, "Come on, let's find some ice."

Chloe and Matt read their phone messages. She stealthily peered at Matt, admiring his strong jawline and the addition of a closely trimmed beard, smiling at how his hair still stuck out in all directions. He was so much more handsome now than in college. *If only...* She quickly looked down as Matt's gaze rose from his phone's screen.

Matt studied Chloe and then turned in his seat toward her. He swallowed and took a deep breath. "Are you ever going to talk to me?"

Chloe jumped. "Of course. Thank you for helping me today." She couldn't quite meet his eyes, uncertain how to interact with him.

"I'm sorry you got hurt. I meant what I said. I will help you in Paris. Look, I don't want things to be awkward between us. After all, we'll be together for a week, so could we call a truce? Maybe start over?" He extended his hand. "Hi, I'm Matt."

Chloe smiled at the gesture.

Matt's grin widened so that both his dimples showed, and his hazel eyes almost twinkled. At that moment, he looked like the younger man she had fallen in love with long ago.

She extended her hand slowly, and they shook. "And... I'm Chloe." When their hands joined, the hairs on the back of Chloe's neck stood up as a spark traveled to her heart. "You were the last person I expected to see at the airport. It's been six years, three months—"

"Twenty-seven days and three hours, with daylight saving time," said Matt, cheeks pink.

They studied each other more closely, taking in the changes—some laugh lines around Chloe's baby blue eyes and tan lines with tiny freckles over Matt's nose. Chloe removed her hand tentatively, blinking a few times, trying to get her bearings.

Matt rubbed his hands on his jeans and spoke again. "We're adults, and there's no reason we can't be civil to each other."

His dimples became deeper—his weapon, her Kryptonite. Chloe felt weak in the knees. Good thing she was already sitting. Then it hit her. Like in the poem, The Spider and the Fly, she was being sucked into him again. "However, this doesn't mean we're friends." She straightened up as much as her ankle would allow. "It means we're on neutral ground for the next seven days. So, if you want to stop helping me at any time, let me know, and I will do the same. Is this acceptable?"

"Sure. Truce?" His adorable dimples were broadly displayed.

"Truce."

She had set the parameters for their relationship in Paris. There would be no misunderstanding or expectations. So, why did she feel it would be problematic to be with him? Why was her heart beating fast? Drops of sweat collected along her neckline. *Stay calm. Focus.* He was her opponent. She was in control. She was strong enough to handle Richards.

Chloe cleared her throat, picked up her cell phone, and read. Matt did the same.

S AM AND B EAU stopped at a newsstand for magazines. He came up beside her, shoulder to shoulder. "How's your love life, Sam?"

She started. "It's great, not that it's any of your business."

"Sure it is. We'll be together for the next week, and it'll be my pleasure to keep you from being lonely. You'd like that, wouldn't you?" He flashed her his killer grin.

"Your ego hasn't deflated since being Mr. College Quarterback. I've taken care of myself all these years without you, and I'll continue to do so, but thanks for the offer." Sam veered away from Beau and reached up two shelves for a magazine. She grabbed one, turned around, and bumped into his chest.

He steadied her, holding her close. Without warning or permission, he kissed her softly at first. She responded willingly, so he continued. He could have kissed her for hours, but an airport announcement brought him down to earth. When they separated, he continued studying her shallow breathing and wide pupils. "Just a friendly kiss, Sam. We are still friends, aren't we?"

"That's to be seen." She cleared her throat. "Don't make kissing me a habit."

Beau moved back and grinned. "We'll see." He winked at her, and Sam rolled her eyes. *She didn't slap me. She didn't call me names. She didn't say not to kiss her. She'll think about that kiss and the next one, and so will I.*

C HLOE SAW B EAU and Sam walking toward her and watched them interact. Beau must have made an asinine comment. Sam slapped his arm and walked on. Beau's laughter made Sam tilt her chin to assume her princess's persona. She had seen that pose for decades and grinned at Sam's response.

Sam tried to ignore Beau and walked faster, but he caught up to her. He walked by her side and then rocked onto her shoulder to plead his case. Then Sam stopped and faced Beau.

Chloe wished she could have heard the conversation, but by their stance, she knew Beau had asked for forgiveness. Then he gave Sam the killer grin. Yep, the one he could use on any female to get him out of trouble or into it. Sam rolled her eyes and shook her head. Chloe read Sam's lips as she said, "Fine."

Great. It was junior high again.

Teasing, laughing, and flirting, Chloe approved. Sam couldn't ignore him. They were back together again. Paris might be a good thing after all.

OVER THE NEXT three hours, two announcements explained that mechanical problems had delayed the plane. "Norwegian Flight 5452 will arrive at the gate at eleven o'clock. Please have your boarding passes ready when your zone is called."

The next announcement said the plane could arrive at the gate by midnight, then another one before midnight said, "Flight 5452 has been delayed again, but we anticipate the plane's arrival soon. Passengers should remain at the gate with boarding passes in hand."

Matt spoke to Chloe. "Your ankle needs to be elevated more. If you move to the chair, I can prop it up with my backpack in the wheelchair." They all helped her move.

Sam handed Chloe Tylenol since the pain was worsening, and again, her baggie was mainly water. Beau and Sam volunteered to find more. Since most restaurants were closed, they jogged a mile before finding ice. Then, panicking, thinking they would miss the boarding call, they ran back without having worked up a sweat.

"Here's the ice. Since we're leaving shortly, it's time to take the sleeping aid for the long flight," said Sam.

Beau looked at Matt and then back at Sam. "Are you sure about this?"

"Dr. Martin prescribed it. You trust me, don't you?" Matt and Beau looked at each other again and held their hands out simultaneously. Sam gave one to each person and then took one herself. Then, they settled in their chairs to wait.

Finally, at four o'clock in the morning, an announcement asked passengers to move to the gate with their boarding passes. Beau shoved Matt awake. "I'll check us all in. I'll grab our stuff while you bring Chloe." Beau gently nudged Sam and spoke close to her ear. "Sam... Sam, give me the passports and boarding passes, and I'll stand in line. Please find some seats for us by the door."

Sam opened her eyes slightly. "I feel like the walking dead." She carefully got up and did as Beau had instructed.

Chloe slept on. Matt lifted her, and she instinctively wrapped her arms around his neck, snuggling her head into his shoulder. His heart melted, torn between what had been and reality. He pulled her closer and kissed her forehead. No one noticed. Matt placed Chloe in the wheelchair and rolled her toward Sam so that they would be among the first to board.

Another hour later, they were called first to board the plane. Matt helped Chloe out of the wheelchair and tried to show her how to use the crutches.

"I can do this," she snapped, hobbling slowly to her seat with Matt silently following behind to put their stuff away.

Contrary to the ticket agent's information, their row wasn't full, and they could spread out. Matt lifted the arm between the seats so Chloe could better rest her ankle over his lap. Chloe blushed. "Matt, I'm sorry I snapped at you. I'm so tired and achy. Thank you for putting up with me."

"Why don't you take another Tylenol, and maybe you'll rest better?" She accepted the pill from Sam with some water. "When they start serving breakfast, I'll wake you." She nodded.

THE PLANE PULLED out onto the tarmac at six o'clock in the morning to line up for takeoff. About four hours later, Beau smelled coffee, and he woke everyone. "Guys, food's coming." When the food cart came by, they were overlooked. "Hey, don't we get meals?" asked Beau.

The flight attendant looked at her chart. "I'm sorry, but you did not order food or beverages online. I'll bring water later."

"That stinks. I was looking forward to some

bad airplane food. Matt, were we supposed to order food and drinks?"

"I don't think so but let me check the travel information." Two minutes later, "Ah, Houston, there's a problem. The fine print says to order our food and beverages for an additional charge. Sorry, gang. It's a good thing we brought snacks." Matt reached for his backpack.

"So, what else do we pay for?" asked Beau.

The others shrugged. While Beau and Matt pulled out granola bars, fruit, and water bottles from their backpacks, Sam read the fine print in the travel documents.

"Apparently," said Sam, "we are responsible for all but two dinners and the breakfasts in the hotel. We are to pay an extra seven euros a day per person for the hotel room, any taxi fares, and extra excursions or attractions not taken care of by the Viator coupons we have."

"What we've got here is a communication failure," said Beau.

"Why are you still quoting movie lines badly? I thought you'd outgrown that in high school," said Sam.

Beau faked a heart attack. "The best and most appropriate responses to every situation are in the movies. I am a connoisseur of the silver screen, from the black-and-white classics of the forties and fifties to modern-day cinema. In fact, I excelled in college theater classes, and if I hadn't been such a stud on the football field, being an actor was my backup plan."

Everyone snickered. The snickers became snorts and then full-blown laughter.

"What? No respect. I get no respect at all."

"Dangerfield, right? Please tell me your father didn't breastfeed you," said Sam.

Beau was sure Sam's eyes twinkled. "Hey, you're okay."

She swatted his arm, and he faked an injury. "Since we missed our flight, we also missed the van that should have taken us to the hotel. We'll have to find our way there and pay for it."

"C'est la vie. Finding a taxi shouldn't be too hard," said Matt. "Speaking of movies, why don't we watch one?" He flagged down a flight attendant and learned they had to buy earbuds. "Cheapskates."

Everyone pulled out their earbuds and chose a movie, but their eyes closed again after ten minutes.

THE DOWN EAST four awoke a few hours later, stretching and yawning. Sam looked to her left. A guy who hadn't been served a meal sat in the aisle seat across her.

"Hi, looks like you didn't preorder food either. I'm Sam. I have some granola bars if you need a snack." She reached into her purse and handed him two.

"Thanks. I'm Simon Brown from Boston. You sound like you're from the Carolinas. Are you staying in Paris or going somewhere else?"

"We'll be in Paris for a week. How about you?"

"I'll stay in Paris overnight," said Simon. "Then try to catch a flight or train tomorrow for the World Soccer games. I missed my connection, so I'm stuck until I can make arrangements." They continued to talk for thirty minutes or so. "I know this great club in Paris. I'll take you there this evening if you like. If I can't find a room tonight, would you let me crash in your hotel room until I can get transportation?"

"Clubbing sounds like fun, but we have an excursion planned this evening, and I'm not sure when we'll head back to the hotel. My friend Chloe hurt her ankle, and I don't want to leave her, but thanks anyway. As far as crashing goes, Chloe and I are sharing an economy-sized room, with twin beds, and there isn't enough space, sorry." As an expert in deflecting unwanted advances and keeping men at bay, she didn't think anything of his comment. "But maybe our hotel has a room available. I'll give you the number." Sam found the information and passed it on.

"Did I hear you say you're attending the World Soccer matches?" asked Beau. "Simon, right? I'd love to hear all about it. Hey, Sam, why don't we switch places so he and I can talk for a while?"

Sam gladly switched, relieved she didn't have to deflect any more flirting.

Beau leaned into Simon and quietly said, "So that you know, she's with me."

Sam pretended not to hear. She should have been angry with Beau for being a possessive Neanderthal, but instead, her cheeks felt hot, and she was glad he had stepped in.

Sam turned to Matt, "We have a few hours before we land, so why don't you start teaching us some good French phrases like, "Hey, handsome, want to buy me a drink?" Beau growled. "Or how much is that? Where is the bathroom? Or, I'd like to see the menu, please."

Chloe took out her French phrase book. Matt spoke in French, and the girls repeated it several times. Then, he asked them to say phrases without looking at the book. Chloe grasped it better than Sam, but then again, Chloe had taken French in ninth and tenth grade a hundred years ago.

Sam was bored. She grabbed her phone, plugged in her earbuds, and listened to music with her eyes closed.

Chloe and Matt continued, trying not to look at each other. "It's a good thing your grandmother taught you to speak French," said Chloe.

"She had to since she refused to speak English. Otherwise, she would have only had my mother to talk to when she moved in with us from Quebec after Grandpère died. What a character. She used to cuss up a storm, and to mom's chagrin, I picked that up, too. Out of the four of us, she liked you best. She always wanted a girl in the family and loved your cooking."

"I enjoyed our time together, but really, you were her favorite." He shrugged. "I was sad to learn she passed away last summer."

He nodded. "Thank you."

Matt read to Chloe in French for the next hour, and his voice lulled her to sleep. His mind went back to high school, when he fell in love with her. They were happy even in college, until they broke up. Could he forgive her for ripping his heart out by cheating on him? More importantly, was it possible to start over as friends?

His life was a mess—two other women had betrayed him, and he sucked at relationships. He had his friends and his work and loved the things he did—he should learn to be happy with that.

Maybe he was destined to be alone.

Now, he was faced with spending time with Chloe. He needed to protect himself and was determined to build a wall around his heart. He closed the book and then his eyes. *I'm so screwed.*

SIMON WAITED UNTIL the group had fallen asleep. Cautiously, he bent down, teased Sam's backpack from under the seat, and carefully dropped the Burt's Bees lip balm into the outside pocket. He replaced the backpack and returned to his seat to take a nap. Now, he could relax knowing the thumb drive was safe if he got searched. He also had people he could count on to watch over Sam and her friends until it could be retrieved.

THE PILOT'S VOICE came over the loudspeaker, "Ladies and gentlemen, we are making our final descent into Paris. The temperature is eighty-one degrees, sunny with winds out of the south. Thank you for flying with Norwegian Airlines. Have a pleasant stay in Paris."

Chloe danced in her seat. She felt the excitement surrounding the four teachers; their hearts must be pounding, too, and their smiles mimicked the ones they wore before an adventure. Chloe spoke to Sam loud enough so everyone could hear, "To think that you wanted to go to New York City to chaperone the senior trip with eighteen-year-olds this week. I'm glad I said, 'no.'"

"In my defense, I wanted to travel and have an adventure. It's still a place we should go."

"Sam has a point," Beau interjected. "It should

be on our list to see."

"I'm game, even for a weekend," said Matt.

"On *our* list?" Sam squinted her eyes at the guys.

Chloe lifted her chin. "If we don't feel like killing each other by the time we get home, I'll consider going to New York City with y'all, but I refuse to do lesson plans." Without warning, her serious expression morphed into a large smile.

"You're on," said Beau. He started singing, "New York, New York—"

"Stop," they all said together.

Beau winked at them, not able to hold back a grin.

Chapter 4

I T WAS AFTER five o'clock in the afternoon when Chloe's wheelchair assistant led her and the others through Orly Airport toward immigration. They were directed to a cubicle devoid of passengers at the far end of the room. A stern-looking immigration officer eyed the group as Chloe was wheeled forward.

"They're with me," said Chloe. She motioned for the others to move closer to her, but the officer held his hand up to stop them and pointed to the yellow line. Like good little children, Matt, Sam, and Beau moved in single file behind it.

Chloe took a breath and handed over her passport. Before it could be stamped, Chloe smiled and said, "Excusé moi." She pulled out the matboard paper doll, Mimi, dressed in paper blue jeans, a t-shirt displaying an American flag, and holding a miniature passport book wristlet. Chloe stood Mimi up on the counter's ledge and opened the wristlet. "S'il vous plait."

The immigration official's steely stare never wavered.

"Matt, m'aide," said Chloe, her voice an octave higher. "Would you please explain that we are teachers, and Mimi is part of my lesson plan?" Surely, the officer would understand that Mimi needed to collect the French passport stamp and then visit famous sites in Paris with her photo taken.

Matt explained their situation. Chloe understood only a few words but smiled, nodding in agreement. He had rescued her once more. *I can't keep relying on him during this trip. He's going to think I'm helpless.*

"*Comme Flat Stanley, peut-être?*" asked the officer.

"Oui," said Chloe and Matt together. She turned to the others and said, "See, Flat Stanley is known worldwide. Mimi will be famous one day."

Still stoic, the officer stamped Mimi's book and then unexpectedly took a selfie with Mimi using Chloe's phone and sent it to his daughter. "*Ma jeune fille joue avec des poupées en papier.*"

"He says that his daughter plays with paper dolls," said Matt.

The stone face returned. He stamped the group's real passports. "Welcome to Paris."

Sam and Chloe giggled the entire way to the baggage claim area.

MATT, BEAU, AND Sam collected the luggage and then moved toward the taxi stand. They were met with a blue sky, puffy clouds, and temperatures in the high 70s. Sam and Chloe removed their lightweight sweaters and added sunglasses while Beau and Matt stretched. It had been so long since the four had felt the sun on their faces or breathed in fresh air.

"Go-oo-od mor-ning, Paris," Matt crooned.

"Isn't that supposed to be Vietnam?" asked Chloe.

"Yeah, but we're in freakin' Paris."

"Uh huh."

They hoped to find a van or large vehicle, but only black taxis lined the curb, their drivers waiting alongside. Chloe's attendant wheeled her to the taxi at the head of the queue, and she tipped him a few euros. "Merci, monsieur."

Matt helped Chloe get into the taxi and turned to Beau. "There's no way we can all fit in here with all our luggage—we need two taxis. You've got the hotel address, right?" Beau nodded. "Okay, then we'll go on and see you there."

Beau and Sam moved to the next taxi.

The driver asked Matt, "Where to?"

"Wait. I've got the address... in here," said Chloe. She dug in her purse, pulling things out and laying them over her lap, finally finding the name and address of the hotel on an index card. "Ibis Paris Montmartre, eighteenth... uh... dix-huitième arrondissement."

The driver peeled away from the curb, horns blowing and hand gestures flying in all directions.

Chloe and Matt grabbed the headrests to steady themselves.

"I am Etienne Boudrow, your driver." He grinned broadly and winked at Chloe in the mirror. "I am a graduate student in English literature, and one day, I hope to go to the United States for my doctorate."

"That's great. Your English is excellent," said Chloe. Etienne smiled again. Matt sighed and stared out of the window. Throughout the forty-minute journey, Matt rolled his eyes and gritted his teeth as the conversation between Etienne and Chloe continued.

Several times, Etienne swerved in and out of traffic without warning. *"Débile! Déplace-tu, connard."* His hands left the steering wheel to gesture to the other drivers as he continued to yell French obscenities.

Chloe's crutches fell across her ankle, and she winced. Etienne took a turn too fast, sliding her into Matt, and her purse fell on the floor, scattering everything across the floorboard.

"Plus lentement. Vous conduisez comme un maniaque!" yelled Matt.

"Yeah, what he said, and I'm getting carsick," hollered Chloe.

"Je suis désolé. It is rush hour, *n'est pas?"* Etienne pointed to the other drivers. "They should go faster to get home. I apologize. I will slow down."

Matt picked up Chloe's wallet and handed it to her. Then he scooped up everything he found and dropped it in her purse.

"If you are looking for things to do or need a taxi, text me," said Etienne. "I will give you my card at the hotel."

Matt casually put his arm around Chloe as she concentrated on what Etienne said. Whether it was jealousy or protectiveness, he didn't know, but Chloe relaxed into him. The driver looked in his rearview mirror to see Matt giving him the eye. Communication understood.

The taxi pulled along the hotel curb. Etienne retrieved the luggage and wheeled them to the front desk.

"Matt, you've been so nice in helping me. Let me pay for the taxi."

"Only if you let me take care of it next time."

"Deal. I need some Tylenol and ice on my ankle before we go on tonight's tour. That was a hard ride from the airport, and I'm worn out."

Chloe located some euros and paid Etienne. He helped her exit the car, handed her the crutches, and kissed her hand, "Au revoir."

Matt rolled his eyes one last time, slipped Etienne a ten-euro tip, and followed Chloe to the front desk.

"Bonjour. I am Claude Montpelier, the hotel manager. Are you checking in?"

"Bonjour. Yes, but we're waiting for another couple to arrive," said Matt."

"Oui, *d'accord*. Please wait in the lounge until the rest of your party arrives."

SAM OPENED THE taxi door and froze. She slapped her forehead with the heel of her hand. "Crap! I left my euros on my nightstand... I need to hit an ATM." She turned around and brightened, "There's one. Be right back." She hurried off to the machine and inserted her debit card.

Denied.

That's strange. She inserted her credit card.

Denied.

"This can't be happening." She inserted her last credit card.

Denied.

"I don't believe this. Now, what am I going to do?" Sam nervously twirled a strand of hair around her left index finger and stared at the ATM.

Beau rushed to her side. "What's going on?"

"All three of my bank cards have been declined. I don't understand it. I notified my bank and the credit card companies two days ago that I was traveling to France, and there wasn't a problem. Now, I can't get any euros."

"Come on; we'll straighten things out in the taxi." He escorted her inside. "Give me a card, and I'll call the company while you call the other one. Explain the problem. If they ask me for a password or other information, I'll swap phones with you."

Sam uncurled her hair and breathed after the first service agent finished speaking. "What do you mean the pin on my card was changed? Well, change it back. I'm in Paris, and I have no money. Fine. I'll do that."

She turned to Beau, "Those idiots locked me out, but they'll allow me to get up to six hundred euros today as an emergency advance at an ATM. I'll have to find one when we reach the hotel. Okay, next card."

"Sorry, Sam. This credit card was canceled, but they said to call on Monday."

"No!" Sam's face turned red. She closed her eyes and fisted both hands as she silently counted. One, two, three, four, five...nine, ten. She opened her eyes to see Beau watching her. She picked up the last card and dialed the number on the back.

"Really? I can't believe it. Thank you anyway." Sam ended the call. "I forgot to set up the PIN for the American Express card to get money advanced...Fortunately, I can still charge things on it." *Breathe.* She felt relieved, stupid, and mad at the same time. Her hands shook as she put her cards back in her purse, and she wanted to rip something or someone in half.

Beau moved closer to Sam and patted her hand. "Relax. I'll help you find an ATM when we get to the hotel. If things don't work out, I'll cover you."

Sam nodded. Beau put his arm around her, and she leaned against his shoulder, taking in the scenery.

"Thank you for helping me through this. If you hadn't been with me, I might still be standing at the airport." He grinned.

"The actress Hedy Lamarr once said something like, I don't fear anything I don't understand. When I think about it, I order a massage, and it goes away."

Samantha sat up and faced him. "That makes no sense at all. Try again, Yoda."

"How about, 'Tomorrow is another day,'" in a falsetto Southern woman's voice, not at all sounding like Scarlett O'Hara.

"Better, but still lame." Sam snorted, and he laughed. *So much time has passed. I wonder if things will be like they used to be while we're here in Paris.*

THE IBIS HOTEL lobby was generic in size and décor, and it was hardly a three-star hotel by

American standards, but it accommodated modest budgets with modest housing. To the left side of the front desk were stairs leading to a small restaurant for continental breakfast and lunch. Below the stairs was a small lounge area with a few chairs and a long sofa for people to sit while charging electronic devices, waiting for taxis or tour buses, or eating an ice cream bar from the freezer cart.

Matt and Chloe were looking at the photos of Mimi while they ate ice cream. Beau and Sam entered the lobby to find Chloe's ankle propped up on the coffee table, draped with a bag of ice.

Matt grinned. "Hey, you two finally made it. Let's check in and rest a while before tonight's excursion." They gathered at the front desk, and Matt told the manager, "We'd like to pay our hotel taxes for the week and put our passports in the hotel safe."

Claude opened the door to a room holding individual safes with keyless entries that lined the wall. The group retrieved their passports and placed them in the safe corresponding to their room number, except for Chloe. She dumped out her purse and then pulled things out of her backpack. No passport. "Matt, did you see what I did with my passport? I had it at the airport when we went through customs."

"You had it in the taxi."

"I suppose so." She sorted through her purse again and shook her head. "Oh well, I'm sure I'll find it somewhere...it's okay."

"Are you kidding?" Beau's voice was loud. "It's not like losing twenty dollars or even a driver's license. This is serious. By now, your passport has been sold in the underworld, and you won't be able to get out of the country."

Chloe's face paled, and tears threatened to fall.

"Hey, that's enough." Matt got in Beau's face while touching Chloe's shoulder.

Chloe wailed. "He's right. I just got here… and now I can't go hoooome."

Sam rushed over to hug Chloe while staring daggers at Beau. "Now look what you've done."

Beau threw his hands up to the sky. "Help me, Obi-Wan Kenobi. You're my one and only hope." He swallowed hard and then leaned down to be eye-to-eye with Chloe. "I'm sorry, Clo, for yelling at you. I'm tired, and I took it out on you. Forgive me?"

Chloe refused to look at him.

"Clo, I'm sure the US Embassy will open early tomorrow morning, and we can tell them about losing your passport. You have a copy of it, right?" She sniffed and nodded. "They'll fix it. I promise you. You'll get home even if I have to put you on my back and swim there."

Matt jumped in. "Things will be fine. There's nothing we can do about it tonight, so let's go to our rooms to rest. I'll bring up more ice and rewrap your ankle. How's that?"

Chloe choked down more tears, nodded, and accepted a tissue from Sam. When she wiped her eyes, most of her mascara came off. She turned the tissue inside out and blew her nose twice. How humiliating. Again. She had done more crying in the last twenty-four hours than in the previous year. Helpless? Is that what Matt saw: helplessness? *Get a grip, Chloe.*

The group headed to their adjacent economy-sized rooms. They had two twin beds, bedside tables, a chair, and a small ledge under the window that served as a desk. The guys brought the girls' luggage inside and placed it by the closet.

Sam gasped, motioning for Chloe to see the view. "You won't believe this, but the Montmartre Cemetery is next to the Ibis Hotel. There must be thousands of funerary monuments in all directions."

"No way." She hobbled over. No Eiffel Tower, no Arc de Triomphe, or even the Seine River. "This gives me the willies," said Chloe. "What kind of teacher trip did we win?"

Sam shivered. "I don't know if I can sleep next to a cemetery."

Chloe laughed. "Girlfriend, you can sleep standing up. I'm more worried about spooks. You didn't bring any sage in your suitcase, did you?"

"No, but we can buy garlic to hang from the window, or maybe the guys would like to camp out in our rooms?"

Matt and Beau peered out the window. "Matt, we may need to protect the girls from supernatural forces. Are you up to the task?" asked Beau, winking at him.

"Fighting the supernatural is what we do best. Bring it on." Matt snickered, and Beau joined in.

Sam slapped Beau on the arm. "Matt, if you don't mind staying with Chloe, Van Helsing promised to help me find an ATM. We'll be back soon."

Matt positioned Chloe on the bed closest to the bathroom with her ankle propped up, the bandage redone and iced. He set his alarm for sixty minutes and then lay down on the other bed.

When Beau and Sam entered the room about thirty minutes later, Chloe and Matt were fast asleep. "They're out. Come on, you can nap in my room," said Beau. "I'm sorry you could only get three hundred Euros from the ATM today, but things will work out, I'm sure."

"MATT, WAKE UP. We overslept." Chloe shook his shoulder twice.

Matt reached for his phone to silence it and put on his glasses before dialing Beau. "Get up. We overslept. I'll get Chloe ready, and we'll meet downstairs. It's too late to get on the Hop On bus for the night-time sightseeing tour. If we find a taxi, we may still make it. Can you call for one?" Matt stood, gathered their backpacks, and helped Chloe stand. "Great. We're coming now."

"You guys look like how I feel," said Beau, rubbing his palms over his eyes. Chloe shot him a nasty look, and Sam punched him in the arm. "Just being honest... let's do this before I change my mind."

The bus tour boarded across the street from the Arc de Triomphe and traveled throughout the city. When the four got to the location, the double-decker bus had just pulled away. It looped around the Arc de Triomphe and returned their way, stopping at the corner stoplight.

The guys looked at each other. "Run," said Beau. "I'll take the crutches. Run, Sam." He flagged the bus driver to open the door.

"Chloe, alley-oop." She was over Matt's shoulder like a sack of potatoes and jogged to the bus.

Oomph. "Put...me... down." Despite the jiggling, an unexpected giggle escaped her.

Matt grinned as he gently lowered Chloe inside the open door. "That wasn't so bad now, was it?"

"You... jarred my insides. Please don't do that—"

"Unless it's absolutely necessary. Got it." He raised both hands in surrender.

"Be thankful it wasn't Beau," said Sam, "He would have farted carrying you."

"Hey. I resemble that remark," said Beau.

Matt and Chloe found a seat on the bottom level and placed the crutches on an empty bench in front of them. Sam found earbuds for everyone, and on channel three, the tour was spoken in English.

Beau spoke to Sam, "Let's go up top." He grabbed her hand and sprinted up the narrow, curved staircase, heading for the best seats newly vacated over the driver. "Toto, I've got a feeling we're not in Kansas anymore." He winked at her.

"I need to pinch myself." Sam turned toward Beau and blushed. "I'm glad you're here with me on this adventure."

"Same here, sugar." Over the two-hour tour, he touched her hand often, pointing out specific things, and without making a big deal of it, he held her hand as the sights went by.

At nine forty-five, the bus stopped across from the Eiffel Tower, which lit up the sky in gold lights. Matt waited until the bus emptied, and then he helped Chloe off. Mimi showed up wearing a beret and a Paris T-shirt, and Chloe posed her as if she were holding the tower in her outstretched paper hand. The four laughed out loud—they had their Parisienne muse.

At ten o'clock, a light show exploded over the Eiffel Tower. White lights danced, and fireworks lit up the sky. Chloe gasped and took a video of this once-in-a-lifetime experience.

"This is so much better than the Magic Kingdom." Even the strangers on the bus laughed.

Beau pulled Sam into an embrace and kissed her. Before he could kiss her again, she gently pulled back.

Sam's eyes lifted. "What was *that* for?"

"This is like New Year's Eve. It's better than New Year's Eve, and I'm going to kiss you again." As he leaned in, she placed her hands firmly against his chest to push them apart.

"Just because we're in Paris doesn't mean you can use your Jedi mind tricks on me. You go through women like water through a sieve."

Beau sobered. She was right. There was no denying it: women were fun, exciting, delicious, and distracting, but he desired something better. He needed to own the comment, be honest, and come clean with her. *No one's like Samantha. She's the perfect woman for me.* "That was in the past. No more water. I want champagne, and you're my Dom Pérignon."

"I doubt it, but getting caught up in the moment is easy. I'll give you that." She patted his face before she backed away, "Good try, though."

Beau's lopsided grin held a promise that he would try harder. He followed her back toward the bus.

Chloe had inched farther away from Matt,

pretending to watch the fireworks until Sam tapped her arm. "It's beginning to rain. Come along, Cinderella."

They were back at the hotel by midnight, dead on their feet. They hadn't had a real meal, and jet lag persisted, but Sam retook the reins. "Remember, the tour bus to Versailles will pick us up at eight o'clock in the morning. Chloe and I will be at the café at seven o'clock. Don't forget your travel diaries."

There was mumbling and grumbling as they waved goodnight, moving like the walking dead to their separate rooms.

Chapter 5

S AMANTHA WAS READY to take charge—her energy level was at maximum. She arrived at the restaurant an hour earlier than expected and finished her continental breakfast with a bottle of Coke as everyone else silently headed to the coffee station. Spread out over the table, taking up most of the space, was Sam's travel book open to the pages on Versailles and a scribbled-in notebook. As her companions ate breakfast, her thoughts returned to their conversation at the Newark airport.

"Paris will be the perfect inspiration for writing prompts using historical figures to tell their stories to people in this century." Sam paced back and forth, thinking aloud and ignoring everyone while maneuvering around the seats, evading the carry-ons and Chloe's wheelchair. "We could also look at English words with French origins."

Matt interrupted her musing. "I could help you with that."

"Hmm.... That would be a big help, thanks.

So, what are you planning for your classes?"

Beau jumped in. "Matt has been enamored with the Eiffel Tower, and I predict he will get all geeky with its engineering. Won't you, Matt?"

Matt ignored him. "I'll teach a semester in building design symmetry from Versailles, hedge gardens with intricate patterns, and paper puzzles. Of course, we'll create the Eiffel Tower and monuments using 3-D printers." He looked at Beau, "You're so jealous that I was given four new 3-D printers, and I was going to let you make that nude model of yourself, but forget it—"

"Pfft." Beau preened. "I'm not jealous, but a statue of me would be awesome. Can it be a life-size replica or merely desk size?"

Sam slapped Beau on the back of the head.

"Why'd you do that?" asked Beau.

"Have you ever done nude modeling, Beau?" asked Chloe.

"No, but for you, darlin', I might think about it." Matt smacked Beau's head.

"What? I'm studly enough."

Chloe couldn't stop giggling, and Matt stared at her.

Sam shuddered. "I need to wipe that image out of my brain… So, Studly, what are you working on for school?"

"We're going to study the significance of the Hall of Mirrors over the centuries. It was used to sign the Peace Treaty of Versailles to end WWI and was instrumental in Benjamin Franklin's efforts for the United States after the Revolutionary War. We'll look at what might have happened if things had been different, and I'll have some guest speakers visit."

"That sounds halfway intelligent," said Matt.

Sam touched Beau's arm to keep him from punching Matt. "Chloe, the guys are going to love what you're planning. Tell them about Mimi."

Chloe opened a large plastic box and pulled out her custom-designed eight-inch paper doll. "Mimi will be visiting all the sights with us as a tourist, wearing different costumes, and I'll photograph her. She has a blog on the school's website and will tell stories about the places she visits and what she's done. I'll need help posing her throughout the trip if y'all don't mind."

"She looks like my baby sister, Morgan," said Beau.

"That's because Mimi is Morgan," said Chloe.

"Huh. You could have drawn a paperboy who looks like me instead," said Beau.

Matt snorted.

"If everything goes well, there will be a family of paper dolls one day, but Mimi isn't my only project. I want to photograph eighteenth-century wall coverings for students to make ink block prints for paper and fabrics. And to photograph landscapes and architecture for my work."

Sam blinked and returned to the present when Beau dropped into a chair next to her with two cups of coffee for himself. He took turns drinking out of each one, saying, "I need both. I don't want one to get cold."

Sam rolled her eyes.

Matt pulled up a chair next to Chloe. "What time does the Embassy open?"

"At ten o'clock. I'll call when we reach Versailles. "The phone number and a copy of my passport are in my purse, so I'm hopeful this can be done without too much trouble."

"Of course, it will," agreed Beau. "Whatever day you go, we'll adjust our schedule to go with you. Besides, I'd like to see inside the Embassy. Students could write about how tourists use them in emergencies."

Sam mouthed a silent "Thank you" to Beau, then added, "Okay, eat, grab some fruit for the trip, make sure you have your backpacks and water, and Chloe, do you have your camera?"

Beau, Matt, and Chloe said, "Yes, Mom."

ABOUT AN HOUR later, the bus pulled up next to the grassy border that delineated the Versailles grounds from public areas and side streets. People strolled on the lawn, enjoying the beautiful early summer weather. The driver recommended the café next to the van for a nice lunch and then pointed to where the group should meet their local guide.

Chloe called the Embassy. If she could have paced, she would have. Instead, she sat alone on a park bench, her hand shaking as she spoke on her cell phone, nodding as she answered questions, forgetting that the person on the phone couldn't see her responses. Since she insisted on doing this alone, the group gave her some space.

About twenty minutes later, Chloe waved to the others to join her. She had a next-day appointment at nine o'clock in the morning to take her photo, fill out paperwork, and then wait until her passport was ready. The weight on her shoulders got lighter, and her wide smile told the others that things would work out. "Now, I can enjoy the day," she said.

Sam motioned for Matt to sit beside her on a companion bench to discuss the background information of Versailles, so Beau joined Chloe and relaxed, watching the people go by.

Using her long-lens camera, Chloe photographed the architecture and people milling around the grounds. She saw two men arguing across the lawn in a shadowed space between two large buildings. The shorter man grabbed the other man's jacket lapels and shoved him. Chloe zoomed in and snapped some photos. The men flew apart, and the bigger guy pulled a knife. More photos. Chloe was drawn into the situation like a TV crime show. The blade slashed across the shorter man's belly, causing him to fall, and blood stained his shirt.

Knife Man lunged, but the man on the ground pulled his leg up and kicked him in the stomach, forcing him back. Then the shorter man picked up a handful of gravel and threw it in Knife Man's face, giving him enough time to scramble up and escape.

Knife Man yelled something at the other man's back, and then he folded the knife and jammed it in his pocket. Chloe kept snapping photos until Knife Man altered his jacket and looked around. He froze and stared directly at her. He donned his sunglasses, raised his cell phone, aimed it toward her, and took a photo. Of her. Maybe the others, too.

Chloe gasped. She attempted to stand up, nearly dropping her camera while grabbing at her bag. "We need to go. Now. Now. I mean, right now!" She reached over and pulled on Beau's sleeve as she struggled to get off the bench, standing on her good foot and hopping around to grab her crutches.

"Keep your shorts on," said Beau. He was busy watching three gorgeous women in short skirts walk by. He winked at them, and they waved back. Chloe smacked the back of his head.

"Hey, that hurt." His smile turned into a thin line.

"I saw something…" Chloe's voice quivered and then got louder. "It's bad… I took photos. I think I'm… we're in danger."

That caught everyone's attention.

Beau went rigid. His eyes focused on hers. "A guy?" She nodded. "What does he look like?"

"Medium height, dark brown hair, and wearing blue mirror aviator sunglasses." She pointed in Knife Man's direction. "Over there."

They all looked.

"I don't see anyone like that," said Beau.

"Me either," said Matt and Sam together.

"He's gone," said Chloe. "Two men were fighting; one had a knife and slashed the other man, but he was able to get away. The man with the knife saw me and took my… our photograph."

Beau touched her arm. "Look at me, Chloe. There are four of us, and we're safe in numbers. We'll stay in public areas until we can return to our hotel. We'll be fine on the tour if we stay close and don't wander off. Keep an eye out, and if you see him again, yell… Sherlock, or Columbo."

Chloe squinted her eyes and mouthed, "What?"

Sam jumped in. "What about Magnum, P.I.? He's hot."

"You've got to be kidding," said Matt. "Gibbs

on NCSI is way better."

"I changed my mind," said Sam. "Since we're in France, I choose Inspector Clouseau."

Chloe quietly said, "I love Wonder Woman."

They all stared at her.

Beau shook his head. "She's an action figure, not a detective. Besides, everyone knows the best detectives are men." He ducked to avoid the swats Chloe and Sam gave him. "Okay, okay. I give. Yell 'Wonder Woman.'"

Chloe appeared calmer, so the four headed toward the guide holding up a closed umbrella like a flagpole. Beau leaned into Chloe, saying, "When there's time, show us the photos, Clo." He squeezed her shoulder. We have your back."

MARCEL, THE TOUR guide, lowered his umbrella to start his speech. "Versailles is a palace with seven hundred rooms. Most aren't open to the public, but what you can see will dazzle you." He pointed his umbrella toward the building. "It was built in the seventeenth century as a palace for King Louis XIV and was the center of French political power from 1682 until 1789.

"The last residents, Louis XVI and Marie Antoinette, lived here until the French Revolution, and then it was permanently closed. Eventually, the revolutionary government moved all the paintings, sculptures, and chandeliers to the Louvre.

"Restoration of the palace to its 1684th opulence began in the nineteenth and twentieth centuries. You will see the private apartments of Louis XIV and Marie Antoinette, public meeting rooms, and others. In 1783, the Peace of Paris treaty was signed in the Hall of Mirrors at Versailles, where England recognized the independence of the United States. Later, other significant treaties and meetings were held there.

"When you reach the Hall of Mirrors," said Marcel, "take note of the three hundred fifty-seven smoky mirrors and the twenty-four crystal chandeliers. However, I challenge you to find the names Renée and Emma scratched in a pane in 1842. Even then, famous places weren't immune to graffiti."

"Kids will be kids," said Beau. "I wonder if they'd notice my initials in ballpoint pen?"

"Don't even think about it," said Sam.

CHLOE TRADED HER license for a wheelchair. The attendant stowed her crutches, and Matt wheeled her around. When the group went upstairs, they rolled off the elevator and waited for the group to catch up.

It took about an hour to tour the bedrooms, sitting rooms, hallways, and other rooms within the palace. Mimi was photographed in various places as if she were living there. The docents placed her on a Louis XIV desk, in Marie Antoinette's bed, then standing by a crystal goblet on the dining room table.

Chloe also photographed Mimi with each docent. She sent them a copy to their phones and gave them her business card, promising to put all the photos on the school's website so they could see Mimi's adventures in Paris.

Marcel asked Chloe to turn in the wheelchair before entering the Hall of Mirrors. At the entrance, Chloe blurted out, "Ooh la la."

Sam sidled up to her, "You can say that again. Wow."

Marcel guided them to a corner left of the entrance so they could take in the best view. "The Hall of Mirrors held soirees and balls which accommodated the large skirts of fashionable women. These exquisite tall mirror panels were costly to make since silver was adhered to expensive glass. The other three sides of the room are lined with gold-leaf pedestals holding crystal candelabras, sitting on intricately designed oak parquet flooring in patterns of squares and diamonds. Now look up and imagine the light from these crystal chandeliers being reflected off the grand mirrors at night."

Beau, Matt, Sam, and Chloe repeatedly murmured, "Wow," as they walked further into the room.

Samantha gasped. "Does my butt *really* look like that?" She said it a little too loud. She cleared her throat, seeing people grinning, trying not to laugh.

Beau took a few moments to admire her backside. "You're a Wonder Woman indeed."

Sam turned to him, blushing, "Thank you."

He winked at her. "Mirrors look good on you, Darlin.'"

"Sweet talker."

"Just tellin' the truth." Beau noticed Matt looking at her, too, and he gave him the evil eye.

Matt turned away to see Chloe examining her own backside. Their eyes held, and he gave her a lopsided grin, "Perfect."

Chloe's face flushed. She waved Mimi in front of her face like a fan. "It's hot in here… and um, I'm hungry. How much longer before the tour is over?"

"It's over now," said Matt, "but I'd like to see the building's façade in the back, and the gardens should be spectacular. We could sit down and look at your photos." She nodded, and they said goodbye to the guide.

Before they could exit, a woman approached Chloe, holding out her business card. "You are Chloe Davis, the artist and photographer?"

Matt and Beau gathered around Chloe as Sam moved to her other side. Chloe nodded, then extended her hand.

"I am Josette Lafleur, Marketing and Guest Services Director," she said in fluent English. "It is an honor to have you with us today—we have been expecting you. Your agent emailed me your itinerary and said you would work on new items while you were in Paris. Your designs are very popular in the gift shop, and I hope you will design more things for us. Do you have some time to chat? It should only take twenty or thirty minutes."

Chloe looked at her friends' faces and nodded, "Of course. We were going to the gift shop anyway."

The director spoke again, leading Chloe away, with the others following slowly behind. "One of the docents sent me a photo of Mimi in Versailles. She would be perfect for a book of paper dolls and fashion through the centuries. Would this be something to consider?"

"Yes, I plan on creating a book," said Chloe.

Matt stopped Sam. "That woman knows Chloe, and she has work here?"

"She does. By day, Chloe is a high school art teacher; by night, she's an international photographer and commercial artist. If you two hadn't broken up in college, she might have never developed her potential, but that's her story, not mine. However, let me say she makes more money in a year selling her art than the four of us do together teaching. Come on. I need souvenirs." Sam caught up with Chloe, followed by Matt and Beau.

The guys were in awe of Chloe's designs. Matt held up a scarf. "This is expensive."

"Yeah," said Sam. "I've seen most of the museum pieces in her portfolio but seeing them in Paris is surreal."

"Imagine that. Our Chloe is famous," said Beau. "*Her* designs are in Paris….in the Versailles gift shop. A Wonder Woman indeed."

Souvenirs were bought, and the director gave each of them additional gifts of chocolate, Marie Antoinette perfume, and a tote bag with Chloe's iconic Paris designs.

"Thank you for all the souvenirs and samples. I'll work up some ideas and email you soon," said Chloe. She pocketed a Hall of Mirrors notebook with the notes from the meeting. The Director escorted the group to the back exit after taking selfies and photos of Chloe for some marketing brochures.

Matt said, "You're an amazing artist, Chloe,

and in Versailles…. What an accomplishment." Beau and Sam nodded in agreement.

Chloe beamed. "Thank you. That was a little weird being noticed by the marketing director, and now, my head is spinning."

"You're like a rock star," said Beau. "Can I have your autograph?"

"It'll cost you," said Sam, grinning.

Matt guided the group past little pools with a fountain in the middle. White swans swam under verdigris turtles and frogs attached to the fountain's base as water spewed over their backs. Colorful flower beds surrounded the pools, attracting flying insects and lots of pigeons.

He pointed toward the vast grounds. "According to the map, these gravel paths lead to statues surrounded by boxwood mazes, and the building in the distance was built for the queen to meet small groups or romantic liaisons. On either side of the long pools are wide paths for horse-drawn carriages or strolling guests, but this is too difficult for Chloe to manage." He guided them to two shaded benches. "Unless anyone wants to go with me, I'm going to take some photographs of the gardens. I shouldn't be too long."

Beau and Sam didn't want to leave Chloe alone. They passed out water bottles and granola bars and chatted about Versailles and her meeting with the director. After several minutes, Matt hurried back. Beau said, "Now, show us the photos."

Chloe accessed the memory card, narrating the images that created a slow movie. "This is the fight. See the knife? The guy grabbed gravel and threw it. Here's the guy looking at me." She enlarged the face.

Sam sucked in air, "He's scary and dangerous. Shouldn't we call the cops or something?"

Beau took out his cell phone, took a photo of the man's face, and then sent it to their cell phones. "In case we think we see him again…. We'll pass off what we know when we go to the Embassy. Until then, we should be careful. Come on, let's get out of here."

They made it to the café and looked at the menu board outside. Matt recommended the onion soup and the croque monsieur, "This is the most decadent ham and cheese sandwich you'll ever eat. I promise you'll love it."

The group arranged themselves at a large table, leaving Sam standing so Chloe could sit down first. A waiter tripped over Chloe's crutch and spilled a glass of red wine down the front of Sam's shirt. Sam shrieked, and all eyes focused on her as a hand reached for Chloe's camera bag. Her other crutch fell, and Chloe instinctively reached for both.

Chloe shoved the camera bag under the table to sit it on her feet and in her periphery, she saw blue mirrored glasses and two other men sitting at a table by the front door. She nearly hyperventilated. She elbowed Matt and rapped her knuckles on the table so that Beau would notice her head tilting in that direction. Sweat beaded on her forehead, and her words came out in a rapid whisper, "Wonder Woman, Wonder Woman, Wonder Woman."

All the restaurant's guests' attention focused on Sam.

"Great. This used to be my best white shirt. Now, it's a wine-stained Rorschach test that will never come out!" She gave the waiter the evil eye as he handed her a white towel and a saltshaker and pointed to the restroom, "*Je suis désolé, mademoiselle.*"

"Yeah, right. You should be sorry." She wagged her finger at him using her best teacher's voice. "You owe me a new shirt." The waiter cringed and hurriedly backed away as Sam huffed to the restroom.

Matt said, "I think we should take selfies with Mimi." Chloe held up Mimi, and Matt aimed his phone at the "bad guys" in the background. He then sent the photos to everyone's phone again… just in case.

Sam returned to the table with her arms crossed over her chest, her mortification complete.

Beau zeroed in on how her lacey bra showed through her T-shirt. Sam would have never participated in a wet T-shirt contest; much less been seen in public like this. He swallowed, removed a jacket from his backpack, and wrapped it around Sam.

"Thank you. I appreciate your chivalry." He zipped her in, and she wiggled her arms through the sleeves. "That waiter did that on purpose. The jerk. Did I miss anything while I was gone?"

"Yeah. Matt is homesick." Beau's words from then on took on the unique Down East Brogue that had been spoken for two or three hundred years. To anyone else, he was speaking another language. Sam tilted her head, squinted her eyes, but she nodded in agreement, and he continued to explain the situation.

His dialect sounded like the others at the table: a little Scottish mixed with Irish, yet more like

Elizabethan English. Combined with elongating syllables like Southerners do, it was definitely a foreign language. The café quieted, straining to listen as Beau stunned them with laughter and prompted the other Down Easters to laugh as well.

"You were right, Matt. The côte monsieur was scrumptious—I can replicate it back home." said Chloe. "But my French onion soup is much better."

"It is, and I'm glad you're my chef," said Sam. The conversation was light because no one understood them, and despite their ordeal, knowing they were fairly protected in a public place, their lunch was heavenly.

They took selfies with Mimi in a soup bowl. "Sorry, Chloe, but Mimi took a dip in my soup," said Beau. "I hope you made her a bib for when we go out to dinner."

"Mimi has several sisters and lots of outfits, but I didn't think to make her a bib."

Matt reached into his backpack and pulled out a red and white paisley bandanna. He fashioned it over Mimi's neck, and the group laughed at his fix. "Now she's ready for anything."

"Our chariot awaits," said Beau, pointing to the driver when he popped his head in to collect them. Beau helped Chloe up, and they moved to the van. "Matt, get everyone settled while I take point and get your phone ready. If we're followed, we need to know who it is. Ladies, I suggest we compare notes on the road."

Chapter 6

CLAUDE RUSHED AROUND the front desk to meet the group as they walked through the hotel's sliding door. "Mademoiselle, your passport..." he continued, speaking rapidly in French.

Matt understood and replied, "Oui, s'il vous plait."

Claude spoke to someone on the phone while Matt waited at the desk. After the conversation ended, Matt smiled and thanked Claude.

"Chloe, remember the taxi driver we had from the airport?" asked Matt. "He found your passport on the floorboard underneath the driver's seat. He'll return it in an hour for the price of cab fare." Without thinking, he grabbed Chloe by the waist, lifted her off the ground, and swung her in a large circle. Her crutches fell to the floor with a clang. She gasped, and he gently put her down. Sam handed the crutches back to her. Tears rolled down Chloe's cheeks.

"Sorry, I got carried away," said Matt. "I'm so relieved."

"Me too. I knew I would eventually get a passport. I hoped I could go home with you all." Tears of relief flowed freely. Beau instantly reacted and pulled her into his arms. Chloe buried her face in his chest.

"Please don't cry, Clo. Everything is okay now. Let's go to the café and have some tea. I'll find ice, and you can put your ankle up. While we wait for the driver, you can show me the photos you took inside Versailles. After that, we'll go to the cemetery and check out the famous headstones."

Chloe nodded between hiccups.

Sam laid her hand on Chloe's shoulder. "I'm so glad this worked out. Now that that's been resolved, we can concentrate on better things. I'm going upstairs to change my shirt and take a nap. There's a souvenir shop next door, and you can buy some postcards to send home. I'm also passing on going to the cemetery, so have fun. Don't let Beau bring anything dead or alive back."

By the time the taxi arrived, their postcards were finished, stamped, and handed to the front desk clerk to mail, and Chloe had canceled her appointment at the embassy. She hobbled to the safe room and deposited her passport. "It's been almost two hours. Sam may feel up to going to the cemetery now, and then we can find a nice place for dinner, but I left tracing paper in my sketchbook and my pencil pack back in the room."

"Don't worry, I'll get everything and convince Sam to go with us," said Beau.

BEAU KNOCKED TWICE, swiped the hotel room keycard, and heard a short "click." He walked into Sam's room. "You who... It's me."

Silence.

Beau shook his head. "Never in a million years..."

Sam was relaxed on the bed, with her back against the headboard and wrapped up in the hotel's plush white bathrobe... naked legs were crossed at the ankles, and Minnie Mouse slippers covered her toes. Her hair was pulled up on her head, and round green things hid her eyes. The rest of her face was covered in black goop, and her earbuds practically danced from the music.

He moved closer to the bed and touched the goop. "What the hell?" How can she sleep like this? There was no response, so he moved closer to the bed, knowing she was listening to music.

Chloe had explained that starting in college, Sam feverishly burned energy the moment she woke up. After a strenuous day, she usually went to bed before nine o'clock and woke up before sunrise, starving for anything Chloe had left behind. Then, she used that time to write local newspaper articles, or ghostwriting short nonfiction books or novels that her agent found for her to do. When Chloe got up, Sam was ready for the breakfast Chloe would make and ensured it was something more than a Coke and peanut butter crackers.

Sam frequently grabbed a nap when she needed to be at peak performance, often in the car as a passenger. Without it, she was hell on wheels—she snarled at people and even made little children and animals run away if they got in her space. But after taking a ten-minute nap, she became the Energizer Bunny, and she slept like a rock when she slept. There was no in-between.

Beau studied Sam in repose. The cinched robe outlined a shapely figure that he tried hard to picture naked. He sucked in a breath and exhaled sharply, "Knockout." The word should have woken her. Still asleep. She was the most beautiful woman, inside and out. *If only she could think of me as more than a friend.*

The thought of a relationship with her wasn't scary—in fact, now he wanted that more than anything in the world. She was perfect for him, yet he seriously doubted he had a chance with her because of his natural propensity to date lots of women.

He moved forward and dared to sit on the side of the bed, thigh to thigh. Despite the black tar, Sam's lips were intoxicating, full, soft, and kissable. He leaned in and kissed her gently. As he pulled back, her lips followed his, so he kissed her again. Her mouth opened slightly, and she moaned. Beau leaned into her, hoping she would wake up wanting more of him. He felt her breath, and his heart beat faster. He peppered her with little kisses, and she smiled. He removed the earbuds and spoke her name, "Samantha."

Whack!

Sam delivered a right hook that knocked Beau to the floor. The green disks hit him in the face, and she scampered off the bed, taking a fighter's stance.

Uh oh. Not fully coherent.

"Sam, Sam. It's me. Take it easy." Beau wiggled his jaw and saw that black goo had transferred from his face to his hand.

"Beau? Why are you on the floor... in my room... and why do you have volcanic mud on your face?"

"You can stand down now, Rambo. You were asleep... I couldn't help myself... I kissed you, and that black shit got all over me."

Samantha tried to relax, but her brows stuck together, and she spoke more to herself than to Beau. "I dreamed I was being kissed... but he didn't look anything like you."

Was that disappointment in her voice?

"Remind me never to kiss you while you're asleep—you pack a wallop." He went to the bathroom to wash his face. Sam followed him to examine the red spot on his cheek and flexed her hand while checking for broken fingers.

"You should never scare someone awake, especially someone that takes self-defense classes... How did you get into my room?"

"We were having coffee and pastries downstairs and finished the postcards as the taxi driver brought Chloe's passport. We were about to leave for the cemetery, but Chloe forgot her sketchbook and pencil pack. I volunteered to pick them up and hoped to persuade you to go with us. So, I used my keycard."

"Your keycard?"

"I have Chloe's room key, and she has Matt's—in case something happens. In my defense, I knocked and identified myself when I entered. *This was a mistake I won't make again. The next time I kiss you, you'll be conscious, willing, and wanting me, not some other guy.*

"Maybe I didn't want company," yelled Sam.

"Then again, what if I had company... male company? Didn't you think of that? The door was locked for a reason. And look at me. I'm not dressed. I could have been naked... My face!" She pulled the robe closer together, tugged at the strands of hair that fell around her neck, and turned her back on him.

Beau was starting to panic. *Guys? Not unless it's me. Think of something quick.*

"I've seen you naked, remember?" He tried to deflect the conversation, but she was right.

She peered over her shoulder. "I was six years old, you jerk, and I had a bathing suit malfunction. I distinctly remember you laughing until Chloe found a towel so I could make it to the bathroom."

"You're right." He moved closer, turned her toward him, and reached out to hold on to the bathrobe belt. "We were kids, but we're not kids anymore. You're a lot curvier and more beautiful. I apologize for using the keycard but not for kissing you. Kissing you is addictive." He was now inches from her, looking at her mouth and eyes. "I need another fix." He waited without her protest, so he leaned in and hoped to kiss her with more passion, but he pulled back, sputtering from the mud that seeped into his mouth.

Sam laughed. "Now you know how pigs feel." She wiped off some goop that had also gotten in her mouth. She wet a towel and threw it at him. "Clean up and leave. You cut into my nap and ruined my facial, but I forgive you.... Okay, I'll rinse off and meet you in the café in fifteen minutes. I'm going to need a croissant and a coke to make it. Chloe's sketchbook and pencils are on the desk. Now, get out."

He managed a two-finger salute, "Here's looking at you, kid."

A hairbrush hit him on the butt as his laughter preceded him out the door.

WHEN SAM ARRIVED at the café, everyone was ready to go. As she wished, her pick-me-ups were waiting. She sat down and gobbled up her snack. She said between bites, "It's kind of freaky that a cemetery is a tourist attraction—it wouldn't be on my list, but hey, we're in Paris."

"This one is interesting," said Matt. "It's a landscaped funeral park like in New Orleans. It was an abandoned gypsum quarry used as a mass grave during the French Revolution. In the early 1800s, it was covered over to make a road. Imagine twenty-five acres with twenty thousand grave sites holding over three hundred thousand people."

"This may be where the Zombie Apocalypse starts," said Beau.

"They'd all grunt in French," said Chloe. Beau high-fived her.

Matt held up a map. "This is an active cemetery with tombstones, monument graves, and mausoleums in various styles: Egyptian, Classical, Gothic, Renaissance, and even Art Nouveau. People take their lunches or stroll around the grounds. Trees line the walkways and sitting areas. Writers, musicians, singers, poets, politicians, and even scientists who have lived or died in Paris are buried there."

"Yeah, but do they stay buried? Hmmm?" said Beau. Matt rolled his eyes.

"I located where the most famous people are buried, and picked the gravesites each of us should be interested in seeing. Chloe will want to see Degas. Sam, Alexandre Dumas. Me, André-Marie Ampère, and for Beau, Charles-Henri Sanson." Heads nodded.

"Sanson?" asked Beau, "How do I know that name?

"He was the royal executioner who beheaded Louis XVI and instituted—"

"The guillotine. Yeah, he ushered in the 'Age of Terror' with the execution of Robespierre and Marie Antoinette," said Beau excitedly.

"Great. Now I'm thinking of Zombies with no heads. Or would their heads walk and talk independently?" asked Chloe.

"You mean like Washington Irving's headless horseman?" asked Sam.

They turned to Beau for an answer. He shrugged, "Return of the Living Dead and Headless come to mind, so I suppose it's possible." He said it with conviction and a straight face.

Matt snickered, and then they all did.

Out of the hotel, they turned left, walked a hundred feet, crossed the street to Rue Rachel, and took the stairs down, under the Rue Caulaincourt, to the entrance. Chloe had a tough time going from step to step, and she felt terrible that the others had to wait for her. From there, it was a five-minute walk to Sanson's tomb.

"You know, the head executioner's job was a family business. His sons and grandson continued the legacy," said Beau.

"And I thought following Dad into law was a deadly business," Matt snickered. "What? That was a good one, right?"

Sam shifted from side to side. "Now, which road do we take?"

"Roads? Where we're going, there aren't roads," Matt interjected. They all squinted at him. "I'm not the only one quick with a movie come-back." He sighed. "Okay, it's going to be a hoof, so I suggest that Chloe gets a piggyback ride unless she prefers the fireman carry again." Matt looked at Chloe with an "I'm waiting, princess" smirk.

Chloe snorted but acquiesced since he asked permission. She mumbled, "Did he use his boy-scout-Jedi art of persuasion on me?"

Matt presented his back to Chloe, bent down, and she got on his back, his arms holding underneath her knees, and her arms wrapped around his neck. Beau's job was to carry the map and crutches, leading them to Degas' tomb while Sam posed Mimi for photos.

Sam tapped Beau on his shoulder, "If Chloe gets a ride, I should too." Sam jumped on his back, and they staggered forward.

"Sam, you're killing me. Have you gained weight?" She smacked the side of his head.

"I haven't gained weight, you jerk. You've become a lightweight since college." He turned halfway around to make some wisecracks and tripped, throwing them both on the grass.

Sam laughed hysterically.

He took advantage of the situation and tickled her until she begged him to stop. "Kiss me, and I will."

"Never."

The giggling became high-pitched squeals, and a tear fell on her cheek; Sam and tears weren't synonymous. Beau stopped, then wiped it tenderly away with his thumb. He pulled her onto his lap and wrapped his arms around her, "I went too far, Sam. I'm sorry." He kissed her cheek. She blushed when they looked into each other's eyes, and he grinned.

Sam pushed off, stood, and extended her hand to help Beau. Halfway up, she let go, and Beau fell on his butt and then she took off running. Beau gave chase until they ended up at Dumas' tomb, where they found Chloe still on Matt's back, waiting for them to catch up.

She turned toward Chloe and took out her phone. *That woman looks familiar.* "Say, "stinky *fromage*." They laughed. She scooted in close enough for all to hear, "Wonder Woman, five o'clock." The four pretended not to notice while studying Dumas' tomb.

Sam spoke again. "Hey, this isn't the Dumas that wrote *The Three Musketeers* or *The Count of Monte Cristo*. This tomb is for one of his illegitimate sons, Alexandre Dumas *"fils,"* who wrote *The Lady of the Camellias*, which became Verdi's opera *La Traviata*, and then was adapted for the stage and film production of *Camille*. Still, this is cool."

Fifteen minutes later, they arrived at Degas' tomb along a beautiful tree-lined walkway. Chloe did a rubbing of the brass portrait medallion bearing his likeness and a quick sketch of the surroundings and tomb. They moved on, stopping at the nearest grassy area for a snack and water. Chloe assumed the piggyback position again while they spent another hour wandering around the grounds. After a while, they arrived at André-Marie Ampère's tomb.

"Let me guess, Ampère had something to do with math or physics, so his last name wouldn't have something to do with amps, would it?" asked Chloe.

"Elementary, my dear Watson," said Matt. "He was a great scientific mind, a savant actually; an inventor who formulated the laws of electro-magnetism, but passionate about other sciences, and even evolution long before Darwin. His tombstone says, "He loved mankind; he was simple, good, and grand." He was also a teacher living a poor life, so I guess he was my hero."

"Blah, blah, blah. Frankly, my dear, I don't give a darn it. If you start shedding tears, I will beat you to a pulp," crooned Beau.

"You're jealous. If there were an NFL football player here, you'd be all over it, taking selfies and peeing on yourself," said Matt.

"Watch your mouth… there's also baseball and basketball. I try not to discriminate."

"Let's not forget horseshoes and corn hole," said Sam.

"Or tiddlywinks," said Chloe.

"How about Dungeons and Dragons or Magic the card game?" asked Matt.

"Magic, that's okay," said Beau. "Magic Mirror on the wall, who is the fairest of all?"

"I am." They said in unison, followed by giggling, snorting, and bold laughter.

"I must agree with Beau; the zombie apocalypse would begin here, headless or with heads," said Sam. "Could you imagine how they would look coming out of their graves? Powdered wigs, silk knee breeches, shoes with silver buckles, and fancy dresses with lace and beads."

Chloe shivered, "Think about Halloween. I wouldn't want to be here or in the hotel watching from our room. It gives me the heebie-jeebies."

"I won't go to the Beaufort Graveyard on Halloween either. What with the ghosts of the pickled little girl, the English Soldier buried standing up, or the dog that tries to bite your butt by the fence? I'm certainly not anxious to have my brain eaten in Paris," said Sam.

"Dead or alive, come with me. All this talk about eating brains is making me hungry. Let's go," said Beau.

The four walked toward the exit while the gatekeeper stared as they passed.

"Other than zombies, what are the scariest movies of all time?" asked Beau.

"*Jaws*," said Chloe quickly. They all said, "Pffft," in unison. "Absolutely. There were five awful scary movies, and I didn't go in the ocean for years."

"No, *Sharknado* and *Lake Placid* were awful," said Matt.

"Agreed, but I hated Wonder Woman meets *Psycho* after school," said Sam. Code for three o'clock, and they all understood, exiting the cemetery as they were followed.

Chloe was perched on Matt's back as they exited the gate. The gatekeeper smiled at her. *He thinks we are a couple.* Her face heated, and she tried to dislodge herself from him.

"Put me down! I can manage from here." She said it a little too harshly, but everyone kept walking. Matt acquiesced, then lagged behind her in silence. She immediately cringed. *Why did I act like that? He was only helping.*

She turned awkwardly on her crutches and slammed into Matt's chest. He grabbed her before she fell, "Whoa, steady there." His arms held her fast. His chest was firm, familiar, but now better. *Home.* She remained in his arms longer than she needed to, then mentally shook herself and carefully straightened away from him, his hands relaxing on her arms, affecting them both.

She sighed. "I'm sorry, Matt. You have been sweet and patient in helping me, and I snapped at you again. You didn't deserve that. I don't like feeling helpless or dependent on anyone, and I don't think I'll get used to these crutches."

"You thought that guard was making fun of you, right? That we were a couple? Don't worry about it." He sighed. "When your ankle is better, you can give me a piggyback ride, and we'll call it even." His lopsided grin sent tingles up her spine.

Chloe had blown things out of proportion, yet he tried to smooth things over like he used to. "I guess fair is fair. Okay."

Matt stuck his hands in his pockets and walked side-by-side with her.

The group exited the cemetery following the sidewalk opposite the hotel, down to Café de Luna on the corner. The mystery "Wonder Woman" continued to walk to the next street, crossing it and turning right.

"She's gone," said Sam. "This is tiresome. I may have to punch the next person following us on principle."

BEAU LED THE friends to the café. "This joint is only open for dinner and into the early morning, so I hope the food's good. However, the kiosk at the end of the restaurant is what interests Sam. This is where she finds her Cokes for breakfast. Isn't that right?"

"How did you figure that out?" asked Sam.

"I'll never tell," said Beau, putting his arm around her shoulder.

"It had to be Claude," said Matt. "I bet she bought quite a few bottles, and Claude has been keeping them cold so she can have one anytime she wants. Right?"

"So, what if he does? He got a box of North Carolina saltwater taffy from Captain Bill's restaurant," snarked Sam.

"That stuff is made in New Jersey," said Chloe.

"I know it, but Claude doesn't."

Beau snickered, "He'll soon realize that Taffy will pull out his fillings."

"I don't understand why you brought Taffy to Paris," said Matt.

"I like Taffy, and I don't have any fillings," said Sam. She stuck her tongue out at him.

The restaurant's massive glass sliding doors opened, so dining was also on the sidewalk. Beau pointed to Sam's closed kiosk, which served hot sandwiches, snacks, beer, and sodas during the day. One of the servers waved at Sam, recognizing her from her morning habit, so waved back.

"It's nice outside. Let's grab this table," said Beau.

Etienne, the taxi driver who returned Chloe's passport, was drinking a draft beer at the restaurant's bar. He saw the friends' reflection in the mirror, turned, and waved. Chloe waved back and encouraged him to join the group.

"*Incroyable. Pourquoi moi?*" murmured Matt. Beau cocked his head in question.

Etienne greeted Chloe with a kiss on both cheeks, then Matt with a handshake. "Please join us," she said.

Matt scooted closer to Chloe and draped his arm over the back of her chair.

Etienne pulled a chair from a nearby table and placed it beside Samantha. He introduced himself to Beau, extending his hand. Beau shook it, but when it was Sam's turn, he brought her hand up to his lips. "*Enchanté mon beauté.*"

Sam grinned—she didn't need any interpretation. She took in his black jeans, black silk shirt with the top button undone and covered by a lightweight black silk jacket, and his Parisian attitude. "It's nice to meet you too."

Etienne gave her a knowing smile and did his best to hold her attention for the rest of the night.

Beau could have eaten glass. He watched Samantha swoon over Etienne's flirtations, perfect hair, teeth, and two heavy gold chains around his neck. *He wears more jewelry than she does. Who will I strangle first, Sam or Don Juan?* He rubbed the back of his neck, and as time passed, he rubbed his thighs up and down. "Grrr." Etienne heard it and smiled.

The waiter took orders for wine and beer. Further down the street, a roar followed by "Yay" and then "Nooo."

Etienne volunteered, "Football. Spain and Chile. You like football?"

Beau leaned in Etienne's direction. "Oh yeah. Matt and I coach high school soccer, and in 2021, we won the men's state championship."

"Et, you play?" Matt and Beau looked at each other and grinned back at Etienne. "Perhaps you would like to play with my friends and me on Sunday?"

"We don't have cleats with us," said Beau.

"No problem. I have extra, and the field is close. We play *á huit heures*."

"Sunday, eight o'clock in the morning?" Etienne nodded. "You're on," said Matt.

"I come for you at seven-thirty and for Chloe and Sam." He picked up Sam's hand again and kissed it. Sam allowed it once more.

Beau casually put his arm around her, "Samantha, are you interested in watching soccer?" Her eyes never left Etienne's.

"I love watching soccer, but I'd rather play. Etienne, if they play, I play. Can you find cleats for me, a European size 42?" asked Sam.

"But of course. You do not mind playing with men?" She shook her head, eyes twinkling, his challenge accepted. Soccer in Paris was an unexpected treat.

"Perhaps you would like to watch some football at Hetfield's Pub. It has great Irish food and dark beer." They all nodded. "A five-minute walk," said Etienne.

Beau gathered their things together. "I'll take our backpacks up to the room and be back in a couple of minutes." He stood and headed to the hotel.

AT THE FRONT desk, a familiar-looking man spoke to Claude. Without stopping, Beau entered the elevator and headed to Chloe's room. After depositing the backpacks, he pulled a piece of paper from a scratch pad, folded it to the size of a gum wrapper, and placed it between the top of the door and the jam. Beau shut the door carefully, securing the paper. It was a cheap burglar alarm he used in his college dorm room to keep from being pranked. If someone entered the room, the paper would drop to the floor.

Exiting the elevators, Beau peeked around the corner to find the man gone, so he approached Claude. "Hey Claude, how's it going?"

"D'accord. How is your stay in Paris?"

"Paris is great. That man you were talking to looks familiar. Is he staying in the hotel?"

Claude made a disgusting sound. "Jean Louis is a detective. I despise him. He tried to arrest my nephew for drugs at a party, and my nephew was innocent."

"That's terrible. Why's *he* here?"

"I should not tell you, but he is checking on you and your friends. I hope you are not doing something illegal—"

"Absolutely not. My friends and I are teachers here on vacation. We aren't looking for trouble, but we won't be harassed either."

"I believe you. If he comes back, I will let you know."

"Just give me the sign." Beau flicked his forefinger across his nose, but Claude didn't understand. "You don't know this? It's from the movie *The Sting*, with Robert Redford and Paul Newman. It was their sign."

"Mais oui. Robert Redford. I remember." He flicked his finger across his nose as Beau had done.

"Thanks, Claude."

Beau texted Matt that a detective asked about them at the hotel. At least their suspicion about being followed wasn't farfetched, but were they really "good guys?"

The ensemble walked less than a block down the Boulevard de Clichy. Like other night-time establishments in nice weather, the pub's sliding glass walls retracted to allow a larger crowd to gather inside and spill over onto the grassy median between the street heading east and west. Etienne waved to the bartender, and they moved to a large table. Food was ordered, pitchers of beer were consumed, and by the end of the second soccer game, everyone cheered with the locals not caring who won or lost. Etienne exchanged phone numbers with Beau and promised to see them early Sunday morning.

On the walk back to the hotel, Chloe spoke softly to Matt about the soccer match. "Matt, Sam has played year-round soccer with two teams since college. She plays hard, but I'm worried about her playing with these guys—we don't know how they play, or even if they play fair. I don't want her hurt. Promise me you'll watch out for her."

"We've got her back. She'll be fine, but if she knows you've said something, she'll be hard to live with." Chloe nodded, willing to take the risk.

Beau walked by Sam in silence. No teasing. No sparring. Nothing. It unnerved her. "You don't like Etienne, do you?"

"No. That guy put the moves on you, and you let him. I can't figure out why."

"Why not? He's a good-looking man. Besides, a little flirting is flattering. It doesn't hurt anyone, but don't think I'm falling for it. Give me a little credit, okay?" She threaded her hand through the crook of his arm and moved closer. "American men are much more interesting, and Etienne is less attractive to me than Matt." Beau stopped walking and faced her. He frowned and was ready to protest, but Sam stopped him. "Do I have to spell it out for you?"

"But you said—"

"Is English your second language? You... are dense." They were already at the hotel elevator when she released his arm. The elevator doors opened, and she walked in. She threw him a kiss. "See you in the morning," she then pressed the button for her floor.

Beau was left behind to think about her words. He studied the closed doors for several minutes before a wide grin spread over his face. Not dense anymore. He'd gotten the green light to pursue her. Paris was looking better and better.

Chapter 7

SAM WAS ALREADY in the dining area, as the others walked in, chatting easily before dropping off their backpacks and heading to the buffet. It seemed like old times as they fell back into a rhythm of easy familiarity spanning two decades. She took a sip of her Coke and then ate part of an omelet with toast in silence to listen to their banter. Like before, Beau was teasing Chloe about something so ridiculous that she swatted his arm as Matt grinned behind his coffee cup.

Sam's mind flashed back to their youth when the four were a formidable force, wholly devoted and attached in ways more binding than blood. They rooted for each other, had each other's backs, and even took the blame when they were blameless. If one of them got into trouble, they all felt it, absorbed it, and were stronger because of it. They could finish each other's sentences, knowing how each person thought, and words weren't necessary because their body language told the story. As a singularity, they were unstoppable, but individually, they were like lost puzzle pieces.

As the self-appointed leader, Sam's job was to create adventures, experience new things, and instigate mayhem in their sheltered Harkers Island life. As such, it was her duty to supply them with harebrained ideas that frequently got them into trouble. She mentally shook it off, thinking of the dares they survived—stupid, dangerous, and many were plain crazy. To them, a dare was the ultimate challenge, the gauntlet thrown down. She relished a dare and could weigh a possible success in a nanosecond, then plowed full steam ahead, usually dragging her compatriots or just Chloe to suffer with her. Sam closed her eyes to reminisce.

Sixth grader Sam told Chloe, "Beau dared me to run a 5K with him and Matt. He said I could never beat them, so training begins today. I need you to spy on them for me, find their weaknesses, and tell me how fast they are." Chloe agreed. Not only did Sam beat the boys, but she also won the race.

"You might think you're a fast runner, but you must be fast, alert, and use your head in soccer. It's a shame you're not cut out for the sport," said Beau. "Matt and I are going out for the team. See you on the bleachers." His smug look, walking away, initiated a challenge she couldn't ignore.

"They're trying to bait you," said Chloe. "I know that look. You don't even like soccer, and you'll have to work with others...not that I don't think you can, but—"

"I get it. The coach will tell me what to do. I won't like it, but that's part of the challenge. Have you ever known me to fail at something I put my mind to? If I stink, I'll have at least tried, but if I make the team, Beau and Matt must admit I have what it takes to be a team player. I will do it, but first, I need to learn how to play."

It took extreme effort to keep up with her teammates, and it was hard not to be the center of attention or give orders. In time, she relished the team camaraderie and learned to help others shine, earning a partial soccer scholarship with an academic one. She learned she could excel on the field, with her best friends rooting her on. Of course, Sam and Chloe were also there to support the guys. *Beau knew soccer was what I needed... that part of the confession will have to stay with me—he'd never let me hear the end of it.* One day, she would thank Beau for pushing her out of her comfort zone. She finished her breakfast and savored the last drops of Coke before writing in her journal.

Sitting across from Sam, Matt leaned back in his chair, nursing his first cup of coffee, and smiling at how Chloe and Beau could resume their antics just like they did when they were kids. *I hope she'll be comfortable enough to joke with me like that. Growing up with them was the best time of my life. What would I have done without them? I guess I would have burned out in elementary school. Mr. Intellectual. Mr. Abnormal.*

"Matt, you're bleeding again, and you tore the knees out of your jeans. Come to my house, and I'll fix you up," said seventh grader Beau. "We'll trade clothes, and Mom can sew up your jeans.... On second thought, you're taller. We should cut off your jeans and make shorts out of them."

"Mom's going to have a fit. She says I'm grow-ing out of my clothes too fast and wants to save them for my brothers. You know she'll ask how I tore them *this* time."

"Tell her you were saving Sam from destruction… again."

Keeping Sam's plans in check meant reading Dad's law books on North Carolina statutes to keep them barely legal. He dove into his memory bank while watching Sam eat her omelet and remembered another egg situation.

"Sam, what you're proposing is illegal," said Matt. "We can't go into Mr. White's chicken house for eggs without permission. I don't care if he is away for the weekend; it's trespassing and theft. However, if you leave a note for him with some money to pay for the eggs, I'll go to his next-door neighbor and explain that Chloe needed them to bake a cake, which should be alright. Otherwise, we shouldn't do it."

He sighed. Brainiac Matt. What a rotten nickname. *Why didn't I make a few "Cs" in math, as Beau suggested? But Dad was right to send me to high school and community college to take math and science classes. Being five or six years younger than everyone else was awkward, but tutoring the older girls who were having trouble was fun.*

Matt snickered out loud, thinking about high school. Back then, Beau had a thing for older women. "Man, you've got it made; all those college girls to choose from. Could I sit in on your classes, or could you set me up with one or ten women there?"

And things with Beau hadn't changed. This morning, he checked out some European women bussing their plates before walking out the door.

Matt shook his head. He picked up his ordered

omelet, refilled his coffee, and sat back down across from Sam, who was studying her schedule for the day. It was a good thing she tutored him in English. Otherwise, he wouldn't have graduated from high school, much less college.

"*Merde alors!* Sam, please explain to me again why we use "me or I" in this sentence. French is so much easier."

"If you have trouble writing your papers, use the edit mode on your computer, or let me look at them before you submit them," Sam beamed. "It feels good that I know something you don't know." *She screamed when I hugged the stuffing out of her, and Beau was ready to pummel me. He had a thing for her then, but why didn't I realize it?*

Matt studied Chloe and remembered her influence. *Helping my brothers with homework and Chloe's idea to turn our kitchen into a laboratory after she tried to teach me to cook inspired me to consider teaching. It was brilliant. We killed three birds with one stone: math, science, and dinner.* "Today, we'll learn about fermentation, and Chloe will teach us to make bread." *Boy, she could cook.*

The laboratory morphed into a tasting kitchen; we were her guinea pigs. Sam and Chloe ate in moderation, always on a diet, but Beau and I inhaled everything and gained twenty pounds before entering tenth grade.

"If we expect to make out with all the women in high school," Beau complained, "then we need to burn mega calories. We should run lots of miles every day."

He was right on multiple levels because running became my sanctuary, but for Beau, discussing history and politics may have been his impetus for going into teaching... until girls became his favorite topic. He taught me everything about girls, or at least what he thought he was an expert on. Matt's cheeks became warm, thinking of times when he had to seek Beau's advice.

"It happened again yesterday. I was on my way to English class, and a gaggle of girls followed me around giggling," said Matt. "They trapped me against the wall, and while one girl ran her hands across my chest, another tried to kiss me... I heard something about a Valentine's Day dance, and I couldn't escape them fast enough."

"I'm confused," said Beau. "Girls were falling all over you... One tried to kiss you, and you couldn't run away fast enough?" He doubled over laughing and then fell on the floor, laughing some more.

"You're not helping... I'll ask Chloe. She'll know what to do." Matt sought her out, "Chloe, I need your help." He led her to a bench and explained the situation. "It was embarrassing. What should I do?" Even then, she turned my world upside down.

Chloe was gentle. "Do you... like any of those girls?"

"No, not at all. I...I like...you," said Matt softly. "I don't want to lead them on, but mostly, I don't want to hurt you. I have strong feelings for you, and I hope you feel the same about me. Do you?"

Chloe nodded.

"I don't want to kiss anyone else either. I hope I'm not presumptuous, but I want to tell everyone we're dating. Is that okay?"

"Yes, and it's about time, Matt. I didn't think you'd ever come around."

She leaned in and touched her lips to mine. Our first kiss was tentative at best, but mind-blowing. *We were our first at everything in love, and being clueless, Sam and Beau knew we were meant to be together. It didn't affect being part of the group, even during the first two years in college. We were so young and idealistic—everyone thought we'd get married, but the breakup was devastating. I lost my soulmate, and part of me died.*

The pressures to hold onto my academic scholarship, graduate in two years, and finish a master's degree in engineering in another two years were the only things that challenged me intellectually. Thankfully, Beau stuck by me as my only friend. *What will I do now that being near Chloe has turned my world upside down? Again.*

THERE WAS A loud belch. Beau. After he'd consumed three plates of food. He'd gotten the moans he was looking for. Grinning, he leaned back in his chair and patted his stomach. "I have an urge to fill a fourth plate. Why not? We'll be on the road all day, possibly hours before the next meal." He went to the buffet line and loaded it up. *Sam will want this apple, and Matt needs a banana. Chloe likes blueberries and strawberries.* The apple and banana went in each front pants pocket, and Chloe got a small plate that he carried in his left hand. He strolled over to the table and gave his presents away before sitting down. He flexed his knife and fork muscles over his plate and ate silently while lost in thought.

Being with Chloe and Sam felt right in Paris, of all places. He exhaled loudly. Losing them in college changed his world. He should have been there for Chloe and Sam. He should have maintained their friendship, and the regret burdened him for years. It was surprising they were speaking to him.

Chloe, Sam, and Matt were like family, keeping him grounded, and growing up with them was the best time of his life. *I was easily angered. I didn't mind using my fists and sported black eyes and bruises, defending my sisters from bullies. Sports contained my inner aggression through wrestling, soccer, and football, making me tough enough to earn a scholarship so that I could explore other facets of myself. They rooted and challenged me to improve, yet I let them down, but no longer.*

Beau studied Matt's profile. He was quiet as usual, but there was something different in how he looked at Sam and even more so at Chloe. Longing? Hope? *Nah, can't be.*

Matt was the brother I always wanted. Samantha, I admired and loved the most, but Chloe was the one I protected at all costs. She looked to me like a brother, trusted me, sought my advice, and shared sensitive things others would have laughed at or condemned us for.

Beautiful, petite, quiet, and shy, Chloe was an easy target for mean girls and bad boys. Matt was mainly off campus, and no one would mess with her when Sam was with her. *When Chloe was alone, she was in the crosshairs until I took care of it. Being captain of the football and soccer teams had its perks—my guys ensured she was shadowed, escorted at school, or even in town when they saw her. Even though she had bodyguards, on occasion, there were problems. She developed secret admirers vying for her attention and frequently had flowers and trinkets left at her locker.*

"Beau, I don't know what to do. My locker was open again, and I found boxes of candy, flowers, and cards inside. There were three invitations to dinner and a movie, and two guys asked to escort me to the Valentine's Day dance. They were all so sweet, and I'm so flattered—"

"But you're waiting for that big lug of a genius to ask you, right?" She blushed, nodding. "Don't worry. I'll handle it—"

"Nicely. I don't want to hurt anyone's feelings, and please tell them I loved the gifts."

"You got it, Clo." She threw her arms around me and kissed me on the cheek.

"Please don't tell Matt, okay?"

"Yeah, yeah, yeah."

I would have done anything for her—until she broke Matt's heart. He hurt so much and needed my support, so I chose him over Chloe and Sam. He shook his head. Matt was worth it then, but not between Sam and me now. Chloe, I'm not sure, but seeing her now means forgiving her so I can be her friend again. I've missed her, so I will. I only hope it doesn't hurt Matt.

CHLOE SMILED AT Beau when he delivered the fruit. "That was thoughtful. Thank you." *Wow, he remembered these were my favorite.* She grinned, realizing he still had the same voracious appetite as he did when he tried my culinary experiments long ago. *Who knew the gang would do almost anything for food? It kept them together and out of trouble more than they knew.*

In some ways, it's natural to be together, yet so much time and experience have separated us. Beau has already tried hard to get us back to where we were, even though he gave me up for Matt years ago. His rationale back then was understandable, but losing him hurt as much as losing Matt. And now? When we leave Paris, will he prefer Matt over me? I can't take the chance. This time, it can only be fun and games... no commitments or expectations. No future.

Chloe watched Matt looking at his phone, enthralled in studying something mathematical. *I loved him so much, and even though long-distance dating was hard, I thought we would make it. When he broke up with me sophomore year, everything changed, and I hated that Beau and Samantha had to pick up the pieces by choosing sides. Yet, without that experience, I wouldn't be who I am today.*

It was a blessing to go to college purely for the love of learning. Grandmother's trust fund guaranteed no pressure to find scholarships, and she even left a nest egg for after graduation, but I had no clear direction. An artist-in-residence internship fostered a passion for my painting and photography. Being required to teach art in the community center made me realize that teaching was my forte. A fire was ignited, and it's never been replaced by anything or anyone.

Chloe rubbed her chest. Her heart twinged, reminding her not to dwell on the past but to live in the present. Paris. *Will I survive them? Him?*

Matt took Beau's tourist map and spread it on

the table. It crinkled as he refolded it, getting Chloe's and Sam's attention. "The day after tomorrow, we have the guided tour of Montmartre, but there's a self-guided walking tour that Beau and I want to run early tomorrow morning. We'll let you know if we find anything interesting." Sam ducked her head, pouting. "What? Sam, do you want to run it with us?"

"No, that's okay."

Chloe jumped in, "Of course, Sam does. You guys like getting up early, and I don't. I can sleep in and have the bathroom all to myself for once. Then we can have breakfast and head out. If you don't mind, please take my little camera and snap some pictures."

"All right, let's do it." Sam was so excited that the three of them were running together. She slapped her hand on the table, shaking the coffee in their cups. They all jumped and then laughed at her.

Taking charge once more, Sam brought out her schedule for the week. "Today would be great for sightseeing, museum visits, and shopping. If that's okay, we should meet back in the lobby in about fifteen minutes."

THE HOP ON Bus stop was less than two blocks from their hotel, across from the Moulin Rouge. The Moulin Rouge. Beau studied the iconic feature, elbowed Matt, and even turned in his seat on the bus to look some more. A broad smile and wagging eyebrows signaled a plan in the works.

"Oh no," said Matt. "Whatever it is, I won't like it."

"Yes, you will."

The bus passed along the Avenue des Champs Élysées, where famous designer houses promised haute couture and sophisticated extravagances for those with disposable income. Chloe sat by the window with Sam sitting next to her. Her camera was ready to take preliminary photos of ideas and things she might want to return to see.

Sam reverently spoke the names as she touched Chloe's arm: "Dior, Cartier, Christian LaCroix, Chanel, Hermès... I know I can't afford to shop in any of them, but you certainly can, and I can drool. I say we take Mimi shopping or have our pictures taken in front of the shops."

Chloe's eyes glassed over. Shopping was the only thing that made her eyes do that, leaving her salivating. It didn't matter if she was broke or in high cotton. Window shopping and trying on clothes were just as good as buying. No, cross that out. Sniffing out bargains, making a purchase, and looking like a million bucks gave her a shopping orgasm.

"I'm in. The summer sales in Paris start on the twenty-fifth, and it's said there are designer discounts for as much as seventy percent off. That's two days from now. Let's do a recon today, ask Claude for some information, and I say ditch the guys for some shopping therapy," exclaimed Chloe.

"We heard that. Where you two go, we go," said Beau.

"Right," said Matt. "Besides, I look good in designer clothes. No way am I passing up a seventy percent off sale." Everyone turned to face him. "What? I modeled in college to help make a few extra bucks, and I need a new Armani raincoat." Their snickers became full-blown laughter, but he shrugged it off.

"It's settled then. We're going shopping," said Sam. Beau groaned. Sam pointed at him. "You can hold our packages." Chloe giggled. "Don't worry, any designer worth their salt will have chairs. Besides, you'll get to see us model things." She wiggled her brows.

Matt continued to rib Beau, "I think it's time you ditch the khaki pants for something less collegiate. I'll help you shop." Chloe giggled again, and Sam joined her. "Then again, you're stocky. I'm not sure European cuts will fit. You could buy a hat or a man purse."

"You talkin' to me?" Matt was at the end of a one-finger salute. "I'll hold the packages, so shut up," growled Beau.

Each person pointed out and commented on things they passed. At a stoplight perpendicular to a lush tree-covered boulevard, Chloe noticed a man walking four designer poodles with exaggerated poufy poodle cuts dyed pink and lavender and matching painted toenails. She smiled and took a few photos as they crossed the street.

Her camera snapped again, catching a young man in his early twenties approaching a black wrought iron trash can. He casually leaned over and dropped in two red boxes with white stripes, each the size of a deck of cards. Strange.

Thirty seconds later, an older man in his thirties, dressed in black jeans and a black t-shirt, with short, cropped blond hair wearing an earring in his left ear, reached into the waste bin, pulled out the two boxes, and kept walking. Again, Chloe snapped some photos. Light reflected off her lens, catching the second man's attention. He looked up, realizing he had been photographed.

Uh oh.

The boxes could have contained anything: money, drugs, or even spy secrets. Chloe had not only witnessed the drop-off and pick-up but also photographed both. She lowered her camera and tried to look away nonchalantly.

The bus slowly moved. The man pulled out his phone and snapped photos of Chloe and the others. He talked on the phone while keeping pace with the bus creeping down the street. The bus accelerated, and the man stopped. Chloe strained to look for the man out the window. He had taken photos of the bus and the bus number. Crap!

She was dumbstruck. What did she witness? She frowned and sat back in her seat to think. It had to be something illegal. "Oh my God, I've done it again."

"What have you done?" asked Sam.

Chloe didn't answer. She scrolled back through the photos she had taken and held the camera so Sam could see as she moved the images forward.

"Chloe... not again. What's wrong with this country? I want to live. Beau, Matt. We have a problem."

Chloe passed the camera to the guys to review. Matt sighed, "Let's think about this. We have two more stops before we arrive at the Louvre."

"The greatest trick the devil ever pulled was convincing the world he didn't exist," said Beau. "Well, the devil's made another appearance. Nothing's changed except the players. We keep calm, vigilant in public, and always stay together."

He pulled out his phone, took a photo of the second man, and sent it to their phones—just in case. "Keep your enemies away and your friends closer."

"That's the first time I've ever heard you misquote *The Godfather*," said Matt.

"*The Godfather* got it wrong. We can't; we won't let anyone hurt them." Matt fist-bumped Beau.

MATT COULDN'T CONTAIN himself seeing the Louvre. "This is the world's most visited museum, so it'll be ultra-crowded. Originally, it was a medieval fortress, but in the fourteenth century, it became the royal palace for Charles V and other kings until 1793, when it became the Louvre Museum. There are steps throughout, and the elevators are in unusual places, so having a guide today will make our visit easier."

"This is research for me, and it's tax-deductible, so the tour is my treat here and at the Musée d'Orsay," said Chloe. Beau rubbed his hands together. Sam rolled her eyes.

Their guide brought a wheelchair for Chloe to the ticket kiosk in front of the Louvre's glass pyramid. Beau winced, hearing their tour would last two and a half hours. "It's a Good thing we brought snacks to tie us over until lunch," said Beau.

They entered an elevator and headed below ground. Under his breath, Beau spoke to Matt,

"Hey, I'm not too proud to receive the VIP treatment. If it gets us out of here faster, why should we fight it?"

"You might be able to fool most people, but I know you want to see the Rose Line and the bottom of the glass pyramid... the *DaVinci Code*, hmm? And then there are the Phoenician, Egyptian, and Grecian works I know you're dying to see," said Matt.

"Well, I've never seen a mummy up close, and it would be pretty cool to see a mummified cat."

"Uh-huh. I bet you can even read Hieroglyphs. Can't you?" asked Matt.

"Not all of them."

"Smart ass."

The tour began on the uppermost level with seventh-century French paintings. Beau and Matt hardly listened to the tour guide when Beau yelled, "Hey, wait. Look at this painting, *The Cheat* by George de La Tour. Check out the woman at the table... It's Meryl Streep."

Everyone around the friends stared as they all talked at once, "It's Meryl Streep." They laughed so hard that one of the attendants at the end of the gallery gave them the evil eye.

The tour guide cleared her throat, then gave them a brief explanation. "La Tour's realistic painting style contradicted other painters then. Here, a young man is exposed to three major temptations admonished by the moral standards of the day: gambling, wine, and lust, which were presented comically. As a result, he became a popular artist in the twentieth century."

"I need a copy of this to go over my poker table," said Beau.

"Yeah, and you love Meryl Streep too. A twofer," said Matt. Sam rolled her eyes.

They took the elevator down one floor to ancient Egyptian antiquities, and Beau was so intrigued with the exhibits that Matt had to drag him forward several times to keep going. The guide explained to Beau, "I think you will like the lower floor of Greek and Roman antiquities with the sarcophaguses and royal mummies of Egypt." Beau's eyes widened, and his hand covered his chest.

"The cats must be there." He slapped Matt on the back. "Wait till you see the mummifying tools they used to smash into the skull, scramble the brains, and pull the pieces out through the nostrils. Ingenious. And the canopic jars hold the organs they surgically removed with sharpened obsidian."

Matt barely managed to keep Beau from ditching the tour and heading down to the next floor.

Without warning, the sounds in the hall ahead became almost deafening, and the space between the walls was so crowded that it was impossible to traverse. Beau and Matt were on the alert. They surrounded Sam and Chloe and scanned the crowd around them. "What's going on? Is there a problem?"

Matt had his phone out, snapping random photos of the crowd. He leaned over Chloe's shoulder and said, "Don't be scared, Darlin. We're watching. Keep your things tightly in your lap."

Chloe scrunched her eyebrows, automatically reaching for Sam's hand and then pulling her closer to the wheelchair.

The tour guide leaned in and yelled, "Don't mind the noise. It's always like this around the

Mona Lisa. The attendant knows we are coming, and he will move the people along so that we can move closer for a better look." She spoke into her walkie-talkie. "Here we go."

The group gasped as they faced the *Mona Lisa.*

Beau was quick to snark, "It's tiny. I was expecting something big enough to hang over the fireplace, not something I need binoculars for." He leaned in to read the sign. "According to the plaque, it was painted on wood. Da Vinci must have been a cheapskate."

Chloe wasn't fazed by his remark, one typical of her students, so she assumed the teacher role at the museum. "This was painted in the sixteenth century. Artists commonly painted over works that didn't sell or when they couldn't afford expensive canvases, which were hard to find, so many artists used wood."

Matt moved in front of Chloe's wheelchair so he could study her. He marveled at her knowledge of painting styles, artists, and art history, but her excitement as she spoke led him and the group to listen intently.

"Degas is my favorite impressionist. He and Mary Cassatt were constant companions. They were considered figure painters, using theater people as their subjects. In the 1880s, she was the only American at the forefront of Impressionism in Paris and America. Sadly, they had a falling out, and both died old and unmarried."

"That's so sad. Do you think there might have been more to their relationship?" asked Sam.

"Possibly. I also believe Degas was jealous of her artistic growth and couldn't get past it."

"That's a man for you," said Sam.

"Hey, we're standing right behind you," said Beau.

Sam gave him the sweetest smile, "I meant for you to hear that."

"Children, no pushing and shoving; I'm getting to the best part." Chloe started again. "My favorite Degas paintings and sculptures are of dancers: ballet dancers, Paris opera dancers, and even the cancan dancers of the Moulin Rouge—"

"Cancan dancers, that's what I'm talking about," said Beau. Sam smacked him. "What?"

Chloe rolled her eyes. "Dancers train from an early age—petite with strong legs, ankles, and feet. Being a dancer from a poor or middle-class family was tough. She needed a sponsor, usually a man, and you can imagine what expectations came with the sponsorship. Degas was sympathetic to their lives. You'll see more of his work when we go to the Musée d'Orsay."

Beau shifted from foot to foot as he played with his cell phone. The guide led them to the lower floor to see the sculptures and antiquities: Venus de Milo and Aphrodite from Greece, and the Rebellious Slave statue by Michelangelo, which got his full attention.

"So, Chloe, why are Michelangelo's sculptures huge with exaggerated feet, hands, and… a smaller, you know… as compared to the rest of him?" asked Beau.

"They're called penis and scrotum. You're a big boy. You can say it, and we all know about them." Beau coughed, and Matt snickered. "The Renaissance artists mimicked the ancient Greek and classical Roman styles thinking that the nude male form was perfection with muscles, body, and facial proportions being the most important features, while the penis was the least important—"

Both Beau and Matt snorted.

She cleared her throat. "Another theory is that the reproductive parts were kept small for modesty's sake. Much of the art was commissioned by the church; sometimes, fig leaf coverings were added, which could be removed later. Experts believe that Michelangelo's hands were sculptured after his own—"

"The hands may not have been the only thing he modeled... size-wise," said Beau, fist-bumping Matt. Sam snickered, and Chloe tried to hide her smile. The tour guide rolled her eyes as they moved on to the elevator for the end of the tour.

CHLOE EXITED THE museum gift shop with two filled shopping bags of mostly Degas souvenirs. She moved awkwardly, holding them against the crutches. Matt's eyebrows raised, learning she had spent over five hundred dollars without batting an eyelash. "It's research," she said.

"I know, tax deductible, but... you'll need a bigger boat." Chloe's eyes widened. "Here, let me carry these for you."

"I didn't even think about that. You're right; I will need another suitcase, and you're willing to carry these? Thank you. I owe you." Matt lifted his fingers to stroke her cheek. She was mesmerized and didn't move. She didn't breathe. He dropped his hand, looked down, and picked up the packages.

Chloe stared at him. She blinked a few times and wondered what it would feel like to have him touch her. Silly girl. It wasn't going to happen. She would never let it happen. She breathed again and regained a casual pose as Beau and Sam approached them.

Matt cleared his throat and looked toward the escalators—there wasn't one going back to the outside. "How do we get out?"

"We'll go through the Carrousel du Louvre shopping center. We can pick up lunch and head to the gardens on the other side of the mall to have a picnic." Chloe pointed to the back exit where people were coming inside the Louvre through security.

They bought sliced cheeses, assorted meats, baguettes, and four bottles of orange fizzy drinks and then made their way to the commonly found green park benches. While they ate, Beau illuminated them on the mummification process, starting with washing the body and then removing the brain and internal organs with specialized tools, except for the heart, which was left inside. Then, the body was surrounded and filled with Natron to absorb bodily fluids. Once desiccated, the body was packed with fragrant oils, wrapped in linen, and covered in resin to seal it.

"The Persian word for the resin is *moumia*, and that's why we call them mummies," said Beau. "After seventy days, the mummy's burial rituals of purification and preparation for the afterlife are complete." Chloe, Sam, and Matt were spellbound, mouths open, staring wide-eyed. His descriptions also took their appetites. "What? I didn't give you all the gory details. See, I can eat." He picked up his baguette and consumed it with enthusiasm.

Beau loved to use ghastly details to make them

squirm. Once their food was packed and purchases gathered, they moseyed toward the Hop on Bus stop for Notre Dame.

"It's hard to believe that it burned. Look at it now, it's fully restored. Let's go in," said Matt. "Would you like to hear about the interior's design?"

"No," said Sam and Beau together.

"Thanks, but I'd rather look around and soak up the atmosphere," said Chloe. "That is, if you'll wheel me around."

Matt grinned and slowly rolled her through the different parts so she could take some photographs. An hour later, holding more gift bags, Chloe wanted to walk outside.

"I think I'll do some renditions of the outside in stages from its original design, through the burned phase, and now. I hope to convey beauty, sadness, and hope." She took photographs and hobbled around the grassy areas where other artists sat sketching, marveling at how they captured the cathedral.

"Should we be concerned with residual lead contamination from the building?" asked Beau.

"Not now," said Matt. "The lead dust in the air and water has been handled. However, if you'd rather drink a gallon of milk instead of wine to keep your fears away, go for it."

"No thanks, I can't eat that much cereal."

Four blocks from Notre Dame was a street of moderately priced shops and the Zara department store. The guys grumbled. Chloe looked at Sam as she squealed, "Look out, credit card, here I come."

They spent two hours shopping while Beau and Matt scanned their phones. The girls found capris, matching tops, skirts, and slinky dresses. The guys weren't interested in shopping, but whistled in appreciation of their models. Less than a block away, they found a sports shop full of soccer gear. Sam, Matt, and Beau bought soccer jerseys, socks, shin guards, and cleats, and rationalized that they didn't want Etienne to keep them from playing.

The cleats needed prepping before they could be worn. When they returned to the hotel, they each took a warm shower with their socks and cleats on and then let them dry on the windowsill with newspaper stuffed in their toes. Once dried, they rubbed "leather food" into the uppers, walked around in them, and jogged around the block a few times to help them mold to their feet.

Without thinking, Chloe left the trio and hobbled to the store across the street that sold scarves, berets, and tourist items. In Matt's periphery, he watched her go. A man and woman, perhaps the same ones from the cemetery, followed Chloe inside.

Matt ran to the door and yelled, "Wonder Woman."

Beau and Sam flinched. They grabbed their purchases and followed Matt into the store, hovering at the entrance. The mystery woman casually reached down, picked up Chloe's backpack, and walked toward the door. Sam pushed a clothing rack in front of the woman, blocking her exit. She fell, and Beau picked up the backpack.

Sam helped the woman up. "Are you okay?"

"Oui, merci." The woman departed, but Beau saw her talking on her cell phone, walking down the street while the mystery man feigned trying on a jacket as he spoke to one of the salesclerks. Beau snapped their photos so they could compare them with the ones from the cemetery.

Chloe took out Mimi, and Matt helped her pose with the scarves. Then, she paid for her items without knowing they had protected her. They exited the building and returned to the hotel.

Chapter 8

"MATT, YOUR ROOM is... clean," sputtered Chloe. He chuckled. The beds were made, the clothes hung, nothing sat on the floor, and even the desk was neat.

"Beau had a major transformation in college, and now he hates clutter unless it's poker night, but once it's over, he won't go to bed until everything is spotless. I can't go anywhere with him without him imposing his rules," said Matt.

Beau appeared at the door carrying Chloe's desk chair, followed by Sam with two bed pillows that would make the room cozy for working on their contest requirements. Everyone grabbed a spot while Chloe reclined on the bed. She uploaded photos to Mimi's Facebook page and the school's website and then accessed the images on the camera's memory card to show the others.

"These are bad guys," Chloe said, pointing to the man with the blue aviator sunglasses and his friend from the restaurant at Versailles. "This man and woman were in the cemetery and conveniently at the souvenir shop. I don't think they wanted to hurt me because there was plenty of time when I was alone."

Beau paced back and forth as he spoke, "In case you didn't know, the woman took your backpack, and we got it back. Your photographs must be important to someone. Could these people be good guys? Police?"

Matt handed the camera back to Chloe. "Let's assume that the man and woman are good guys," stroking his beard, thinking aloud. "But we spotted them. So, I suspect other people will pick up where they left off. We need to remain vigilant. The moment something happens, we report everything."

Sam's eyebrows furrowed, "I don't like having to wait until something bad happens."

Beau rubbed his neck. "That detective from the hotel deals with narcotics. The red and white boxes from the trash cans could have been drugs or drug money—"

"You mean ill-gotten booty or ill-booten got-ty?" Chloe giggled. They stared at her in amazement. "I like *Mash* reruns."

Having Chloe deadpan a line had them laughing.

Beau kissed her on the forehead and tried to reel them in. "Right. Then we should test the theory that good guys are following us, protecting us from the bad guys. We should keep doing what we're doing and watch each other's back. In the meantime," He twisted a pretend Hercule Poirot mustache, said in his best French accent, "We need to feed "...the little gray cells."

"Your gray cells are always hungry," Sam challenged. "Come on. Pizza should do the trick." The others enthusiastically agreed. Sam grabbed her purse and Beau's hand, then headed for the elevator.

While they walked two blocks to the pizza parlor, Sam was quiet. *What was she thinking?* Beau feared she would say they needed to keep things friendly without getting involved. He needed to get the conversation going positively while he still had a chance with her.

"It's a shame that we didn't do more stuff together in college," he blurted out.

"Uh-huh. You had your hands full with school, football, and women. If you forgot, you only paid attention when you had papers due. As I recollect, you still owe me."

"I guess I do. Name it, and you can collect anytime, anywhere."

"In the old days, I could come up with something outrageous, but I can't think of anything right now." She looked away from him to focus on the people passing her.

"That's not like you.... Then collect when we get home."

"Who's to say we'll even see each other then? After all, we haven't spoken in six years." She shrugged and lowered her head.

"That's true, but I've missed you," said Beau. Sam stopped in the middle of the sidewalk—her face questioned the comment. "Junior and senior years, when I could get away, I watched you play soccer. I even saw Chloe a few times in the stands, but I didn't want her to feel bad or the situation to be awkward, so I never did anything about it. I regret that. You were an excellent player."

"Huh! I *am* an excellent player and play at least twice a week. Nevertheless, in the past, with things as they were, I didn't want to hurt Chloe by keeping in touch with you, as you couldn't hurt Matt by associating with us. I'm sorry, too."

Beau placed his hands on her shoulders and turned her to him. "*We* screwed up, and we've wasted too much time. I don't want to keep going on like this. Paris will be good for us, you'll see. I'm predicting that when we get home, things will be better, and we'll be better than friends so that you can collect then."

Samantha cocked her head to the side, raised an eyebrow, and for an instant, Beau saw her eyes twinkle mischievously. "Okay, Vinny (his middle name as a nickname). Since you're so positive, I'm going to be positive too. I have several days to think about how I'm going to collect. Be afraid, be very afraid."

CHLOE'S ANKLE AND foot were painfully swollen. She had two pillows propped under her foot, a bag of ice on top, and she had taken Tylenol. Matt shared the bed's headboard but had scooted over to the edge to give her more room and remained there. So close. It was hard to ignore Matt's masculine scent teasing her subconscious.

She sent a long email to her agent about product ideas and Mimi's book. "Marty, I'm excited about developing the Versailles paper doll books. I got to meet with the director of guest services, and she thinks it's a wonderful idea, too. There will be dresses for girls, costumes for boys, and wigs for both. In fact, I can see this done with different historical sites, such as Mt. Vernon, Monticello, and Williamsburg. Let me know when we can start."

She downloaded all the photos, and her fingers flew over the keyboard. When she reached a stopping point, she snuck a look at Matt. His eyes were closed. A few minutes later, he spoke quietly in French. Chloe stopped working and listened. It was fascinating. *If I asked him questions, would he answer me?*

"Are you having fun with Chloe?"

"*Oui.*"

She giggled. "Do you still have feelings for Chloe?"

He answered, "*Oui.*"

Her heart stopped—her hand flew over her mouth to suppress a gasp. A few seconds passed before she whispered another question. "Do you... still love Chloe?"

"*Oui. Je l'aime.*"

Chloe's breathing became labored. She couldn't take her eyes off his mouth. She whispered back, "*Je t'aime, aussi,*" knowing he wouldn't hear her. "Would you like to see Chloe after Paris?"

He sighed, "*Oui. Elle m'a manqué.*"

Her brows scrunched together. She whispered to herself, "*Elle m'a manqué.*" What does that mean? She grabbed her French phrase book to look up the verb. *I have missed her.* OMG.

Chloe didn't have time to process the conversation. The door to the room opened with a click. Beau and Sam carried in three pizza boxes and lots of beer.

Beau yelled loud enough to wake Matt. "Chewie, we're back home." Matt ran a hand over his face and sat up. "Chloe, there's a message for you from Claude." He handed her an envelope. "He hired us a driver for our shopping trip on Friday morning. The driver will take us wherever we want and handle our packages. Here are the instructions." Chloe pulled out a letter and the receipt for the driver's bill. "How much will it cost for the driver?" asked Beau.

"Don't worry," said Chloe, "I've got it covered." Matt looked stern, and Sam had her hands on her hips; they wanted to pay their part. Chloe held up her hand to stop them from arguing. "How would I manage shopping with my foot? This is Paris. It's not like I'll get back here again. Besides—"

"It's tax deductible," the gang finished the sentence together, making Chloe giggle.

Chloe spoke to the three as she read the letter. "Claude says we need to go to the designer websites, sign up for their newsletters, look at their sale items, and hold what we want with a credit card. When we go to the store, we should try on things before we buy them. He also suggests we focus on the "Golden Triangle" of designers with showrooms in the eighth arrondissement; there are sixteen. We have four laptops, I say, divide and conquer." Chloe gave them each four names from the list. "Yell if you find something one of us might like."

They spent the next few hours surfing for and reserving items, laughing at what they could buy for Beau to make him fashion-forward. Matt went through the Armani site and called Beau to check out the clothing.

"I like this tan-colored crew neck sweater with

the gray Armani letters knitted in. It goes with my khakis," said Beau. "Wow, it was originally 1,750 Euros, and now it's on sale for 250 Euros. At seventy percent off, that's still almost three hundred dollars! I've never spent that much money on a sweater. Um, I don't know—"

"It goes with these gray pleated trousers," offered Matt.

"You're nuts. Those pants have a band around the bottom that hits above the ankle. I wouldn't be caught dead in them."

"You're right. You couldn't pull it off, but I could."

"You wear those with me," said Beau, pointing at him, "and I'll write you out of my will." Sam and Chloe looked at the picture and immediately agreed with Beau. They might work in Paris, but Matt would be a laughingstock back home.

Sam found Beau a belt bag. "Oh, hell no. I'm not wearing a fanny pack. You're hilarious... Hey, stop. Scroll back. Right there. I like that leather belt. See if there's a size thirty-eight because I want it, and it's only fifty Euros. Put my name on it, will you?"

Beau took the ribbing well and laughed along with them. Once he found a few items, he helped Sam find several slinky, sexy outfits. He toured the lingerie sections, hinting at things he wanted to see her in. Occasionally, he whispered naughty things in her ear; as expected, she swatted him often. Without her knowledge, he saved her a teddy, panties, a silk nightgown and robe, and some slippers from Dior as a late birthday present. He only hoped that he would get her size right.

Matt never found an Armani raincoat but reserved a black Gucci one instead, a Yves Saint Laurent gray suit, Italian loafers, two pairs of Armani pants without the ankle bands, a Givenchy brown sports coat, and two ties. He asked Chloe her opinion on the colors, and he reserved whatever she picked out.

Chloe went wild over a Dior asymmetrical dress, a coordinated skirt, blouse, and short jacket ensemble with laser-cut perforated fabric, two Chanel purses, two Givenchy scarves, a pair of gold wedge sandals, a pair of mules with criss-crossed pieces of leather in vibrant colors from Gucci, and lastly Yves Saint Laurent funky jewelry.

Each person found what they considered bargains and narrowed their selections to five designer stores. They finally said goodnight past midnight, happy about the shopping but grumbling that they had to get up for a six o'clock run the next day, except for Chloe.

Chloe tried not to boast about being able to sleep in, but in the end, she had less sleep than the others. She tossed and turned, thinking about Matt's conversation and her confusing dream. She was jealous of the woman he had been dreaming about because he wasn't dreaming of her. He told the woman he loved her, but she didn't have the right to be jealous. She had her own life, he had his, and they weren't destined to merge. Sometime in the early morning, she cried herself to sleep.

Chapter 9

SAM AND BEAU found Matt in the lobby, stretching his legs for the Montmartre run.

"You got up early. I thought I'd have to drag you out of bed," said Beau, yawning. "You look… different. I can't put my finger on it. What gives?"

"Nothing." Matt turned away from the others, trying to hide his burning cheeks. "I felt like getting up early." Beau shook his head and joined Sam in stretching.

"I highlighted the map where we should run this morning," explained Matt, showing them the route. "We'll go over the cemetery to Van Gogh's apartment, down to the Pink House, up to the Moulin de la Galette, then to the Renoir Gardens, up the hill to Sacré Coeur, past Artist's Hill, down to the Wall of Love, and at last to the Boulevard de Clichy, past the Moulin Rouge.

"We can cool down by walking back to the hotel. Most of the famous sites are in neighborhoods with small shops and restaurants. At this time of the day, it should be clear, and it's hilly going up to the basilica, so it should take us a little over an hour."

Beau stuffed the map in his pocket while fixing their water bottles.

Matt slapped Beau on the back. "I'll race you to Van Gogh's." He took off.

Beau looked at Sam. "He's in a good mood. He's hiding something, and I'll find out what it is." He winked at her, and they took off racing to catch up to Matt.

IT WAS A glorious morning to run at a comfortable jog: with a blue sky, puffy clouds, and a slight breeze. Beau ran beside Sam most of the time but preferred staying behind her, watching her move, and never taking his eyes off Sam's sexy body.

"I know what you're doing. Get up here," yelled Sam as she turned toward him, catching him drooling. "You're such a perv."

"I'm sightseeing, and I like what I see." He tripped over a rock. Sam laughed at him and then sprinted ahead to run beside Matt.

"Oh wow, look at these old houses. I need to take some photos for Chloe." She stopped in the middle of the road and snapped a few photos, then continued to walk the sidewalk, peeking around each corner as she went. She approached a flower-covered trellis and pulled a yellow flower toward Beau. "Ooh, smell these." He sneezed. He sneezed again. "Poor baby. Serves you right for looking at my derriere. You wouldn't do that, would you, Matt?"

Matt was jogging in place, patiently waiting, and on cue, looked at Sam's derriere.

"You're a perv, too. I'm out of here." Sam pocketed the camera and took off running.

Beau fisted Matt's shirt in between sneezes. "You better not have looked at her butt."

Inside the fence, a dog growled and advanced toward them, snarling and showing his teeth. Matt pushed Beau aside and sprinted toward Sam, "Dog. Run."

Before the beast had time to escape his quarters, the three runners had gained a lot of distance while laughing hysterically—another successful escape.

ON THE WAY to Sacré Coeur, Paris was waking up. Shops were slowly preparing for the day. Brooms swished over sidewalks, windows were washed, flower boxes watered, and board signs announcing café specials were prominently placed by the doors. The scent of fresh bread wafted from patisseries while espresso machines hissed. Sam thought about what she would eat when she returned to the hotel.

"Beau, take some pictures, will you?" Sam handed him the camera, and she led Matt to sit on the wall at the edge of the basilica. "You and Chloe have come to an understanding. I'm glad. The past can't be undone, but despite everything that happened, I've missed you."

"I've missed you too, and I hope we can still be friends when we get back home."

"That remains to be seen…I warn you not to hope for anything more than friendship with

Chloe. She has changed significantly since college and has an active social life. You might say that she has taken a page from one of Beau's playbooks to date often and with several guys simultaneously."

"I see." His face turned to stone.

Sam's voice squeaked. "Wait a minute. Don't tell me you were thinking about getting back with her. Are you nuts? Absolutely not! That ship sailed long ago."

"What if I want to try? What if I still have feelings for Chloe? What if she... might... still have feelings for me? Then I must try."

"Jeez, maneez. You're crazy. You two may have struck a truce while we're in Paris, but she has a life back home, and you're not in it... Don't look at me that way. I had to talk her into letting you and Beau hang out with us here. If you stir things up and it goes south, it will be my fault, and Chloe will hate me. I can't let that happen."

Matt turned toward her and pleaded for her to listen. "What if we could put the past behind us and start over? I know it's asking a lot, but we were thrown together in that airport. Chloe needed help; deep down, I needed to be there for her. Call it fate, karma, or divine intervention, but this is our chance to make things right. Samantha, I need to try, and I need your... your blessing.... You could help things along."

"Oh no... If you do this, you are on your own. I'll always have Chloe's back, and if you hurt her, I will make sure your battered, lifeless body is dumped in the Seine River. Understand?"

Beau walked up and faced Matt. "That goes for me, too. Even if you are my best friend, on this, you're on your own, and I'll even help dump your body. Make damn sure this is what you want to do because I want to keep Chloe as a friend when we get home."

Sam faced Beau, realizing he was sincere about continuing their friendship, as well as with Chloe. *Could she hope for more with him?*

"I don't plan to hurt Chloe, so turning me into fish food won't be necessary, but I'm glad Chloe has you both to look after her." Matt pulled Sam into a sweaty, stinky hug. "I want to keep being your friend too, so I'm going to be extra careful, and I promise you, if she's not receptive, I will back off... forever."

Sam shook her head. Matt's promise was enormous and one she was willing to hold him to. Was any of it possible? She sniffed and wiped the sleeve of her shirt across her nose. She shouldn't get her hopes up. It wasn't fair to her, to Chloe, or the guys. Forever was a long time.

"You've been warned...I'll be watching. Let's go. I'm ready for some breakfast and a Coke." *Chloe and I need to talk.*

At seven-forty-five, the trio walked into the hotel elevators. "The tour guide will meet us at half past nine," said Sam. "We get lunch on the tour, but it'll be late when we return, so bring some snacks and water. Chloe and I will see you for breakfast."

Matt and Beau walked into their room. "You know Sam is going to talk to Chloe, don't you?" asked Beau.

"I'm counting on it."

IT ONLY TOOK Samantha three seconds to start talking after entering their hotel room.

Chloe was out of the shower, a towel wrapped around her, sitting on the bed, and combing her hair.

"You look like you had fun," said Chloe. "Did you get any good pictures?"

"I did, but if they're good, it's because of the camera, not me…. It felt like it used to be when we ran in high school, but that's not what I want to discuss." Sam pulled out a chair and sat across from Chloe. "Matt and I had an interesting conversation. He wants to stay friends with us after we get back home. I'm open to that, but how would you feel?"

"I'm certainly not opposed to him being your friend, but I don't know about him and me. I guess it depends on how things are going for us in Paris. It feels weird being thrown together, but I don't know. What about Beau? I want to stay in touch with him when we get home. What do you think?"

"We've talked about it, and Beau wants to continue being friends, but as you cautioned, we'll see."

Samantha omitted Matt's intentions of wanting to start over with Chloe—she would have hit the ceiling. Keeping quiet may have felt like lying, but Sam needed to protect her friend now more than ever. She was confident they could handle Matt and Beau as friends, but protecting their hearts would be tricky. If they weren't careful, it would devastate them all.

JEANNETTE BAKER, AN American ex-pat living in Paris for twenty years, met the group in the hotel lobby while the tour's small white van and driver parked along the curb. She pointed to Chloe's crutches. "Are you good to walk?"

"My ankle is sprained, but I have help." She smiled at her friends.

"There's a wheelchair in the van, and as a group, we will have handicapped privileges. If you ever get sick or need health advice, visit the pharmacy. It's the building with the white sign and a green cross, only three minutes away. The pharmacist can help with prescriptions or recommend a doctor or hospital to go to." She pointed down the street from the hotel.

"I understand you won a teacher's trip to Paris," added Jeannette. "Congratulations. Is this your first visit?"

Chloe said, "Yes. For all of us."

"Wonderful. I hope your stay here will be memorable. I'll be your tour guide for two days, and since you are teachers, I will add more information than normal if that's what you would like."

"Perfect," said Sam.

Jeannette passed out a map of the area with typical tourist sites highlighted. "I'll point out the most interesting areas, so ask me anything. Things generally don't open until ten o'clock, so we have some time. Follow me to the Montmartre Cemetery pedestrian walkway for a great vantage point for photos, and it's only a five-minute walk. Chloe, are you good?"

"Yes, thanks."

"This cemetery was once an open grave for the rioters of the French Revolution. In 1792, hundreds of Swiss guards were massacred defending the Paris imperial palace across from the Louvre."

Chloe shivered. "Now I'm envisioning hordes of zombies in clown uniforms, grunting in Swiss."

"Not Swiss," added Sam, "German—"

"It could also be French, Italian, or Romansh," corrected Beau.

"Ah. "Multilingual grunts," quipped Matt.

"Do you think zombies understand other zombies?" asked Chloe.

"Maybe they sound like Arnold… I'll be right back," offered Beau in the actor's accent.

"Arnold would control the zombies," said Matt.

They all nodded seriously, then laughed heartily.

Jeannette watched the four interact with her hands on her hips, eyes squinted, and she tried hard to follow the conversation. Teachers, huh? This was going to be a long tour. She cleared her throat to regain control.

"Montmartre was the most populated district in Paris, where the middle-class, working-class, and artists lived side by side for the last two centuries. This cemetery is the final resting place of many of those artists. Visitors should maintain a respectful attitude in silence."

Beau, Sam, Matt, and Chloe looked at each other with "oops" being mouthed, and then snickered.

"Why do I think you've already treated the cemetery like an amusement park? Please tell me you didn't get kicked out," pleaded Jeannette.

"Of course not," said Beau. "We're upstanding teachers…besides, that guard needs glasses. There's no way he could identify any of us."

Jeannette heard snickers. She cleared her throat once more.

"Relatives and visitors honor the dead with flowers and tributes. There are four other cemeteries in Paris, but the most visited is Cimetière du Père Lachaise, where the singer Jim Morrison is buried. He gets the most visitors and tributes than any other gravesite—"

Sam touched Beau's arm, "Don't say it."

"I volunteer for tribute," crowed Matt. Beau smiled as Sam rolled her eyes.

"Uh huh…. Now I get it… Away from school, you all act like kids." Jeannette clicked her tongue and steadied on with the lecture.

"Père Lachaise cemetery is the only one with a moulin, but it doesn't work. Moulin means mill. They look like windmills because they are wind-powered and have been used all over Europe to grind grain, press grapes, and crush seeds and flowers. Without wheat being ground, Paris wouldn't have the flour to make bread, delicate pastries, or create the essences for perfume, and you cannot think of France without thinking of wine. Let's head back to the van."

Jeannette stopped several feet from the van, and the group stopped behind her. A strange man waited by the bus driver's door; the regular driver was absent. She approached the man and chatted in French. He opened his hand, flashed something, and spoke once more. Jeannette frowned. She hurried to open the van door and explained to the group as they entered that their original driver had an emergency—this man was the replacement.

Matt had heard the exchange and calmly stated, "Wonder Woman is *Driving Miss Daisy*." The others stared at the new driver.

"This is Gaston." Jeannette tried to stay calm, but her voice cracked as she spoke again. "At one time, there were over three hundred wooden windmills in Paris, and even into the twentieth century. Technically, there are three windmills now; we will stop at two situated side by side, called the Moulin de la Galette, but first, we'll pass by the Moulin Rouge, famous for the Cancan.

"Cancan! That's what I'm talking about," cheered Beau. "What? It's a dance." Only Matt found the humor in it.

Sam and Chloe looked out the windows as they passed rows of lingerie stores and sex toy shops along the boulevard around the Moulin Rouge, only a few blocks from their hotel. Chloe elbowed Sam, and they both fanned themselves. Sam grinned and wiggled her eyebrows. Chloe whispered, "No way. Don't ask me to go in there."

"Chicken," whispered Sam.

"Bawk bawk."

"Three famous artists lived in Montmartre: Toulouse-Lautrec, Degas, and Van Gogh. They knew each other and admired each other's work. Degas and Lautrec were associated with the Moulin Rouge and influenced how the public viewed Paris, especially Montmartre. Where Degas was enamored with dancers, Lautrec loved the nightlife, painted people in a caricatural style promoting stereotypes, and cast cabaret women with the bourgeois men who watched them. Their art was adapted to new printing techniques, so posters became graphic art. Once Lautrec's posters were hung, they became souvenirs and brought him instant recognition. His most famous subject was the dancer, Jane Avril. Were they more than friends? Who knows?"

Gaston checked his mirrors. He spoke rapidly to Jeannette while maneuvering through traffic like a racecar driver, speeding through two red lights. Jeannette turned in her seat to talk to the group. "Gaston spotted some road construction ahead, so we're going to take a detour to see the apartment building where Van Gogh lived with his brother, Theo, from 1886 to 1888. Seatbelts, everyone."

Matt eyed the others and nodded. He held up three fingers on each hand, forming WW. By the time everyone understood, Gaston had returned the vehicle to the speed limit and in front of the apartment, where he had double-parked.

"It's privately owned, so we can't go in, but there isn't anything to see except for this plaque on the outside of the building," announced Jeannette.

"I am disappointed," said Beau. "I thought we'd see blood spatters on the floor from where he cut off his ear."

Chloe swatted Beau's arm. "Ewwww... Besides, that didn't happen in Paris, so he won't be in the zombie apocalypse either." Beau shrugged.

The van moved through narrow, one-way cobblestone streets, around and around like they were driving inside a maze. "Ah, we are in luck. La Maison Rose is open. We will make a short stop, and Gaston will park on the next street. I'll tell you more when we get out."

"Wow. It's… Pepto Bismol pink," said Chloe.

Beau frowned. "Is this a subliminal message for the public to eat elsewhere?"

Jeannette chimed in, "Yep, it is."

"The Pink House has been a restaurant since before 1850 and was frequented by Picasso. Sadly, the food is expensive and terrible, so we're only here for coffee and a pastry. At the top of this street, you will see the Sacré Coeur Basilica on Montmartre's highest point.

"This area used to be covered in vineyards. In the eighteenth century, one vineyard had a garden with a pond that Lautrec and Renoir liked to paint, but now only one vineyard has survived, Clos Montmartre. It produces only seventeen hundred bottles of wine a year. We will sample some of their amazing wine during lunch, and I know you will want to purchase a few bottles before we leave. Don't worry; they will bubble wrap them so you can carry them on the plane."

JEANNETTE WATCHED GASTON position himself in front of the Pink House entrance, wearing sunglasses and surveying the street area, speaking on his cell phone. He got Jeannette's attention and signaled to her, holding up five fingers before retreating to bring the van around five minutes later. Although their next stop was only minutes away, Gaston took a circuitous route, and twenty minutes later, they arrived at Moulin de la Galette for lunch.

Gaston drove to the lower parking area, semi-hidden from the main street. Everyone exited, and he was the last to enter the restaurant. The group sat on the outdoor patio under shade from the willows that bordered the river. Gaston distanced himself at a corner table with an iron fence at his back. He faced the front door, keeping the others within sight while being privy to their conversations. His protective posture mimicked what mobsters and police did in the movies. Beau caught Matt's eye, then raised his chin in Gaston's direction.

Jeannette noticed the action and quietly stated, "Drivers seldom eat with passengers so they can take care of business that might disturb the guests. Restaurants usually have a set plate and price for them to eat quickly and to prepare their buses for the passengers' departure."

Chloe nudged Sam, "He's as bad as you for needing a caffeine fix." Gaston had consumed several espressos, a chocolate mousse, and espresso cream for dessert. Sam picked up her glass of Coke and clinked it to Chloe's glass of water.

"I take it you all teach at the same high school?" asked Jeannette.

"Oh no," said Sam. "Chloe and I teach at East Carteret. Beau and Matt teach at Croatan in the same county, but we're about fifteen miles apart."

"So, how do you know each other?"

"We grew up together and were best friends for a long time... until... the second year in college—" said Matt.

"Until two days ago," said Beau, "we hadn't spoken to each other in six years."

"Seriously? But you live so close." Jeannette

leaned in, not wanting to miss anything.

Beau explained the situation as Matt and Chloe chose to look elsewhere.

"Six years… is a long time not to talk to someone who used to be your best friend." Jeannette took her time looking at each face as she spoke. There had to be more to the story; she was nosy enough to find out.

Sam sighed and cleared her throat before divulging the truth. "Honestly, when Croatan played East in sports, I went to the games and looked for Matt and Beau… they looked great and were doing well. My parents filled me in on all the gossip, so even though we hadn't spoken, over the years, I kept up with them."

"I didn't know that," whispered Chloe. "You never told me you went to the games."

Sam mouthed, "I'm sorry."

Beau spoke up. "I knew when you were there because someone from Harkers Island would tell me. I always scanned the crowd, and sometimes saw you, but a coach can't leave the team, so I never spoke to you. I'm sorry. I should have done more to stay in touch."

Sam studied Beau intently, their eyes locked with so much more to say. He mouthed, "Later," determined to make time for them to talk and work things out. Sam nodded slowly.

"Since this seems to be confession time, I guess I'm next," said Matt. "My dad is friends with Chloe's dad, and I got periodic updates." His face turned red, "I even own two of Chloe's paintings of old shrimp boats… They were auctioned off to benefit the Core Sound Museum, so I bid on them."

"You did? Why would you want them after what happened in college?" asked Chloe.

"They reminded me of growing up on Harkers Island and our great times together. They're beautiful and… because you painted them," said Matt. He shrugged, embarrassed at divulging the secret. Chloe looked away in time to wipe at a tear before it fell.

Jeannette turned to Chloe and assumed the role of a therapist. "Weren't you curious about Matt and Beau?"

"I suppose so. It's hard to live close and not hear about their accomplishments, what they were up to… and even about their girlfriends. We may have gone our separate ways, but I've only wished the best for them."

"Interesting…Then, how did you all get together in Paris?"

Sam explained the contest and the rules. "We called a truce in the airport, and we're trying to rebuild our friendship. So far, so good." She fist-bumped Beau, and Matt laid his hand over Chloe's. "We're a work in progress, but I think we'll get there if we don't kill each other before we fly home." Beau winked at Chloe, and in an instant, they were all smiling.

Gaston pulled out a small notebook and jotted down a few things.

"Well, I wish you all the best of luck. It looks like lunch has arrived," said Jeannette. The conversation gravitated to the history of the restaurant, and the discussion of famous paintings by Renoir, Toulouse-Lautrec, and Van Gogh, inspired by this location. They sampled several wines, each choosing a different bottle to share later, and Sam's and Chloe's backpacks were perfect for returning them safely to the van.

An hour later, they stood at the bottom of the hill below the basilica. "The van will meet us at the top after you visit Sacré Coeur. Now, we'll ride the Funicular, or…" she said, challenging them, "you can climb the three hundred steps to the basilica."

"Huh! No sweat," crowed Beau. "Three hundred steps are nothing. I can easily beat Matt."

"In your dreams."

"What about me?" asked Sam. "I can beat you both."

"You're on," both guys said together.

"Go ahead, get sweaty," said Chloe. "I will enjoy sitting in an air-conditioned trolley, and then you three can take a taxi back to the hotel because no one will want to be near you. Then again, maybe you're afraid to ride the funicular."

"Huh!" said Beau.

Jeannette winked at Chloe. "Beau, this is a safe, modern funicular, but it has a lot of windows. I love the panoramic view, but sometimes, it can leave people weak in the knees. Don't worry; there are benches inside." Beau's mouth fell open, and Chloe snickered, patting his arm in a motherly way.

"I don't have problems with heights… Fine. I'll ride the trolley and look out the back windows."

Sam patted Beau's other arm. "I happen to have a barf bag from the airplane. Here you go." A low grumble emerged from his throat. He snatched the bag and tucked it into his back pocket.

Jeannette tried not to laugh as she led the four inside the waiting car. "These tickets will allow you to go to the front of the line at Sacré Coeur. I am not allowed to take groups inside, but there are information plaques at various stations and a shop for souvenirs. We'll be here for one hour, so look for my umbrella. I'll be in the shade by the wall."

Chapter 10

S ACRÉ COEUR'S WHITE travertine limestone walls gleamed in the sunshine. Matt was awestruck. He had studied all aspects of this basilica with the round domes, flying buttresses, gargoyles, grotesques, and two patron saints sitting astride bronze horses guarding the entrance to the main vessel. The building looked like it should have been from a long-ago century, yet it was completed in 1914 and fooled the visitors.

Beau opened the main door and held it for everyone to enter. The pipe organ played liturgical music carried to the back of the church and grew louder as they entered. This basilica was built to withstand a millennium of visitors, pilgrims, and a worshiping congregation. The friends entered in silent reverence and then moved to sit in a back pew to take in the surroundings.

Beau, Sam, and Chloe watched Matt closely.

Matt's eyes glazed over. He studied the travertine forming pillars, walls, and window casements for the Biblically inspired stories within the stained-glass windows: form and function. Architectural designs and mathematical formulas were spinning in his head. He mumbled, "Arcade...clearstorey. Transverse rib meets the longitudinal ridge... to a beautiful boss."

Beau touched Sam's arm. "If I have to listen to this brainiac, I'm going to knock him out, and when I do, an old nun half my size will bend my ear, haul me off to an alcove, paddle my hands, and I'll have to confess to a priest and then say ten Hail Mary's."

"You're having flashbacks, aren't you?" asked Sam.

Beau shivered. "Yeah. Come on." He exited the pew but waited for Sam to get Mimi from Chloe, and then they went off together.

Chloe scanned the interior, thinking about what she would photograph, not bothered by sitting in the wheelchair and waiting for Matt to return to earth. Glancing toward the main altar, she watched Sam and Beau walk swiftly through the basilica, stopping only a few times to read plaques and take photos of Mimi shaking hands with a statue or two and pretending to drink from an altar chalice before they were shooed away. Laughing, Beau and Sam hurried along before heading toward the gift shop to buy souvenirs and, more than likely, a Coke for Sam. She calculated they lasted all of twenty minutes.

"Matt." She touched his arm. "Matt." No answer. She touched his face with her fingertips, and he jolted back into the present. "Hey. I'm sure you know a lot about the architecture, so would you give me a short tour?"

His face lit up like a Christmas tree. "Of

course." Matt maneuvered Chloe's wheelchair down the aisles, stopping to point out unique features, assuming his teacher's persona. He moved away from her periodically to point at something that Chloe couldn't touch.

"Sacré Coeur was built in the Romanesque-Byzantine architectural style. Look at the vaulted ceilings and archways and how they are suspended in the air. I'm sure you want to look at all the stained-glass windows—my favorite ones are the rose windows." His deep voice, authoritative stance, and intelligence took center stage.

Chloe was mesmerized. "Tell me everything. I'm really interested." If she wasn't careful, her eyes were going to glaze over in admiration… and lust, listening and looking at him.

He couldn't have smiled any larger.

Chloe studied him as his head was slightly turned. His physique was more athletically defined, even since college, more handsome, and his voice was deep and sexy. Her eyes focused on his sensuous mouth. *No one has ever kissed me like he did.* She touched her lips, and her heart beat faster. As he spoke, she heard only about every fifth word. *I'm so screwed.*

Chloe had never confessed her artistic secret—Matt's lips, face, and other body parts had inspired her commercial artwork. Now, she focused on his hands, their size and strength, and remembered how he used to touch her. Hold her. Focus only on her. Make love to her. She shivered.

She raised her camera to take photos of what Matt pointed to. Only *he* became the focal point of each one. So what? Chloe rationalized that she would use his image as inspiration in future artwork. But if she were honest, she wanted to remember everything about him when they returned home, ultimately going their separate ways.

Chloe studied Matt's broad shoulders, his muscular arms, down to his waist, and lower. His soft, worn jeans molded to his backside like a second skin and down further to well-defined muscular thighs—her hands itched to touch all of him. If she could paint him, he would be the perfect male. *Naked. Oh boy.*

Her face felt warm from the images she had captured, and no architecture in focus. She looked up in time to find that Matt had finished talking and was walking toward her. Sitting in the wheelchair, she had the perfect view of the front of his jeans pulled tight. Since she had been staring, he knew she had been checking him out. Thoroughly. The corner of his mouth turned up, and his eyes twinkled. Her effect on him was unmistakable. More importantly, it affected her equally. *Snap out of it. He's a gorgeous man. Nothing more.*

"Is there anything else you'd like to talk about... or touch... before we move on?" purred Matt.

"Uh... no. That was... very enlightening. Lead on." No one would ever see the photos, and his image was burned into her brain. She casually wiped the moisture from above her lip.

Matt leaned down and whispered, "Let's go find some gargoyles and grotesques. You'll like them and they will photograph well." She sighed. His breath was warm. It tickled her ear, and the hair on her skin stood up. Thankfully, she managed to gather her composure exiting the church—

it would have been embarrassing to have the others notice. Outside, she photographed about a dozen icons, convinced they could be used as caricatures or cartoon-like images on tote bags or other souvenirs.

At noon, the tower bells rang, and the friends met on the stairs leading to the meeting place. "When a bell rings, an angel gets wings," announced Chloe. "I think angels are all around us, protecting us, especially on this trip." Matt, Sam, and Beau looked at her and nodded. "People can be guardian angels, and I'm thankful you all are mine."

Sam hugged her, "You're my angel, too. What would I do without you?"

"Probably starve," said Chloe.

Jeannette yelled their names, frantically waving the four to her. Gaston was agitated and briskly directed them to an empty mini train parked on the road by the basilica.

"Vite! Get on the train." Gaston led them to the front benches. He spoke to the driver while extending something in his hand and told Jeannette, "When you reach Pigalle, a black van and the driver, Pierre, will be waiting for you. He will take you to the Wall of Love, and I will meet you there." The four complied without asking questions.

Gaston handed Chloe's crutches to Matt and told the train driver to hurry. He placed the wheelchair in the van and followed the train to the top of the one-way street, parking it diagonally so no cars could follow. Then, he turned on his emergency flashers and propped open the hood, feigning engine trouble.

Chloe sat in the first compartment close to the engineer. Her boot took most of the room, so she was side-sitting from Sam, while Sam made herself as tiny as possible in the other corner.

"This train was designed for children in an amusement park," griped Beau. "It's going to kill my legs." Twelve separate compartments were coupled front to back so they could snake along the road, and each compartment had hard benches facing each other.

"It takes mostly families and tourists around this area," said Jeannette. Beau and Matt moved to the third compartment behind her. Knee to knee and body to body, they all twisted in their seats to watch as a black car stopped behind Gaston's van, and several young men jumped out.

Gaston leaned against the bumper, smoking a cigarette while looking at his cell phone. Suddenly, there was a heated discussion that could be heard everywhere. He remained calm, pretending that the van had broken down, pointing to the front of the van with the hood raised, both arms extended out, and palms upward. He shrugged. Chloe snapped a few photos with her phone.

"Good thing Gaston's van conveniently died. That was close," said Sam.

Minutes later, the whine of skateboard wheels over cobblestones grabbed Beau's attention. "We've got company. I think they plan to board us. Any suggestions?"

"Sam, what do you have in your purse that's a lubricant?"

"What are you thinking, Matt?"

"I'm not sure; I'm making this up as I go along."

Beau smirked, "Good one, Indiana."

Sam and Chloe looked frantically through their things. "We both have sunscreen spray and hand lotion." Sam handed them over.

"SPF 50. Really?" asked Beau.

"We're both fair-skinned, and I burn easily," said Sam.

Beau snickered. "Redheads get freckles, and I've always liked your freckles."

"I'm a strawberry blonde," said Sam, raising her chin. He snickered again.

Matt and Beau hurried to the back of the train and climbed through the open window to stand on the outside ledge.

Matt yelled to Beau. "Coat the top with lotion and then spray the railings with sunscreen. Hurry." Matt demonstrated, and Beau followed suit; seconds later, they were empty-handed. As the train steadily descended around a large curve, they managed to move back to the front compartment area behind Jeannette.

Matt pointed to the backpacks, "Find anything else that can be used as a weapon or that can be thrown in their faces, but they'll have to be close for that to be effective. If they reach the front, do whatever you can to push them off the train. Use the crutches. We'll move farther back and try to get rid of them there. If we get separated, call 999 for the police and head back to the hotel. We'll meet there." Matt tapped the conductor on the shoulder and spoke to him in French, "Drive as fast as you can and take the curves hard. We need to lose these guys." The driver understood, and so did Jeannette.

"You're fluent in French... Don't worry, I

won't tell." Jeannette pulled out a can of hairspray and a lighter. Instant flame thrower. She grinned as a distinct accent emerged. "I was raised in the Bronx." Beau fist-bumped her.

Chloe grabbed Matt's hand. "Be careful." He nodded, "You too." He kissed her hand before moving back a few seats.

Beau's hands cradled Sam's face. "Remember when we used to play king on the mountain?" His eyes twinkled. "This is just like old times." He kissed her softly.

"We'll take care of things up here, and I'm counting on you to kick some ass, like old times," said Sam. He winked at her and headed toward Matt.

IT DIDN'T TAKE long before four young skateboarders caught up to the train. They grabbed the metal carriage, trying to let the train pull them along. One guy hit a pothole that flipped his skateboard up on its nose and shot out from under his feet. He crashed face-first into the metal caboose—lip split, blood spurting from his nose, and at least two fingers were jammed or broken. With agonizing moans, he fell to the street.

The second guy grabbed hold of the back-end corner rail. He held out his other hand to catch the next guy, who managed to pull himself onto the top of the train. The lotion made him slip and slide, but somehow, he crept forward.

The two guys climbed on either side of the train while the one on top kept moving. Their slipping and sliding caused the train to bob and sway with their weight, and often they lost their footing. The fourth guy took a flying leap and landed on the bench in the last compartment. Chloe looked back and screamed.

The train driver watched the guys' movements in the rear-view mirror. He took the curves rapidly, hoping they would lose their grip. Then the driver whipped the train from one side of the road to the other, aimed for a low-hanging tree limb, and jerked the train into it. The guy on the top was hit and slid off, landing in a patch of thistles and brambles, screaming bloody murder, then he fell silent.

Two down, two to go.

Beau and Matt squared off with the last two guys, one on one.

Chloe struggled to get to her knees. She armed herself with apples and trail mix. Sam took a stance facing the guys, ready to use what she had learned from her self-defense class and street-smart commando tactics growing up. Jeannette had her hairspray ready while the driver whipped the train back and forth. One guy stumbled as the train switched to the other side of the road. Beau punched the third guy in the stomach and then finished him off with an uppercut to the jaw. The guy fell off the train and into an open garbage can butt first, head landing against his chest. Lights out.

The fourth guy swung into the compartment on Matt's side and kicked him in the shoulder; Matt fell to his knees. This guy scrambled over Matt reaching for Chloe. She yelled, furious at what the guy did to Matt and threw everything she had at him, but to no avail. Panicking, her hand touched the wine bottle in her backpack, and she swung it as hard as she could. It bounced off the guy's ear and smacked into his nose with two big thuds; his eyes crossed.

Matt grabbed the guy's ankles and pulled him off his feet as Jeannette sprayed hairspray into his eyes. He brought both hands up to his face, writhing in pain. Matt threw the guy off the train and watched him land on someone's front lawn. A large, growling dog moved toward the guy and, without warning, attacked his leg. His shouting could be heard for the next five minutes.

Beau high-fived Sam. "The name's Mr. Bond. James Bond."

"Nice moves, Mr. Bond."

Matt grinned at Chloe's hand still wrapped around the wine. "Great move, babe." He removed the bottle from her shaking hand and gave it to Sam to put back in the backpack.

Chloe quaked with an adrenaline rush. "I was scared, and yet I wasn't. The four of us are still great together, aren't we?" She reached for Matt and hugged him tightly.

"Yeah, babe. We'll always be good together." Matt gently pulled away but slipped his hand into hers over the back of the seat as they sat down.

"What do we do now?" asked Sam.

"Pigalle is about five minutes away," said Jeannette. "We'll get in the van and meet Gaston at the Wall of Love. I don't know what you all are involved in, but Gaston is a detective who will keep you safe."

"I think we can keep ourselves safe," snarked Beau. He and Sam fist-bumped each other.

Chloe turned toward Jeannette and explained everything that had happened.

"I see, wrong place at the right time," said Jeannette. "Considering today's run-in, I'm not sure you should take the Eiffel Tower tour or the river cruise tonight. It could be dangerous." The friends exchanged quizzical looks.

The mini train arrived at the Pigalle roundabout and stopped at the red light. A black van was parked to the right, with the driver standing by his door. He opened the sliding door for the group to get in, and they headed to the Wall of Love.

"I'm sorry about the train ride," said Jeannette. "The streets it travels on are lovely, and there are many small restaurants and shops to peruse. You can take a taxi there when it's safer to get a look."

"No thanks," said Beau. "Our trip was a lot more fun." The others grinned.

Gaston had cleared the area of tourists, so the group was alone by the time they arrived at the Wall of Love. He motioned for them to take a seat on two park benches. "My name is Detective Gaston Marvell, and your van driver is Detective Pierre Durand. We are here to protect you. Mademoiselle Davis, you took photographs of two dangerous men. One hasn't been seen since he went underground to get a facial reconstruction. Your photographs may be the only record of his appearance now. These men will not stop until they get the photos. I plan to give them a camera filled with tourist photographs to make them think you do not have the right ones. Once they have the camera, you should be safe."

Sam cocked her brow. "In other words, you used us as bait at Sacré Coeur, and now you're going to use us as bait again, so they get the camera?"

"You will not be in danger. I will protect you."

Sam laugh-snorted, "No thanks, we can take care of ourselves from these hooligans."

"Nevertheless, let me show you the photos on my camera," he said.

Chloe looked at photos of generic tourist sites showing Sam, Beau, and Matt in them. They had been followed from the beginning, starting with Versailles. Why? How? She turned away from Gaston, her lips formed a thin line, and her eyes squinted. "We've been played, y'all, from the very beginning."

"Detective, you know I'm a photographer, but my memory card won't help you. Each day, I download my photos to my computer and send them automatically to my agent or a cloud storage site to empty the memory card. That way, I never lose my photographs, and my agent can suggest what to photograph next. If you look, there are only a few photos on my camera now."

Gaston took her camera and scrolled through the memory card. He was stunned. "Is this the only one you have?

"Yes, of course." He studied her face. She gave him the best 'I'm telling the truth' look possible while looking him in the eye. She and the others had perfected that look at an early age, and they also mastered many other looks helpful in dealing with their parents, students, and the principal.

"Very well. My camera will be the decoy, so give your camera to your boyfriend." Chloe blushed, and Matt put her camera in his backpack and placed it on the park bench next to Sam's. Chloe laid Gaston's camera on top of that. "Now we wait," he said.

Jeannette sensed the hostility and took control to redirect her group's attention. "Since we are here, let me tell you about the Wall of Love." She motioned for them to follow her and beckoned them to touch the enameled lava tiles. "This monument was created to show that love can unify and reunite. Over six hundred tiles say, "I love you," written 311 times in 250 languages from ninety-two nations. People worldwide come here to find their language of love, and many marriage proposals occur here."

Sam handed Jeannette her phone to take photos of the four friends, which morphed into silly poses. Chloe and Sam jumped on the guys' backs, the guys picked up the girls like they'd carry them over the threshold, and then the guys pretended to beat their chests as they were thrown over their shoulders. The giggles and laughter were contagious; even Pierre and Gaston smiled at the antics. When Chloe and Sam landed on their feet, the mood changed again; each couple encapsulated in a private world where only the other one existed.

Beau pulled Sam into his arms, circling her waist, and she rested her hands on his biceps. He tried to kiss her, but she laughed at him as she pushed him away, "A public display of affection isn't appropriate." He frowned.

Sam's heart couldn't take it if he were only playing her, and she couldn't risk letting her guard down. She felt guilty and needed to make things better. She crooked her pinky up, challenging him to join his pinky to hers. "Friends?" she asked.

"More than even best friends," said Beau. "You want more than that, too, don't you?"

"Maybe. We'll see. I guess so…. I don't know."

She turned away from him, and he slapped her on the butt.

She lifted one eyebrow and tilted her head, "You're playing with fire."

"I like it hot, like you." He tried to grab her again but missed. "Sam… Grrrr."

She escaped from him, laughing, but what else could she do? They had fun together, and that was all she should have expected. It was better to be flippant than sorry, because things could get out of hand if she didn't keep her head straight.

Jeannette gave Sam her phone back, and then she and Beau moved to the bench to send copies to everyone.

"I didn't know you could be such a tease." Beau put his arm over Sam's shoulder.

"I'm having fun," said Sam, "and you're driving me crazy. So cut it out."

He whispered in her ear, "Never." Beau attempted to hold her hand. "You have such kissable lips."

Sam rolled her eyes. "Pfft."

"What? I'm trying hard to woo you, and you laugh. My self-esteem is shrinking."

Sam snorted.

Jeannette watched their actions and concluded they were in love, but Sam was fighting it. She turned back to Chloe and Matt to see how they interacted.

Chloe ran her fingers along the blue-black tiles and then over tiny red specks across the wall. "Are these significant?" She looked at Jeannette.

"When the red marks are put together, they form a heart, but as it is, the heart is broken because, according to the artist, there isn't enough love in the world," said Jeannette.

"That's so sad," said Chloe.

Matt covered her fingers with his. "I believe that a second chance at love can be greater and sweeter than love the first time around... Chloe, do you believe in second chances?"

She couldn't look at him. Their love had been a first love and a true love. They shattered like the red specks across this wall when their hearts broke.

"Sometimes second chances aren't deserved." She spoke without thinking, with enough venom to hurt. Why did she say that? What he did was in the past. They had gone their separate ways. They were older, more experienced, and more mature. *No matter what she did, she didn't need to be such a bitch. What harm would it do to meet him halfway?*

His face was unreadable.

She lifted her eyes to his. "If two people thought having a second chance was worth it, I believe it should come with a healthy dose of skepticism and a guarded heart... It would also take time to work things out."

"I agree... I believe fate brought us together in Paris for a second chance. Don't say anything. Think about the possibility, okay?"

He had planted the seed in her head and heart. "I'll think about it."

Being thrown together by winning the same contest for the same destination was uncanny. Matt's probably calculated the odds to be astro-nomical. *It's destiny to revive our friendship, but is it my destiny for a second chance at love with him?* She felt her eyebrows scrunch together. Matt squeezed her hand, and she squeezed back.

Skepticism and a guarded heart. She would take her own advice.

Whining, gravel crunching, and tires squealing over the sidewalk caused the group to turn that way. A guy on a bicycle was heading straight for the bench. The cyclist coldcocked Gaston and then reached over him, grabbing the camera. Before he could ride off, Matt took one of Chloe's crutches and threw it like a spear into the tire's spokes, throwing him off the bike and mangling the crutch.

Gaston grabbed the cyclist by the shirt, leaving the camera on the ground. Speaking in French, he said, "You're under arrest for assaulting a police officer." He quickly handcuffed him and moved the guy into the black van. A second cyclist rushed past, picked up the camera, and then took off. Gaston did nothing to stop him.

Two more cyclists moved in on either side of the bench and grabbed Sam's and Matt's backpacks. Chloe and Sam screamed at them to stop. Matt sprinted to the downed bike and yelled to Jeannette, "Stay close to Chloe." He jumped on it and went after the guy who took his backpack.

Sam pointed at the last cyclist, screaming, "He has our journals! We have to get them back." She and Beau took off running after him.

Having run the one-way streets all over Montmartre, Beau and Sam had no problem ambushing the cyclist by cutting through yards and jumping over low rock walls. Sam sprinted forward ahead of the bike, leaped into the air, and landed a flying sidekick into the biker's ribs. The guy had the breath knocked out of him as he rocketed off the bike and tumbled to the ground.

Beau picked the biker up by the collar and

clocked him before retrieving Sam's backpack. He took the guy's wallet and the bike back to the black van, leaving the guy in a heap, hoping the police would pick him up.

When Beau and Sam returned, Matt was sitting on the bench with Chloe, not breathing heavily, and holding his backpack with Chloe's camera inside.

"Hey man, looks like you were successful too," said Beau. "Any trouble?"

"Nah, I managed to pop a wheelie over his back tire, and he lost control. The rest was a piece of cake. You know, riding bikes in Montmartre is invigorating. We should do some biking here because it's perfect for cycling." He gave Chloe a killer smile as Sam and Beau shook their heads.

Matt faced Gaston. "You knew they worked together in gangs. Tell me why you let the guy with the camera get away?"

Everyone turned to stare at Gaston. "They needed to take the bait. They have the camera, and now, I think you all will be safe."

Jeannette turned to Gaston. "This is intolerable. We could have been hurt, and I intend to call your superior." Gaston laughed, extending his arms out and open palms. Jeannette wagged her finger at him, "*Ne te moque pas de moi, détective!*" Matt snickered. She returned to the group, "I told him not to mess with me! You all are with me, and it's my duty to protect you."

She turned back to Gaston. "They have a tour planned for the Eiffel Tower at six o'clock tonight and then a river cruise. Are they safe to go?"

"Of course."

Chloe whispered to Matt. "I think that was

code for Wonder Woman." Matt nodded.

"I don't know about the rest of you, but I need a nap," said Sam.

"Me too," said Chloe.

"I need a hot shower and a change of clothes," said Matt. "So, take us back to the hotel." Beau nodded.

Pierre dropped everyone at the hotel at about four o'clock in the afternoon. As soon as they entered the lobby, Sam pulled Chloe into the lounge, and the guys followed. "Chloe, you never delete your photos. You always keep your memory cards because you claim that the pixels are reduced when they're transferred. Spill it."

Chloe lifted a finger and started counting. "First, I don't trust that detective, Gaston." She lifted a second finger. "I don't think it was a coincidence that he put us on that train, and the guys chased us. So, I swapped out the memory card on the train and put the real one in my boot." The third finger popped up. "Gaston miraculously has a camera with photos of all of us starting from Versailles. Then…" Fourth finger. "He wanted us to wait for the bikers to show up… How did he know the bikers would attack the Wall of Love? I'm not sure he's a good guy, but I think he bought my story."

Matt put his arm around Chloe's shoulder and squeezed. "That was quick thinking. We still need to be vigilant, but going on the tour tonight should be safe. I'll go to the pharmacy to get another crutch for you. When I return, I'll bring ice and check on your ankle."

Claude saluted Beau with a finger across his nose. Beau nodded and escorted Sam and Chloe to the elevator. "Ladies, go on and I'll meet you in a few minutes."

The elevator door closed, and Chloe turned to Sam. "You're going to think I'm crazy, but I thought I saw the Boston guy from the airplane inside Sacré Coeur."

"Simon Brown? Did you take his picture?"

"Uh, no... I guess I was distracted."

"With everything going on, we've all been distracted. Don't worry. Perhaps it was someone who resembled him."

"I suppose you're right."

CLAUDE SIGNALED BEAU to enter his office. "Hey Claude, how's it going?"

"Our visitor came back today. He wanted to see inside your rooms, but I refused. He may come back tomorrow with a search paper. Then I must let them in."

"Thanks for telling me. People have been following us since we arrived in Paris, and we had trouble with some punks today. It's time to visit the American Embassy. Claude, do you have another hotel safe?"

"Oui. There is a safe for changing money and for packages that come for guests."

"Is it possible to leave our cameras in it while we go out?"

"Of course. No one will know."

"Thank you," Beau called the American Embassy and received an emergency appointment for the following afternoon.

Chapter 11

J EANNETTE MET THE group in the lobby at six o'clock, anxiously shifting from one foot to the other and carrying a large, weighted tote as her purse.

Beau sidled up to her, grinned, and said, "I know women's purses. Small ones hold the essentials, medium-sized ones are for every day, and big ones, the size of a tote bag, mean she's on a mission. Your bag suggests you're loaded for bear."

"Damn straight. Firearms may be illegal in France, but *MacGyver* was my tutor, and chemistry is my best friend." She patted her bag but refused to let Beau see inside. He winked at her. She opened the van door, and they got in. "We have another hotel stop to pick up more dinner guests. Everyone, say 'hello' to Gaston."

There was groaning in the back, followed by a sing-song unison of voices, "Hello, Gaston." Pleasantly surprised, he looked back and said, "Bonsoir." They were stuck with Gaston for the evening. Should that be comforting or dangerous?

Once the other passengers climbed into the van, Jeannette spoke to everyone.

"For the 1889 World's Fair in Paris, there was a contest to design a structure to commemorate the hundredth Anniversary of the French Revolution. Over one hundred designs came in, but Gustave Eiffel's design won. You may not know this, but he was already famous for designing the world's longest single-arch, wrought-iron railway bridge in Porto, Portugal.

"The Eiffel Tower was only supposed to last twenty years and then get dismantled, but it became a symbol of French industrial power, so it stayed. The top section was used for scientific experiments and housed wireless telegraphy for the military. Today, over one hundred antennae are at the top for beaming radio and television broadcasts worldwide.

"It is as high as an eighty-one-story building, was painted brown, then yellow, but today it's painted black every seven years, and nearly seven million people visit yearly… Okay, we're here." The van pulled up on a back street into a gravel parking area.

Matt, Sam, Chloe, and Beau had seen the Eiffel Tower from a distance the first night in Paris, but up close, it was magnificent, gargantuan, imposing, and Matt was catatonic. Sam, Chloe, and Beau watched his eyes dilate, and his lips moved silently. They knew numbers were running in his head— weight, height, and steel strength. Matt knew about Eiffel, his studies, engineering, and design capabilities. He had even done extensive research translating French documents into English for his master's degree thesis, but this wasn't the time to explain what he knew. It was the time to absorb everything around him, soak it all in, and touch it.

He emerged from his stupor as Jeannette opened her door, beckoning them to follow. A gravel pathway to the structure's base housed shops for souvenirs, candy, drinks, and ice cream. Jeannette guided them to benches overlooking the Champ de Mars Park, a green space area with trees surrounding a lake, and told them to wait for her while she picked up their tickets.

Matt couldn't sit. He examined the massive concrete slabs embedded with black steel legs spread out at the bottom and bent together at a pivotal point, creating a cantilever design. The curve continued upward, climbing to the highest station on the tower, forming an obelisk called the cupula. An engineering feat of the nineteenth century, it was aesthetically pleasing and was artistically designed, accentuating the negative space between the girders—a timeless creation.

"It looks like a drunken pagoda," said Sam. "Or how a steel giraffe gets ready to drink water."

"I see that," said Chloe, "but the edges are lacey."

"This design pushed the wrought iron's strength as a sculpture," said Matt, "but it also had to appeal to the senses, an illusion of fragility with strength."

"Uh-huh," said Beau. Matt slapped him on the back.

Jeannette gave each passenger group envelopes containing tickets for dinner and the cruise. Sam volunteered to hold onto theirs as they climbed into the elevator, carrying about thirty people.

"Rather than walk several hundred steps, we are taking the elevator to one of the two restaurants, but not on just any elevator. Since the tower's legs curved, a typical elevator wouldn't work, so all the workers, including Eiffel, had to use the stairs. Imagine if you left something or if there was a problem. Climbing the stairs was unpopular, and until the Otis Elevator Company from the U.S. invented an elevator system that worked, Eiffel had his office in an apartment at the top. If you return to Paris, consider dining on the second floor in Le Jules Verne with their Meilleur du Ouvrier, *the* best French award-winning chef, but you'll need to make reservations months in advance. Or continue up to the third floor to the Champagne Bar, where you can have a glass of champagne with a view.

"We will stop at the first floor, and the overlook will give you a panoramic view of Paris from this side of the river. Walk around. Touch the wrought iron and take lots of photos. Opposite the elevator is our restaurant, 58 Tour Eiffel. Dinner begins at seven thirty, so you have about an hour. We have reserved tables, and I will wait for you inside.

"The van will pick us up at the drop-off location at eight forty-five, and from there, we drive to the dock for the nine o'clock cruise. If for some reason, you aren't on the bus at that time, you will have to make your way to the docks on your own. It's a short eight-minute walk, but the boat will not wait for you. If you have food allergies, I need to know now."

Sam motioned for Jeannette's attention. "I don't eat seafood. Is that a problem?"

"The appetizer is shrimp, then there is a small salad, and the main course is fish or chicken. We can substitute a soup for the appetizer, and I presume chicken is fine?"

"I'd rather have the soup, a large salad, and vegetables without chicken."

"That can be arranged. Wine comes with dinner, and several desserts are available. Let me make a phone call."

"You're still a picky eater?" asked Beau.

"I have a refined palate," said Sam.

"Oh, yeah. Coke and coffee fit in a refined palate—"

"My food and drink choices are to my liking. So, bite me," she said.

"I like that idea," said Beau.

She punched him on the arm. "Besides, you're with me, aren't you? I'd say my palate is very refined. Don't you agree?"

Beau gave her a high-wattage smile. "When you put it that way, I agree."

BEAU FOUND THE observation deck overwhelming. The structure was like nothing he had ever seen before or would again. Although he wasn't afraid of heights, he pitied any person with that phobia or the fear of open spaces. He was thankful that they were standing on a textured steel floor that gripped his shoes and surprised that the open-girded steel crisscrossing beams didn't move with the constant wind, and that additional railings kept people safe. A person would need to be a contortionist to get to the farthest railing, yet in the past, people tried to "fly" off the tower in makeshift flying apparatuses.

The area was filled with couples, families with children, individuals, and small parties like theirs. People strolled around after an early dinner at the restaurant, while others waited to go to the next dinner time, and others took photos or looked at the view. Beau noticed two young men stumbling around, having had too much wine with dinner or no dinner and wine. It was a party.

He also noticed that Chloe wore a sailor outfit—a navy blue and white sailor top, navy blue bell-bottom long pants, and one white shoe. She held up Mimi, who was dressed identically in a French boating outfit and a beret, ready to be photographed climbing the girders of the tower or with a panoramic view of Paris in the background.

"Chloe, it's not Halloween, so what gives with the outfit?" asked Beau.

"Pfft. We're dressed for a cruise, and I wanted our pictures taken together. I wish we all had sailor hats."

They snorted and snickered, with a collective "No."

Chloe took many photographs of the tower's architecture and then looked to pose Mimi for her shots. She had a Nikon fixed-lens camera small enough to fit in a pocket and worn around her neck, and then attached Mimi to a selfie stick and beckoned the others to move the paper doll around the tower. The wind kicked up, causing Mimi to fold in half. Sam doubled the ticket envelope and placed it behind Mimi to keep her straight, which worked beautifully.

After Chloe took many photos, she wanted some of her and Mimi together. Sam held the selfie stick while she removed the camera and handed it to Beau. Holding it by the strap, it dangled to the ground. Chloe then asked Matt to remove her sailor hat from her backpack and place it on her head. He tried to get it straight but putting it halfway over her eyes was more fun, tilting it over one ear and then back on her head. She tried to sound irritated, but it didn't work. A gust of wind blew the hat off her head, and they all scurried to keep it from floating away.

They laughed so hard that no one saw one of the drunk guys grab the camera from Beau's hand before tripping over the foot of disguised Detective Gaston Marvell. The would-be thief righted himself and made a speedy getaway down the stairs, chased by Gaston.

Beau spun around. "Hey, what happened?" He bent over to retrieve the camera and bumped into Sam. The selfie stick holding Mimi on top of the ticket envelope took a nosedive over the edge of the Eiffel Tower. The four watched in rapt fascination, staring at the objects' descent, unable to stop it.

"It's infinity and beyond."

They all stared at Matt. It *was* the perfect movie quote for this situation.

"You have to stop watching animated films," said Beau.

Matt shrugged. Sam giggled.

"Great. We lost Mimi and our tickets, but it shouldn't be too difficult to find them since the selfie stick is bright pink with bedazzled gems that reflect light well," said Chloe.

"What are you proposing? That one of us goes back down and hunts for Mimi and the selfie stick?" asked Beau.

Sam poked him in the middle of his chest. "Not anyone, you. I know the general location. I can use the light on my phone to guide you in the right direction while Matt calls or texts to direct you more. We need Mimi and the tickets."

Beau scanned the area. There were two options, the stairs or the elevator, but a crowd had been waiting several minutes for the elevator to appear. If they had had all day, Sam, Matt, and he would have challenged each other to race down the stairs.

"The elevator is taking too long." Sam's mouth turned up at the corners. "So, you'll get there faster using the stairs... Besides, you want to be able to say you climbed the Eiffel Tower, don't you?" asked Sam.

Beau shook his head. With hands on his hips, he sighed loudly. *Am I going to do this?*

"There are six hundred seventy-four steps down to the bottom," quoted Matt. "It should take about twenty minutes if you jog, but *you* can go faster. It'll be like running sprints on the stadium bleachers when you played college football."

"That only happened once, and I wish I'd never told you. Blabbermouth."

"Well then, lesson learned, right? Who knew the coach's daughter was underage?"

"I know, right? From then on, I always ask to see a driver's license," said Beau. Sam and Chloe were shooting eye daggers at him. "Hey, it's not what you think. We were at a party, and she said it was her twenty-first birthday, so I bought her several beers. Later, she asked me to drive her back home… to the coach's house. I didn't know he had a daughter, and for sure, I didn't know she was only nineteen." *Good thing nothing else happened.* "He made me run the bleachers with full gear for an hour before practice. I never did that again."

"Served you right," said Sam.

Matt cleared his throat, "Once you find the selfie stick, take the elevator back up and meet us in the restaurant. Jeannette will save our seats; the appetizers will be waiting. I'll order a nice bottle of wine."

Beau looked at the three standing near the railing. The wind caressed Sam's hair around her face. *She's so beautiful and has me wrapped around her little finger. They know I'll go after Mimi since Sam told me to. After all, I bumped into her, but I refuse to look pathetic.*

"The things I do for you. I deserve compensation," snarked Beau.

"You'll have our gratitude," said Sam.

"I need more."

"We'll see. Now go. I'm getting hungry."

He pulled Sam in for a kiss and headed for the stairs.

Beau let them think they had set him up, like old times. Fine. The laughter behind him was the telltale sign that they were enjoying his predicament. He was enjoying it, too, especially since he would save the day.

He knew he had to hurry. Fortunately, no people were on the stairs, so he could take the corners like the building was on fire. Beau arrived at the right side of the tower's base in good time. He bent over to catch his breath, hands on his burning thighs, and looked at his watch—only fifteen minutes, but he was running out of light. He hurried to the grassy area outside the tower facing the Seine River, where boats lined the docks, and waved his hands over his head.

Sam's light moved from right to left to get his attention—it continued to move left and stayed there. Beau flashed his light in acknowledgment. Matt texted him to keep moving left and then to turn right. More. More. To the left again, then right. More. More. Their directions were confusing.

He looked up. Sam's light jiggled. Either her hand was shaking, or she was laughing so hard that her hand shook. Fine. He was being played, so he'd play along, following their direction while he searched. About ten minutes later, he found Mimi after shining his light over the ground. The pink selfie stick's gems sparkled like Chloe said they would. He texted Matt that he was on his way back up. So, Matt and Chloe headed to the restaurant while Sam waited for Beau to return.

Beau popped out of the elevator, finding Sam at the top of the stairs looking down. His arms encircled her waist. She jumped and then relaxed into him. "You know what I want, Sam. I want more with you." He pressed her tighter against him as his body gave itself away.

"A kiss, but nothing else. Renewing our friendship is too important to me. Please don't ruin this."

He stilled, squeezed her tight, and released her, knowing he couldn't speed things up any faster than she was willing to go. "I'll wait," he whispered, "but I'm serious about us. Think about it."

She turned and kissed him lightly, hoping her heart pounding wouldn't give her away. It wouldn't hurt to be honest. "I will... I'll think about it. Thanks for getting Mimi."

He extended his hand, and they walked to the restaurant with their fingers entwined.

The sun went down as gold lights illuminated the Iron Lady. Somewhere in the distance, romantic music wafted up from the riverbank, and there was hope for the beginning of a beautiful relationship.

ON THREE SIDES of the restaurant, large windows revealed stunning views of the Seine River and the twinkling lights of Paris. Matt hoped Chloe would see it as magical and romantic. Yet, like any restaurant open to tourists, it had more of a pub atmosphere. Diners weren't afraid to converse in their normal voices, and the din became even louder, sounding like a party.

When Matt and Chloe entered the restaurant, the window seating was taken, and only four seats remained together. Matt seated Chloe at the end of a long table filled with a dozen other guests so that she could stretch out her booted foot. He chose to sit across from her to flag down Beau and Sam as they came in.

Beau held up Mimi and presented her to Chloe as he sat beside her.

"Where's Jeanette?" asked Sam.

"She's with the other passengers that came with us in the van... She said we could handle ourselves and felt she needed to be with the others. If you look near the entrance, the group has already finished several bottles of wine, and they aren't feeling any pain," said Matt.

"I hope they don't throw up on the boat." Beau snickered, "We don't need to worry about that. Do we, sailors?"

They all said in unison, "No."

The conversation was lively as they rehashed losing Mimi and Beau's efforts to retrieve her and the tickets. Beau pretended to be wounded as they teased him, but he preened being the center of attention and even helped Mimi pose several times in the restaurant before Sam put her back in her purse.

The appetizers, salad, and main course came with a bottle of wine. For dinner, Sam received French onion soup, two salads, and some root vegetables.

"It looks like you got today's roughage allotment." Matt laughed. "I think I speak for the others in saying that since we ate like kings, you can share our desserts to make up for your dinner."

"I'm glad you said that because I had intended to taste them anyway." Sam started with Beau's dessert and then moved to the others' once or twice.

All around them, strangers became friends. Friends became friendlier, tablemates became conversationalists, and inhibitions disappeared. In a brief time, the noise level rose even higher. Two heavily drinking men tried to strike up a conversation with Sam and Chloe. The women were polite, but from the men's gestures, it was apparent the men were after more than conversation. They spoke in French and made rude, suggestive remarks to and about the girls, laughing and elbowing each other. Chloe was the first to be uncomfortable.

"Ignore them. It's the wine talking," said Sam as she stomped on top of the man's foot sitting next to her, hard. "Sorry."

The lewd gestures continued. Sam turned her back on them, giving them the cold shoulder, and faced the three friends at an angle. Beau's hands were in fists. Trying to rise, Matt touched his shoulder to restrain him from beating the guys to a pulp. Matt understood it all, and it was too much.

"Enough!" Matt shouted, rising from his chair and getting in the man's face, sitting beside Sam. Both men moved back in their chairs. He spoke to them rapidly in French. "Shut up! You're talking about my sister and my girlfriend. Neither deserves your vulgar speech and obscene gestures, and I'm sure you would be upset if your sister or wife were insulted like that. I demand an apology from you."

The men were shocked and embarrassed, thinking the two couples were dumb Americans used to being treated that way. In turn, they spoke to Matt in French, "We were rude and out of line," and then in English, they spoke to Chloe and Sam, "Please accept our apology for our actions." With red faces, they rose from the table and flagged down a waiter. Words were spoken, and one of the men handed over one hundred Euros before leaving the restaurant. A few minutes later, the waiter returned with a bottle of Chateau Rieussec

Sauternes 2014, an expensive bottle of dessert wine, to further their apology.

Chloe extended her hand to Matt over the table. "I only understood some of what was said, so thank you for standing up for us." She squeezed his hand.

Beau fist-bumped Matt. "I didn't understand a word, but you took care of things. Thanks." Then he rubbed his hands together. "Those jerks were obnoxious, but they know good wine. Try this." He poured everyone a glass, and with a sip, the mood turned festive again as they shared desserts. They were having so much fun that they forgot about the time until groups of people were leaving the restaurant.

"I hate to break up the party," prompted Matt, "but we have only fifteen minutes to get to the van."

They hustled to the elevator, but only two or three people could get on when the door opened. Unfortunately, this elevator also served the upper-level restaurant and champagne bar. It would take much longer to get down, so Matt called Jeannette.

"We are stuck waiting for the elevator... No, Beau and Sam will wait for us to go together. I see. Okay, thanks."

"What did she say?" asked Chloe.

"Gaston blew a gasket. He will take the other passengers to the dock and return to get us. We may miss the cruise; if we do, he'll take us back to the hotel."

It was after nine o'clock before they reached the bottom of the Eiffel Tower. "The cruise would have been nice, but *C'est la vie*," said Matt. "Once we get to the hotel, we'll find something to do or chill out."

When the elevator door opened, Gaston was waiting for them.

"Hello, Gaston. Are you going to take us back to the hotel?" asked Chloe.

"Non. I asked the captain to hold the boat until your arrival. It was the least I could do to make up for this afternoon."

Matt stared at the others. Had they been wrong about Gaston, or did he have other motives? Curious. The van pulled up in a no-loading zone by the gangplank. Sam brought out the tickets and then helped Chloe on board. As the boat pulled away from the dock, Matt saw Gaston retrieve his cell phone, enter the van, and drive off.

Chapter 12

"I STILL DON'T trust that guy," said Chloe, "but at least we're going on a cruise. Okay, any preference for where to sit?"

"Yeah," said Sam, turning away. "I'm headed to the pilot house. I want to steer the ship."

"You've got to be kidding me! Wait, Sam. You can't go up there." Beau chased after her. Chloe giggled, and Matt's mouth formed a thin line.

"She's going to get us in trouble, like when we were kids. We're going to get thrown off the boat," said Matt.

Chloe patted his cheek. "Not this time. She's legal. Come on, let's get a seat on the bow, and I'll explain."

BEAU TALKED SAM into touring the upper deck before trying to speak to the captain. On the boat's top deck at the edge of the bow, Sam braced herself on the railing, threw her arms out wide, and yelled, "I'm queen of the world."

"Don't you have to be crossing the Atlantic on the *Titanic*?" asked Beau.

"I play along with your stupid movie quotes, humor me," said Sam. Beau snickered. "I want to steer the boat. Come on."

"Just because you passed a couple of boating classes when you were twelve doesn't mean you can steer a cruise ship."

Sam talked to Beau over her shoulder as she walked on. "We should find the captain, and I can ask him to let me steer. What's the harm?"

He trotted to catch up to her. "Apparently, you forgot how much trouble we got into the last time we skippered a boat." He shook his head, watching her eyes twinkle. "Remember borrowing my uncle's wooden spritsail to picnic on the water? The wind picked up, the currents were fast, the shoreline looked different, and the water had deepened quickly. We all panicked, thinking we were heading toward open water and eventually to the ocean.

"Seeing that Coast Guard boat was a Godsend. We all stood up, waving and yelling to get its attention. You and Chloe were hanging on to each other, crying. It was a miracle you two didn't capsize the boat."

"That's not right, you were the one crying, and Matt had to console you."

"Tomato, to-ma-toe."

"Yet, it was a win/win situation," said Sam. Beau's eyes narrowed. "We had to take boating classes and then go to the Fort Macon Coast Guard Station in Atlantic Beach to demonstrate our skills with the two Coastie hunks... I think I drooled the whole time."

"You did—it wasn't a good look... Fortunately, Matt and I worked the sailboat like pros."

"I admit it, you did. Chloe and I were amazed," said Sam with a smile. Beau wrapped his arm around her waist. "As I recall, you and Matt got to crew for sportfishing boats and even the marlin tournaments. You guys made a boatload of money."

He directed her to a bench, and they sat down. "And what did you get out of it?"

"Motivation." Sam unzipped the inside pocket of her purse and proudly handed Beau an orange passport revealing her 100-ton boat Captain's License, making her legal to captain a large commercial vessel.

He whistled. "I'm impressed. When did you get this?" asked Beau.

"My journey started the summer after sophomore year in college. Uncle Ray wouldn't let me use his sailboat because I didn't have the experience, so I took two sailing classes from the Maritime Museum and was hooked. He said I didn't have the smarts to pass the captain's test—If I passed it, he'd give me his 23-foot sailboat. It needed lots of work, so he and Chloe helped me. By the end of the summer, it looked great. I passed the Captain 6-pack test and then earned the Sailboat Captain's license."

Beau closed the orange passport and handed it back to Sam. "So, you could take six people out on a fishing boat or a sailboat and get paid."

"Yep. Except no one would hire me. The word got out, and rumors spread that I'd sink the boat, or the Coast Guard would have to rescue me. No one took me seriously."

"You proved them wrong, didn't you?"

"When I turned twenty-one, before senior year in college, I studied to get my 50-ton Master License and realized that with a little more studying, I could get the 100-ton Master License. The Wildlife Federation was looking for captains to ferry people to Cape Lookout Lighthouse for the summer, and I applied. I was overqualified but needed the experience, and I knew those waters like the back of my hand.

"I was hired then, and after graduation. The pay was good, and finally, word got out that I didn't ground the ferry, start a fire, destroy property, or needed to be rescued by the Coast Guard. Sadly, there was a betting pool against me at the marina, and even after all these years, the board hangs on the wall. It reminds me that I need to be vigilant on the water and never take safety for granted.

"I've kept up my license, and occasionally, I get called in to sub for the captain or first officer on the Harbor Princess for dinner cruises or on the local ferries and even more work in the summer," said Sam, polishing her nails across her shirt.

"No kidding. Then why teach? You could have a job on the large ferries full-time."

"I like doing it, and the pay is great, but I love teaching more, and it gives me time to write, which is what I love the most. Once I publish a few novels, I will buy a big boat and travel everywhere." Her eyes twinkled the same way they did just before trouble found her.

"Take me along. I could be your cabin boy." He wiggled his eyebrows.

Sam snapped out of it and blushed. "Are you licensed?"

"I'm licensed for all sorts of things… especially for love." He pulled her to him and tried to kiss her, but Sam snorted and wouldn't stop laughing.

"You had me there. I'm going to the pilot house. You coming with me?"

Even with a bruised ego, Beau wouldn't miss seeing her in action.

Sam knocked on the outer door of the pilot house. A man dressed in black pants and a white shirt with one bar on his epaulet opened it.

"Do you speak English?" asked Sam.

"Oui. How can I help you?"

"I would like to speak to the captain." She introduced herself, and Beau then presented her license to the man. "I am visiting Paris and would like to steer this ship on the Seine River. Is it possible?"

The man turned to another man with four bars on his epaulet, the captain, and they spoke rapidly. The captain met Sam and Beau at the door and allowed them inside. "I am Captain Brock. Regrettably, the insurance company only allows employees to steer the ship; however, you may come inside to watch for a few minutes."

Sam was beaming, and Beau was impressed that she could sweet-talk her way into the pilot house of a French cruise ship. The captain explained that he had never met a woman captain, and he shook her hand. He gave them a short tour of the instruments and showed them the chart for their cruise so they knew what they would see and in which direction.

Before they left, Sam pulled out Mimi and her cell phone. Explaining Mimi's role, she took lots of photos and then passed on Mimi's information so the crew could follow her on Facebook. Sam and Beau left the pilot house on top of the world.

They toured the top deck again and found a nice spot on the bow to watch Paris drift by.

"I can't believe we did that," said Beau. "You are fearless. I don't think there is anything you can't do... Do you know what we should do? We should rent a boat and go cruising when we get home. We could go to the Bahamas or the British Virgin Islands. What do you say?"

"You're not afraid I'll ground the boat or have to call the Coast Guard?"

"No. We don't even have to go that far. We could head down to Charleston or Smith Island in the Chesapeake Bay to eat their famous cake... Hey... I'm serious."

"If...*if* we go, we'll have to take Matt and Chloe too. I can only open a can of soup and make sandwiches, and Matt's great at calculations—I could teach him how to plot a course, but we'd need to do some short runs first, like to Ocracoke, Little Washington, or Wilmington." She was excited, and Beau let her talk so that she would agree to spend more time with him.

"Whatever you say. I can do stuff too, you know." He held out his hand, and she shook it. Things were looking up. Samantha never reneged on a deal. It was resolved; they would see each other when they went home.

Beau and Sam spent the rest of the night looking at the lights of Paris, the bridges, seeing the Eiffel Tower glowing in gold, and passing Notre Dame while talking casually. He put his arm around Sam and kept her close. Beau kissed her as often as she would let him. It was the best date

Beau ever had, even if his date didn't know they were on a date.

MATT AND CHLOE inched along the main level toward the bow, laughing while trying to find their boat legs. They found an empty bench seat illuminated by ambient light and got comfortable. In front of them, a double glass door led to a wraparound deck with large sliding glass windows on both sides. For now, stars couldn't compete with the city lights, but a full moon rose slowly as a prelude to a romantic night.

Despite the muffled engine propelling them along the river and the noise from the people in various parts of the boat, Matt and Chloe seemed alone, silently watching.

It was too perfect. Staged.

Chloe shifted in her seat. She and Matt weren't in a relationship, and nothing from the past had been resolved. Old feelings and hurt bubbled up. Time to talk, to somehow find closure to six years of wondering. She needed to approach this in her diplomatic roundabout kind of way. She turned toward Matt and cleared her throat. "Sam told me about your recent breakup. I'm sorry it didn't work out for you."

"I'm not. Missy was wild… she reminded me of Sam in her heyday; only Sam took responsibility for her actions, and Missy didn't. But she pulled me out of my shell to try new things. She thrives on noise and people, and I need quiet time after being with teenagers at school all day." He shrugged. "You know how I get—I need peace to calm things in my head." Matt hesitated to reveal more.

"You don't have to tell me about it. I'm sorry I asked."

"No, that's alright. Missy said I was dull, and she was right. I couldn't give her what she needed. I should have broken things off when I found out she was dating other guys behind my back... it reminded me of us in college... and I didn't want *that* to happen again, so I tried harder to make things better, but it didn't work. I caught her in the backseat of some guy's car in the high school parking lot, so I ended it."

"What do you mean it reminded you of us in college?"

"When I found out you were dating other people...I knew you'd find someone who was... a normal guy. I didn't fight for you... I let you go." His voice shook.

Chloe spat out her words. "Back up. First of all, I wasn't dating anyone else, and you were the one who said we should date other people, not me!"

"But the guys told me. Caroline told me." Matt wasn't a good liar. Chloe knew he was telling the truth.

"Someone... told you... I was dating other guys... behind your back?" Venom oozed from her mouth. "Wrong! Never happened. Hold on... because of what people told you, that's why you wanted to date other people?" She glared at him, and Matt barely nodded. "Tell me the truth right now." Her breathing accelerated, and her nostrils flared. "Why did we break up, and who in the hell is Caroline?"

Matt rubbed his chest; his face contorted as if his heart would explode. "One weekend, I got drunk and called your dorm room. Some guy named Kevin answered and said you were unavailable. When I asked him to give you a message, he said you wouldn't be interested in hearing from me because the two of you had been seriously dating for a couple of months." Matt rested his arms on his thighs. He refused to look at her.

Chloe rose from her seat and hobbled to the window and back, standing on her crutches to listen. Her eyes narrowed, her lips pressed together, and she panted hard. "Go on."

"I called back to speak to Sam, but this other guy, Nathan, answered, and he told me that you and Kevin were dating and not to call back. I grabbed my car keys to find you, but my roommate stopped me. His cousin, Caroline, was visiting, and she said she had friends at ECU who could find out. The next day, she confirmed that you had a new boyfriend."

Chloe dramatically rolled her eyes, "Unbelievable."

Matt faced Chloe. "I should have gone to see you, but I didn't. I should have made you see how much I loved you... But I was so hurt. Caroline urged me to save face by telling you I wanted to date other people—I didn't want to do it. She convinced me I needed to move on. A few months later, Caroline and I started dating."

Chloe hobbled closer to Matt, took the crutch from her side, and whapped him hard on the thigh, yelled, "What a manipulative bitch—she lied!

Everyone knew how I felt about you. Kevin was an art major and a chronic liar. We worked on a couple of art projects together, but that was all. Nathan was his sidekick and would say anything to cause trouble. You...you... stupid...guy!" She whapped him again and then once more.

Chloe screamed out. "I was always faithful to you. You should have talked to Sam... You didn't trust me... and that hurts most of all." She sat down and slapped him repeatedly while the tears flowed. Matt grabbed her wrists and held on to them until she settled down. She jerked from his hold, turned her back, wiped her face, and blew her nose. She refused to look at him.

Chloe's words were almost too soft to hear. "When you broke up with me, I was devastated. I didn't understand how you could throw me away... I had done nothing wrong. I became a shadow of myself... Sam helped me pick up the pieces, and I don't know what I would have done without her.

"Then, I got angry. I hated you for the longest time. I don't know when, but I felt sorry for you after a while because you didn't see my transformation." She swallowed, squared her shoulders, and faced him.

"I threw myself into my painting and photography. I became the artist I was destined to be. I didn't date for over a year because I didn't want to be sucked into a distracting relationship or have another man influence me. During my senior year, I was discovered by Margaret Bishop in Morehead City, and she sold several of my pieces. My work is in her three galleries, and she even hooked me up with an agent that sells my work commercially." A rivulet of tears rolled down her cheeks.

Matt didn't move, listening intently.

"Since you've been out of my life, I've become successful. I've also found great satisfaction in teaching. I'm happy, and it's taken me years to say that... Do you know the saddest thing about this? We've lived the last six years based on lies."

It was true. Matt was mortified that he'd been so gullible. "You're right. How could I have been so blind? Chloe, I'm deeply sorry that I put you through all that... I hope one day you'll forgive me."

He got up from his seat, paced back and forth, then turned to Chloe to kneel before her. He slowly shook his head and forced the rest of his story out. "It didn't take long until Caroline became upset with me—I introduced her at a university math faculty function as Chloe Davis. She slapped me and walked out. She didn't speak to me for three days, and I didn't even realize what I had done until a colleague explained it to me."

"Served *you* right."

"I suppose so. What ruined things was... I'm embarrassed to say... I called out your name at an inappropriate time."

"You don't mean, umm...?"

"Yeah, during sex... three separate times."

"Served *her* right!"

Chloe couldn't help it. She blinked several times, looked at Matt's face, and grinned. It shouldn't be funny, and it wasn't funny, but it was funny now. Her grin turned into a broad smile, and Matt mimicked her. Then she burst out laughing, and so did Matt. "That confession doesn't make up for things, but it helps."

They watched the lights along the river for a while, thinking about what they had learned and how much time they had wasted.

Matt spoke in hushed tones. "Just so you know, my arm stings, and I have at least three subdermal hematomas on my leg, so you may have to help me get back to the hotel."

"Suck it up, buttercup... You'll live."

"You're going to continue to make me pay, aren't you? It's okay. If I can be with you, I can handle whatever you dish out... Still friends?" He held his breath.

"For the time being. You deserve to pay for a long, long, long time, and I want to be around to watch." She sighed loudly. "I could really use some chocolate."

His smile took her breath away. There was a chance with him after all.

"Uh... I happen to have some. Call it a peace offering." He pulled a bar of French chocolate from his jacket pocket. "You know, this is supposed to be a romantic cruise. Could we pretend we're okay and enjoy it together?"

She unwrapped the chocolate bar and sucked on a large piece with her eyes closed. Her mind whirled, yet her heart was opening to him. *I need to be careful. It would be too easy to get caught up in him.* She searched his face as he waited for an answer, "I can pretend if you can." He nodded.

Chloe broke off a piece of chocolate and held it to his lips. Matt ate it. She rationed the chocolate so that she ate most of it, but he didn't mind. Sometime later, after the chocolate was gone, he wrapped his arm around her shoulder, pulled her close, and laced his fingers with hers. There would be other things to say later, but they watched Paris drift by for now.

AS THE BOAT docked, Beau noticed a white van parked close to the gangplank. A lone figure stood beside the van door, waiting for the Down East group. He elbowed Matt, cleared his throat to get the girls' attention, and pointed his chin toward the driver.

Chloe groaned. "I should have known he'd be waiting. Still, we have a ride back to the hotel... Hello Gaston." He nodded to her and the others as they piled into the van.

Gaston dropped the friends off at the hotel about midnight. Before they could walk into the lobby, a resounding din came from the direction of the Irish pub down the street. Beau eyed the others, "Anyone feel like a beer and soccer?"

In ten minutes, they were surrounded by boisterous fans.

Two large televisions mounted behind the bar showed the last minutes of a soccer game. The glass panels were open, allowing the crowd to stand in the pub, on the sidewalk, or on the lawn. People rooted for their teams, and as one scored, sounds erupted in groans or jubilation. The bartender made room for Chloe on a bar stool while the other friends stood around her.

At halftime, people moved away from the television to talk and refill their mugs. Matt brought out his phone and put it in a glass on the bar to amplify the beach music he wanted to hear. He and Chloe sang together while Beau and Sam danced on the sidewalk. Soon, a crowd gathered to watch them dance, encouraging them with shouts, clapping, and laughter as Beau dipped Sam.

Before the match started again, the crowd turned feisty. A rowdy Irish folk song competed with an English bawdy tune as both groups tried to out-sing each other, swaying, locked arm in arm. Sam and Beau moved back into the pub.

"Hey, beautiful, come join us." Two rowdy drinkers pulled Sam into their group and handed her a draft. They urged her to sway with them and cheer when a goal was scored. Sam was having a terrific time.

"Son of a…" Matt held Beau back. He tried to get Sam's attention without success. Before he could wade through the frenzy to get to her, a guy grabbed Sam and tried to kiss her.

"Son of a brain-eater," Beau pushed people aside. The other guy was doubled over when he reached her, and she walked toward him.

"Sam, are you alright?

"I'm peachy. Let's get out of here. I've had enough of soccer, men, and beer." She stomped out of the pub and didn't wait for Beau or the others.

Beau jogged to catch up with her. "You should be more careful in how you interact with men. This isn't Down East. These guys have been drinking all day, and I don't want to get into it with some guy over something stupid—"

Sam raised her hand to cut him off before he had time to finish. "I can handle myself." She was fighting mad and looked at Beau, ready to bite his head off. "What I do isn't up to you." Beau placed his hand on her arm, and she jerked away. *I don't need him to fight my battles. I was stupid for not adhering to self-defense protocols, but I don't need a lecture from him.* "Since when are you my keeper?"

"Since we were in the second grade. I've always had your back—"

Matt butted in, "That's true. We've always had your back, Sam… yours too, Chloe."

"Name one time," said Sam. *Why did I say that? Me and my big mouth. Now I'm being childish challenging them.* She stood with her hands on her hips, daring either of them to say another word.

"How about the time before ninth grade began, you and Chloe dyed your hair green?" Sam and Chloe groaned simultaneously.

"That was an accident," said Chloe. "Sam wanted to put some highlights in her hair, but it was my fault that it turned green… I misread the instructions, and I didn't know it was permanent. I felt so bad that I dyed my hair, too, so she wouldn't be alone."

"That's it," said Beau. "The four of us had the last summer competitions against Billy's crew. There was watermelon seed spitting and rowing out to Brown's Island and back. What else, Matt?"

"It was my idea to have a bike race to Marshallberg and the dart throwing contest, but it was Sam's idea to have a water balloon war and a bowling tournament for the last challenge."

"In school, Billy called me 'spaghetti legs.' I hated him for that," said Chloe. "I wanted to beat him."

"Darlin,' by tenth grade, when you wore those short skirts, he drooled looking at your beautiful legs, and Beau had to keep me from beating him up," said Matt. Chloe blushed.

"As I recall, we were tied until the bowling tournament," said Sam.

"Yeah, but you two refused to go because of your hair. Matt and I promised to dye our hair green and even go to school looking like that if you two went bowling with us."

"That's a lie." Matt smacked Beau in the chest. "I didn't say any such thing. You volunteered me like you always did. I had no choice—the girls wouldn't have had anything to do with me unless I dyed my hair too.

"My mom had a stroke, and my brothers picked on me for months. We were the butt of every joke until Christmas, and it was so humiliating being asked to dress up as elves in the Christmas parade. I got a buzz cut after Christmas so that by the time school started again, I was back to normal," said Matt. He put his arm around Chloe and pulled her to his side.

"My point is… ladies, we've always had your backs. We dyed our hair; we beat those guys bowling and won the competition. If we'd do that, we'd come to your rescue any day," said Beau.

He approached Sam slowly. "You know I'm right, and we are more than friends. I'd do anything for you, and I know you'd do anything for me. Admit it."

Sam looked from Beau to Matt and back to Beau. "You're right about everything. We are more than friends." Samantha put her arms around Beau's neck and kissed him like she was starving, and he was dessert. Beau joined in enthusiastically until she gently pulled back. "How much more than friends are we?"

"We should explore our options." Beau's eyes looked dreamy. She had initiated the kiss. She had knocked his socks off, and at that moment, he would have said or done anything she asked of him.

Sam looked at Chloe. Her hands were still around Beau's neck.

"How about a 'more than friends' bonding experience?" Sam's words were soft and sweet. Beau nodded. She gave him one last feathery kiss and released him.

Chloe winked at Sam, "We'll think of something." She smiled at Matt coquettishly.

A deal was in the work. Chloe and Sam whispered as they walked.

Beau fist bumped Matt. "We're in Paris. What could go wrong?" asked Beau.

Chapter 13

CLAUDE MET THE friends in the hotel's restaurant with instructions about designer fashion sales. He had booked a professional driver to stay with them from when the stores opened until midafternoon. Chloe would use the wheelchair to avoid having her foot stomped on, and they could hang their purchases on the handles, then Beau and Matt could help take the packages to the car.

"Pickpockets are everywhere. Leave your purses and backpacks with the driver. Take only a credit card and passport and stay together to finish your purchases. If you saved items online, a clerk will ask for your name and take you to try them on. Do not expect chairs," said Claude.

Beau snarled at Sam. "You owe me, Sam."

Sam threw Beau a kiss.

Claude continued. "Do not be alarmed if men and women change in the same area or even in the open—this is natural, the shops are small, and it is how we do things here."

Beau snickered. Sam growled.

The handsome thirty-something driver, Victor Martine, arrived promptly at seven thirty. He joined the friends eating breakfast and noted their shopping choices for the eighth arrondissement: Dior, Ralph Lauren, Givenchy, Chanel, Yves Saint Laurent, Gucci, Armani, and Kenzo. Sam passed out B vitamins, the teacher's vitamin for energy and stress reduction.

Victor pulled out a paper map to locate the shops and organize their schedule—they had six hours to shop. "This will be a long day." His English was perfect, with a slight French accent that Matt recognized as Quebecois, like his grandmère. "I suggest you try on the reserved items first. If you can't decide, don't buy it, because you cannot return anything. These sales can be brutal, and your feet will swell, so try on shoes last. Don't be surprised if someone tries to take your items. It's up for grabs once you hang up something or give it back.

"If you feel claustrophobic or anxious, I will bring the car around for you to sit in the air conditioning. You will need your strength. Stay hydrated and eat snacks in the car. Is there any designer on the list that you have not reserved items?"

"Kenzo and Ralph Lauren," said Sam.

"Good. If you feel up to it, they will be the last two we visit. You have about one hour in each shop. That's not long, so we should get in and out quickly to allow more time in the shops with more items being held. Which shops have the most items?"

"In order: Dior, Yves Saint Laurent, Armani, Gucci, Givenchy, and Chanel," said Matt, demonstrating his brainiac abilities. "I'm assuming that we will also get VAT refunds."

"Purchase at least 175 Euros in one shop and show your passport and round-trip tickets. You will get twelve percent back. Keep the items together, unopened, with the receipts, and show everything at the VAT refund center in the airport before your flight. The refund may be instantaneous or sent to you later, but it may be enough for a trip back to Paris."

Beau was now enthusiastic. "Sam and I will get the return flight tickets while Matt and Chloe get the passports."

"I will keep your documents safe," said Victor. "*Bien*. We are ready."

Chloe held her hand up. She introduced Victor to Mimi. His mouth dropped, learning that he would also be responsible for photographing her with the group.

"I will join you in the shops," Victor sighed. "I'll also take photographs, take charge of Chloe's wheelchair, and help her in the changing areas." Chloe grinned, and Matt growled.

Claude gave Victor a large picnic basket of sandwiches, fruit, bottles of water, a thermos of coffee, and two Cokes for Sam. Chloe kissed Claude's cheeks, Sam gave him a whopper of a kiss on the mouth, and then they all piled into the limo.

"I can't believe these sales occur in the middle of the year," said Sam.

"In the past, because of French law, clothing that wasn't sold by the end of the year could not be donated, so they burned them."

"No way. Why?"

"It helped control original designs from getting

on the black market. In 2019, the laws changed so clothing could be donated for a tax deduction. However, the designers would rather get money, so the mid-year sale allows clothes from fashion week to be brought into the stores for buyers to place orders. Good for them and good for us." Chloe wiggled her eyebrows.

THE GROUP'S FIRST stop was Dior. Sam and Chloe picked up their saved items and headed to the dressing area. Jackpot—everything looked fabulous. They modeled the dresses for Beau and Matt, embarrassed by their wolf whistles.

"Sam, this is my favorite store," said Beau. He showed her the saved lingerie selection. Sam lightly touched the Belgian silk lace framing the neckline and wrists on the translucent pale pink silk robe, nightgown, and matching slippers. She blushed. The pieces were covered in white tissue paper and sealed with a gold Dior sticker, then enclosed in a white box and a large bag embossed with Dior in gold. "This is to remember our time together in Paris." Sam blushed.

"I can't accept this. This is something a woman would save for her trousseau."

Beau pulled her aside. "Exactly. I'll save this for your trousseau. Think about it."

She blushed a beautiful shade of pink. "I will," she whispered.

In Armani, Matt had the nerve to try on the pants with the band around the ankle, only to receive hoots and hollers from the others. Much to their surprise, two young men watched Matt model the pants, and each purchased a pair for themselves. Beau bought the funky sweater and leather belt, and Matt bought two regular-styled pants.

Chloe rolled the wheelchair over to an area with umbrellas and rain hats. She had given Victor her camera to take pictures of Mimi in the men's area, and he promised to return swiftly. A woman approached Chloe from behind and unceremoniously moved her to a more secluded spot. Her strange voice demanded the camera. People turned and stared. Chloe stiffened and yelled, "I don't have it."

Victor's voice boomed through the store. "Allez-vous-en." He had seen the encounter and jogged toward Chloe as the woman ducked around men and women standing in line to pay for their items. She left in a black van that waited by the sidewalk, tires squealing as it peeled away.

"Are you alright?" Victor asked Chloe.

"I'm fine. She wanted my camera."

He nodded, "If you don't mind, I will hold the camera for you. I doubt there will be any more trouble. Let's find the others. We have four more shops unless you'd rather not go."

Chloe looked at Victor suspiciously.

"You... *doubt there will be any more trouble.*' Let me guess: you're one of Gaston's men. I should have known...Very well. Let's keep shopping. Please don't say anything to the others."

"I don't like keeping this from them, but I will until I need to tell them." He pushed the wheelchair towards the others standing at the counter. Matt and Beau had their arms full of clothing and spotted Armani sunglasses for forty-five Euros.

"These were originally 285 Euros. I'm going to

get this pair. We couldn't buy these at home for this price. Why are they so cheap?" asked Beau.

Matt held up two pairs: "They must be last year's models. I don't care. I will get this tortoise-shell pair and the black ones for prescription lenses."

"You two look like you're having fun," said Chloe.

Sam laughed, "I would never have believed it. Beau's getting into designer clothing."

"Land's End and L.L. Bean are designer clothes," said Beau. "What?"

The snickers were so loud that the salesclerk blushed.

MATT ACQUIRED HIS raincoat under Chloe's supervision in Gucci while Sam found Beau in the fragrance area. Sam encouraged Beau to try on different scents until he found one that almost made her swoon. When he put it on, she wrapped her arms around his neck and nearly licked the smell off him. He bought every product in that fragrance because of Sam's reaction. Shopping was growing on Beau.

Cruising through Givenchy, Chloe loved the scarves and shoes but didn't like the jewelry. Matt called her. "Chloe, I need your honest opinion."

Victor pushed her over to see Matt trying on a suit. A female salesclerk hovered over Matt, assessing more than his suit. She checked the fit of his waistband and then casually smoothed the fabric over Matt's tush. He was oblivious, but Chloe nearly jumped out of the wheelchair.

"*Mademoiselle, s'il vous plait.*" Chloe's hand

beckoned the clerk to walk toward her. When the woman approached, Chloe used the universal sign language: two fingers pointed at her eyes, to the girl's eyes, and then with both hands, made claws and hissed like a cat. Message received.

The salesclerk spoke rapidly. She nodded slightly and then found a male clerk to finish with Matt. Beau grinned and then high-fived Chloe. Matt was clueless about what happened, but Chloe's jealousy mortified her.

In Chanel, everyone looked at jewelry, purses, shoes, and clothing. At the perfume counter, a young salesclerk was enamored with Beau and Matt and presented them with samples of everything. Beau picked up her hand and kissed it before saying, "*Merci.*" Matt followed his lead and spoke to her softly in French for a few minutes. No one heard what he said, but it was saucy enough for her to blush when she removed her hand. She handed them each a Chanel shopping bag, and after they had walked away, Sam and Chloe watched the girl fan herself.

"Looks like Matt learned a thing or two from Beau," said Sam, grinning.

"Apparently so. She'll have something to dream about tonight, I suspect." Matt used to speak to her in French when they were younger. She unconsciously fanned herself. *Oh boy.*

SIX DESIGNER SHOPS in six hours. It had been a rush, eye-opening, and exciting. Finally, the adrenaline and B vitamins were depleted, but Victor was the best-kept shopping secret. Chloe vowed that the next time she wanted to do significant shopping damage, she would hire a driver to take care of everything.

The limo stopped at a red light several yards from the Moulin Rouge. Beau asked Victor to stop in front of the building. He got out and told the others to follow him, then pointed to large photos inside a glass-encased bulletin board by the entrance. "Ladies, Matt and I have a special treat for you tonight. We're taking you to dinner and then to see the nine o'clock show at the Moulin Rouge."

"What kind of show?" Sam turned to Beau as she looked at some of the wall posters.

"It's like a Vegas show. You know, showgirls, singing, dancing, and magic acts."

Matt explained things to Chloe on the other side of the entrance. She raised her eyebrows and then hobbled over to Sam. "I understand this is France, and the Moulin Rouge has been famous for its cabaret shows for over two hundred years, but I'm not so sure it's something I'd enjoy seeing."

Beau picked up the conversation. "Where's your sense of adventure, your desire to experience French culture? You can write about this in your diary and tell your grandchildren. Come on. Dress up for an elegant dinner and then go to a one-of-a-kind show." Sam faced the guys with both hands on her hips.

"We are trusting you two, not only tonight but with our reputations... and yours. Remember, we know both your mothers." Sam and Chloe turned toward the car and slid inside.

It was a toss-up as to whose face, Beau's or Matt's, turned red first. Sam didn't make an idle threat; it was the ultimate threat, rarely given. Southern women, specifically girlfriends, wives, and mothers, could make life on earth heaven or a living hell... forever. Their memories endured a lifetime and could be revived at any given moment. If things didn't go well, what happened in Paris wouldn't stay in Paris.

Chapter 14

"CHLOE, YOU DON'T think Beau and Matt believe that tonight is a date, date, do you?"

"I'm not sure, but there are so many sparks between you and Beau like I knew there'd be, and... things have been going well between Matt and me."

"But what if... Beau thinks..."

There was a knock on the door. Chloe hobbled to open it while Sam finished her hair, still muttering. The guys stepped in dressed to kill, both wearing dark slacks, white dress shirts, sports coats, ties, and a clean, woodsy, masculine scent. Beau must have given Matt guidance on what to wear, including aftershave.

Chloe's heart stopped as she took in Matt's features. *Wow. He looks good enough to eat.* She had always found him to be extraordinary and handsome. He used to be her best friend and lover, and unknowingly, he set the bar for her to compare all the other men to. Yet, no other man had ever measured up. *Stop. Get control.*

Matt complicated things now. She was grateful they had resolved the reasons for their breakup. The pain lasted a long time, longer than it should have. Now, they could openly rebuild their friendship. *Baby steps. Could it be more?*

The corners of Matt's mouth turned up. "Hey, beautiful." He leaned in and kissed her cheek. "Ready to go?"

She nodded, her cheeks pinkening. "Come in. Sam's almost ready." She moved back toward the bed to get her cameras and handbag.

Chloe had taken time with her appearance. Her hair was styled in a ponytail pulled to the side, exposing a beautiful, long neck adorned with a short, braided silver chain and matching earrings. Her blue, shimmery, low-cut top with long, see-through sleeves that fanned out at the elbows picked up the silver sparkle of her jewelry. She hadn't anticipated difficulty using the crutches with the long navy skirt that kept getting caught in the boot. She leaned over to adjust it, and Matt was treated to a beautiful view down her top. If this happened all night, every man in Paris would see.

Matt cleared his throat. "Honey, why don't you lift your skirt and hold it in your right hand as you use the crutches? That way, your skirt won't get caught."

"Excellent suggestion. I suppose I flashed you, didn't I?" She grinned, not the least embarrassed.

His face heated. "Well... no harm done. Here, let me help you."

"Would you mind putting my phone in your pocket? My clutch is only big enough to hold my lipstick."

"That's all it holds? Sorry for asking, but why did you buy it if it only holds lipstick?"

"It was on sale… Don't worry. I put my keycard, ID, credit cards, and memory cards in my boot. When I get home, I'll buy the larger purse to put the clutch in."

"Uh-huh."

Chloe turned toward the bathroom, "Sam…We're heading to the lobby to give Claude my cameras and to wait for the taxi." She and Matt left Beau pacing the room, waiting for Samantha.

"What if… he…" Sam's voice was loud enough to bring Beau to the bathroom door. She continued to rock back and forth in front of the mirror.

"What if, what? What has you bumfuzzled, sugar?"

She jumped. "What makes you think I'm bum-fuzzled?"

"You're twisting your hair the same way you did when your credit cards were declined."

She barely realized that Beau had lifted her fingers from her hair as if in a dream. She watched as he kissed each fingertip and intertwined their hands together. He was so close. *I can't think straight. Breathe.*

"You're so beautiful. I've always been a sucker for your red hair. You should wear it down like this more often."

The fog lifted. *He's not teasing. He's serious and genuinely concerned.* She couldn't respond. *Beau is the only man to make me lose control, and I don't know what to do. I want to put my arms around him. Kiss him. Love him. If only he could love me, but that's impossible.* She swallowed.

Their eyes locked, and from the depths of her being, she willed her voice to calm and to present her usual persona.

"Humph. You're late. I thought you'd come to get us fifteen minutes ago. We might not make our dinner reservation if we don't leave soon."

"I think you were worried that I would consider this a date, right? Of course, you did. I'm glad you've been thinking about me because I can't think of anything except you. So yes, I consider this our first official date."

Sam blinked a few times and backed into the sink's counter, the solid surface jolting her. "You're so full of yourself."

Beau's confident personality was mesmerizing. He moved forward to stand inches away, his hand still holding hers. He leaned in and kissed her lips softly, then moved closer, breathing in her signature fragrance—the same expensive perfume he had worked and saved for as a present for her eighteenth birthday. He whispered, "You still wear Poppy."

He remembered, after all these years. "It's my favorite, so I wear nothing else."

"It's you, sweet like cotton candy." He leaned back and gave her a killer smile. "When you wear it, you think of me, don't you?" The cockiness was pure Beau and the spell was broken.

"In your dreams, Vinny." Sam corrected her posture, lifted her chin, and dropped his hand, moving toward the other room. "Let's go."

I'm back. No need to fret. Beau is Beau. This date, or whatever he wants to call it, is back on track. Tonight, she would show Beau her sophisticated side, dressed in a simple black dress and low heels that brought her closer to his height, the perfect height to kiss him if she dared. She sashayed to the bed, knowing he was watching her, and reached for a colorful silk shawl.

Beau swiftly picked it up and helped her put it on. Then he picked up her purse and handed it to her. Their hands touched briefly, and their eyes locked again. He kissed her cheek and smiled. "You look like a million bucks."

"Thank you." She tilted her head and scanned his features, from his shoes to his combed hair. "Coat and tie. I'm impressed. It looks good on you."

"I know. I even shaved again, for you."

Sam rolled her eyes. "I should never compliment you—it always goes to your head." She glided toward the door. "Stop looking at my backside."

Beau snickered and rushed to open the door for her.

THE TAXI ARRIVED on time on time at one of Paris' most romantic restaurants, the Grand Colbert. Sam cut her eyes toward Chloe and winked. It was an elegant restaurant, ultra-expensive, and in high demand. Surely, Claude had something to do with the restaurant selection and the reservation. Samantha put her arm through Beau's as they headed inside.

"Reservation for Jacobs. Four people." Chloe and Matt eased up behind Beau.

The Maître d' frowned. "I'm sorry. There has been a mistake. Table for two for Jacobs."

"And, Richards, table for two," Matt said instantly. The corner of his mouth tilted up, and he shrugged. "I called the restaurant after Claude had made the reservation."

This evening, two couples will be on a romantic dinner date. The maître d' gave two waiters the menus, and they led the couples in opposite directions. Finally, each guy was alone with his girl. Beau saluted Matt.

Sam and Beau were seated in the corner on the same side as the entrance, away from the front picture window. They couldn't see passersby, but they could hear faint noises from the street. The afternoon light was changing into soft twilight, classical music played softly, and the table's candlelight created intimate dining—the perfect setting for romance. In silence, they studied the menus. Beau suggested a glass of Lallier Grand Rosé brut. This was definitely a date.

"Since I'm going to be adventuresome and trust you tonight by going to the Moulin Rouge, I think you should be adventuresome with dinner; maybe try something you'd never eat, like frog legs."

"Hmm..." He didn't look up but still scanned the menu. "I'm not eating frogs, snails, raw meat, smushed liver, or "it's alive, it's alive." Think again."

"Point taken, me neither. However, we should have something uniquely French, so I will let you order for me." She folded the menu and put it aside as the waiter appeared at the table. This was a test, and Beau was up to the challenge. She didn't eat seafood, preferred beef over chicken, and loved salads. She loved every kind of salad. He nodded.

"We would like the charcuterie board, Châteaubriand for two, cheese on a green salad with balsamic vinegar, and water with dinner." She picked up her glass of wine in salute, and he did the same.

"I'm glad Matt tricked us. He and Chloe need time together. I hope they can work things out," said Sam.

"Things look promising. He went through a tough time after Chloe broke up with him. I don't think he ever recovered."

"What do you mean by the way Chloe broke up with him? That's not how it went. I was there. I know what happened. It was after the midterm exams. Chloe had a bad sinus infection that nearly turned into pneumonia. She spent almost three weeks in the dorm except for going to classes, and she didn't get to see Matt during that time. Unexpectedly, he calls Chloe and says he wants to date other people. It broke her heart. She didn't eat or sleep and wanted to drop out of school."

Beau stared at her like she had three heads.

"Before she failed all her classes, I talked her into taking incompletes and staying in the dorm until the semester's end. When we got home, she went through withdrawal. Then, she became angry. She tore up every photo of Matt, burned everything he had given her, and then she had a sage cleansing done on her house and car. That didn't go over well with her parents—they wanted to eviscerate him, and she would have helped.

"Before the summer ended, she knew she had to start over and create a new life. She made up all her classes and morphed into a different person.

Chloe refused to get involved with anyone and put all her energies into classwork and art. The breakup started her career.

"She didn't start dating again until halfway through her senior year, and since then, she only dates older men. She's never gotten over Matt, but Paris will decide their future."

"This makes no sense," said Beau. "She broke his heart, and he started dating Caroline, the bitch. He went through an anti-women spell until about a year ago, and even that girlfriend cheated on him, so he's been burned badly three times. If Chloe breaks his heart again, I'm not sure what will happen to him."

Sam tried to continue the conversation, but the waiter appeared. Small plates and a charcuterie board of assorted soft and hard cheeses, thin slices of ham and beef, olives, butter, and relishes, with a basket of bread slices, were placed in the middle of the table. The waiter refilled their wine glasses before retreating.

"You have to try this." Beau spread soft cheese on a piece of bread and topped it with beef. Sam closed her eyes and moaned in appreciation.

Once she swallowed and sipped some wine, she asked, "Who is Caroline?"

"She was Matt's roommate's cousin. She visited often, and the three would do things together. She flirted with him constantly, hinting that they should date. She was the one to find out about Chloe's boyfriend and told Matt." He dropped his fork. Stunned. "No, it can't be. If Chloe wasn't dating another guy, which I believe now she wasn't, then Caroline set Matt up."

"Bingo. She did this. She broke them up. Holy

cow. All this time, they've suffered because of her. Beau, we need to tell them. They need to know."

"Hold on, sugar. We shouldn't interfere. You and I had to take sides when Matt and Chloe broke up." He reached over and took her hand. "Not only did it ruin their relationship and the one the four of us had, but it also ruined the one between you and me. I've missed seeing you, Sam. I've missed our friendship and what could have been between us as a couple. Promise me that whatever happens between them doesn't affect what happens between you and me. They must find their way by themselves, just as we need to. I want to give *us* a chance, please."

"How can you say this since you've only been with me for the past few days?"

"I understand you're skeptical, but it's true, I swear it. I've wanted this for a long time… only I never thought you'd be receptive to it, and I didn't have the guts to do anything about it until I saw you in the New Bern airport. I realized that if I didn't take a chance this time, I'd regret it the rest of my life."

Sam couldn't speak. The waiter cleared the dishes to serve the main course. She refused to look at Beau or talk about the food, so they ate in silence. Beau's confidence level dropped considerably. He couldn't read her and may have scared her by speaking so boldly. "I shocked you. I'm sorry."

"Yes, you did. I thought you were flirting, pretending I was someone else, another one of the women you're attracted to."

"How I've been with you hasn't clued you into what I've been thinking? Have I read you wrong? Are you toying with me to see how far I'd go? Is this a game? You're going to have to clue me in, Samantha. I'm on a precipice here and starting to feel foolish... I'm serious. I've laid it all out, and it's up to you now." He pulled at his napkin, stretching it back and forth, hoping it would provide him with some comfort. It was placed back over his lap before he rested his hands on the table.

Sam touched his hands and searched his face. She took a breath. "Paris isn't home. I don't want to jump in feet first and realize once we get home that it was the excitement of being here... that what we're feeling now isn't real. I only have one heart. If you break it, I won't survive."

"Do you trust me?"

"Of course I do."

"Then trust me not to break your heart. Will you try? What if we have a trial run?"

She studied her wine glass and took a sip. "A trial run to be together... say four weeks?"

"I'm thinking a year. That takes us through the next school year and into summer."

"Or by the end of this summer."

"Six months takes us through the summer and Christmas vacation."

"To the end of this summer... by Labor Day weekend." Sam's left eyebrow went up, and a wall began forming. This was the end of her negotiation. She looked at Beau and smiled. He smiled back, then extended his hand for her to shake. She did. No matter how silly it appeared, it always came down to making a deal.

The waiter came back for the dessert order and cleared the dishes. "We'll have the cheesecake with fruit sauce and coffee with cream," said Beau.

"Today's his birthday." She winked at the

waiter, and he nodded.

"It shouldn't surprise me that you'd remember, but I'm touched that you do."

"I've never forgotten anything about you, but we have six years of history to catch up on."

"You're right. We should take things slow, but I'm not a slow kind of guy. Why don't I give you the CliffsNotes version, and you can fill in your blanks as we go along?"

The efficient wait staff appeared before the conversation continued. Beau's cheesecake was topped with a sparkler, and they sang "Happy Birthday" in French. Rather than be embarrassed, Beau was exceptionally pleased when the restaurant applauded. He stood and bowed. Samantha shook her head. In the back of the restaurant, Matt and Chloe clapped.

MATT AND CHLOE sat next to each other in a quiet corner booth hidden from the public areas of the bar, kitchen, and other tables. "This is a delightful surprise. I assume the food is good," said Chloe.

"Not only is this restaurant noted for its food, but it is also considered one of the most romantic restaurants in Paris... I wanted to have dinner with you alone. We need time to catch our breath and talk."

"Okay, let's talk, you first."

"I thought I'd gotten over you after all these years, but I haven't. Chloe, I want you back in my life."

"Like old times? No. So much time has passed, and we don't know each other now. I doubt you'd even recognize or like the woman I am today."

"Granted, it's only been a few days, but deep down, I know who you are: compassionate, generous, and devoted to your friends and family. You fight for what's important, and you're true to yourself. You're the most remarkable woman I've ever known, and I want to know more. So, tell me about Chloe Davis, artist extraordinaire." She blushed and then looked at him directly, with no hesitation and no apologies.

"Very well. I'm not the shy, reserved, dependent girl you once knew. You said jump, and I did because I trusted you implicitly. I used to hang on your every word, whether I understood it or not." She chuckled. "I'm independent and career-minded now. I refuse to be taken for granted, and I go after what I want."

"You're amazing. Without sounding condescending, I'm so proud of you. You're an incredible artist and businesswoman. What do you do for fun? Have you gotten to travel like you always wanted to? How about teaching, do you like it? What about your personal life? What about—"

"Hold on." She grinned. "I love teaching, I've traveled some in the south for work, I still like yoga, and I love shopping. However, I'm not sure I want to tell you about the personal side, which I assume is another way of asking about the men in my life."

"Men? Wow. I should have known. You're so beautiful, and you have this charisma that attracts guys to you... I've seen how men look at you, even with the crutches, so don't try to deny it."

"Am I hearing right? Don't pull the jealousy card on me because it won't work. If you must know, I have been in two serious relationships, been proposed to once, and I only date older men who don't live close to home—I like my privacy. I've been dating a professional athlete, a law clerk for one of the NC Supreme Court Justices, and a Delta pilot. That is when our schedules mesh, and yes, they all know about each other."

"Incredible. All those men, and you're not serious about any of them."

"They're wonderful men, and I have feelings for each of them—"

"But you're not serious about any of them?" She shook her head. "Then I'm going to assume that you are open to us spending more time together, to start dating... then we'll date exclusively, because hopefully in a little while you'll fall in love with me again, and from there—"

"Oh no. Don't think you can waltz back into my life and start making demands, Mr. Richards. What I do isn't up to you. Try that controlling shit as you did in college, and I'll cut you off at the knees and toss you to the sharks, do you understand me?"

"Yes, ma'am." He scooted in closer, wrapped his arm around her waist, and pulled her into him, his other hand holding hers. "This new you is... so hot. I can't tell you how much you turn me on." Chloe's eyes opened wide, and she felt her cheeks get hot. "You bring out the real me so that I've never had to pretend to be something else or feel the need to restrain my... geekiness. I don't want to dominate you... unless that's what you need me to do… but I want you to want me… more than any other man."

Holy…. This wasn't happening. It was both erotic and frightening. Her breathing became shallow and quick. "I… I also don't want someone who's submissive, clingy, or unwilling to be an equal partner, because I've ended things with men on less." Her breathing stabilized. She had to tell him exactly what she felt. "I don't think you know what you're asking, and I won't fall into an exclusive relationship until it's right for me."

"I appreciate that. We'll find what works for us if we try. You said you go after what you want. Do you want me?"

"Don't ask me that."

"You're challenging me to meet you halfway, and I'll do that and more. I want to. You already know that I never stopped loving you… Do you want me?" There was no desperation, just a simple question to the point, like Matt, a question that deserved an honest answer.

"God help me… I do… I've always loved you."

Without hesitation, he kissed her with enough passion to steam up the booth, and when they separated, she was almost faint. The man could kiss her into unconsciousness, and she could let him kiss her for days.

Reality hit.

"Hold on." She pushed away from him. "What did you mean by 'you already know I never stopped loving you'?" His face flushed.

"*Je l'aime. Elle m'a manqué.*" He repeated the exact words he had said before.

It only took a second for her to understand. "You weren't asleep." She whacked him in the stomach. "What a terrible thing to do to me." She hit him again. He took the hits, and then he brought her against his chest.

"You're a strong woman, another quality I love. You're passionate and decisive. I apologize for pretending to be asleep, but it only confirmed my suspicions. It made me so happy. You make me happy, Chloe. Can you forgive me for that and maybe… other things?"

They studied each other. He was sincere. She was toast.

"Beg me… in French," she whispered. His mouth millimeters from hers, so she closed her eyes.

"*J'ai désolé. Pardonne-moi. Je t'aime tellement, mon cher.*" He repeated it closer to her ear, "I'm sorry. Forgive me. I love you so much, my dearest." He placed tiny kisses below her earlobe, moving lower on her neck. She melted into him as he continued to kiss her.

"Justin." The only name she called him when they were intimate. "I forgive you."

"*Merci, mon amour.*" His lips found hers.

Fireworks exploded. When they separated and the room stopped spinning, she swallowed, finding her voice. "What now?"

"Correct me if I'm wrong, but we should use our time in Paris to keep talking, be together as friends, date, and renew our love. When we get back home, we'll continue on this path. Is that acceptable?"

"That sounded like a business proposition."

"I want all the romance too… I don't want to mess things up this time because I want everything with you. I will rely on you to tell me things, not clues, be frank with me."

"I can do that, and we will talk. What about the other men I've been seeing?"

"I don't like being jealous, so I will concentrate on us and not worry about them. You'll tell me when I no longer have competition."

"That's arrogant," said Chloe.

"No. I'm willing to wait because I'm confident in us."

"You're that sure?" His dimpled smile confirmed it. "Then kiss me like you mean it."

"Yes, ma'am."

After dinner, they shared a warm chocolate cake covered in raspberries and thick raspberry sauce with a glass of champagne. On the other side of the restaurant, they heard "Happy Birthday" being sung to Beau; he stood and bowed. Matt and Chloe clapped.

The waiter brought the bill, and Chloe realized it was too extravagant for a teacher's salary. She pulled out her credit card and laid it on top. "The dinner was lovely, and I'm glad we are working things out, but I'd like this to be my treat."

"Thank you, but no. This is more than a date; you're worth all this and more." He placed her credit card in her hand. "Let me tell you a secret. You're not the only one who makes a good living. Since we turned eighteen, I've invested in the stock market and small business ventures with Beau. Like you, we're quite solvent and teach because we love it."

"Since you're the math genius, I should have suspected that. You spent a fortune today, and with all the designer shopping bags, you'll need another suitcase too... I hope you don't take offense, but I'm proud of you." His smile said it all.

Chapter 15

THE FRIENDS RECOGNIZED the Moulin Rouge by the red windmill on top of a red building. The photos and posters of some of the acts shown in photographs inside the sidewalk marquees didn't reveal anything outrageous or provocative. Yet, this was Paris, and one should have suspected otherwise.

The friends entered a terraced-style theater. Red and white striped fabric draped from the ceiling gave it the illusion of a circus tent, while strings of lights inside reproduction 1890s-style hanging lanterns gave off soft ambient light.

Most of the audience sat at tables in tiers, five levels high. Two more VIP tables were situated at the two highest levels in the middle of the room, enclosed with glass walls. The stage took up most of the lowest level, with an orchestra pit in front. Yet, the most expensive tables were near the stage, set up for dinner and to watch the show.

The group was escorted to a table for four people on the third level on the right side, closest to the server's station. Each section on every level was surrounded by a thick, ornate gold-painted iron railing with posts shaped into right-sided up and inverted hearts. Samantha and Chloe sat by the railing on opposite sides of the table, their dates sitting next to them.

Beau and Matt took an awful risk coming here, especially after their romantic dinners. They had more to lose now than to gain. Suddenly, two bottles of wine appeared on the table. "Matt, tell the waiter to keep the bottles coming," said Beau nervously.

For a fleeting moment, Beau wondered if this was a colossal error. He knew what the Vegas shows were like since he had seen several. He only hoped the Paris show would be less risqué in Sam's eyes. Yet he would have never taken Samantha to Vegas, so why did he want to bring her here? This could ruin any headway he had made with her. Beau whispered to Matt, "Are we making a mistake?"

Matt's brows pinched together. He nodded. "We should leave. Uh oh, too late." The lights turned off, illuminating the table with a small brass lamp in the center. The Announcer welcomed the audience in several languages, and the orchestra played before the large curtain rose.

In the first number, the entire stage filled with women performing an intricately choreographed dance. They dressed in a G-string attached to sheer sparkling tights. Of course, they were topless. It might have been the Rockettes on stage; only more flesh showed.

The women were beautiful, perfectly trained dancers, the essence of every man's wet dream.

Sam and Chloe were shocked. Their mouths dropped open, their eyes widened, and they hardly blinked or breathed as their hands twisted the tablecloth edge in their laps. Sam and Chloe looked at each other, ready to bolt should the other one make a move to stand. They cleared their throats and drank heavily.

Matt and Beau studied their dates more than the stage. This *was* a mistake.

Chloe spoke first. "I've sketched and painted a lot of studio nudes, but I've never been subjected to a situation such as this. Am I blushing? Because I'm uncomfortable."

Sam lowered her voice, but the whole table understood her discomfort. "Beauregard Vincent Jackson. How could you bring me to such a show? This is the kind of thing you and your buddies would see in Vegas at a bachelor party, but *pulease...* we're ladies. I never imagined you would take me to a venue like this. Chloe, I think it's time to leave."

Beau missed most of Sam's tirade and only latched on to the leaving part. "Samantha, I'm sorry this offends you. I would never have suggested we come if it weren't an iconic Parisian show. Perhaps if you don't think of these women as topless wearing G-strings and view it as art, it would help."

"And are *YOU* viewing this as *ART*?"

"Y-yes, I do." Sam whacked him in the stomach. "Chloe would be the first to say that the human form is beautiful, and these women are beautiful."

"And I suppose you get girly magazines for the articles.

"Sure, I do, and of course, for the photography." She smacked him again, but he was teasing her and expected it. "There are other acts and performers besides these dancers. Why don't you try to make it till intermission? If you still feel the same by then, we'll leave, and I'll make it up to you."

"Chloe, what do you want to do, stay or go?"

"I'm willing to give this a chance, but if I see the first sign of arousal, I'm out of here. Matt, Beau, understand?"

"Understood." The guys said in unison.

"Fine, but I'm staying under protest. Pour me a glass of wine." Sam squinted her eyes at Beau, and he refilled her glass. "Wipe that smirk off your face, mister, or I'll wipe it off you."

"Yes, ma'am."

The guys knew they had crossed the line, but it was too late to quit. Sam would never respect a wishy-washy attitude, much less a course of action they wimped out on once a plan was in motion. Chloe might be more lenient with the semi-nudity if it were artistically done, and both men hoped it would be so as the show progressed. In their research, the guys only found a video of the rehearsals in ballet attire with more benign acts shown on the website, buried deep within the content. Cameras or phones weren't allowed during the performances, so they didn't know what to expect. They had to make the best of the situation.

More wine.

The curtain closed to applause, leaving a narrow stage for the next act to appear out front, a magician. The girls relaxed and enjoyed it. Each time the curtain fell, for at least ten minutes, a fully clothed act appeared. There were singers, clowns, acrobats, contortionists, girls dressed as jockeys parading miniature ponies, and even large snake handlers. Sam and Chloe could breathe then and even laughed. Beau and Matt were hopeful. More wine.

When the curtain rose, the stage changed into vignettes or period scenes where clothed male dancers interacted with female dancers who might or might not be dressed. Dancers representing other countries, like Russia and China, appeared. Some costumes depicted figures from a masked ball, and singing pirates took over the stage. Swings, slides, staircases, and little villages appeared around the stage, allowing the dancers to move around, to leave, and return.

Elaborate costumes with hats, headdresses, boas, giant feathered fans, beads, and sparkling jewels grabbed the viewers' attention under colored spotlights. Outfits varied from contemporary to historical, while the music changed from fast-paced, toe-tapping beats to sensual, sultry rhythms that taunted the audience. Four bottles of wine were consumed before intermission, followed by a pitcher of water with bowls of pretzels and nuts. Sam took her program and created a fan—it had to be a hundred degrees in the room.

Thirty minutes into the show, the stage became a circus ring with jugglers, acrobats, and half-clothed women riding horses and performing unusual feats while their body parts jiggled. On center stage, women in sparkly see-through body tights wrapped their legs and entire body with long red strips of cloth as they shimmied up to the ceiling. There was a drum roll, and they tumbled downward, unrolling themselves.

Beau pointed toward the women. "That defies the laws of physics." Sam punched him on the arm. He snickered, knowing the reaction that he would get out of her.

"No, that's physics at work," said Matt. He got the evil eye from both ladies.

The lights came on for intermission, and the guys escorted Sam and Chloe to the restroom, prepared to take them back to the hotel. They checked their watches. Chloe and Sam had been in the bathroom for twenty minutes—way too long. They were toast.

A bell rang, signaling the end of intermission, and the girls exited the restrooms. Without speaking, they walked back to their table and took their seats. The show had only thirty more minutes left, so they ordered their fifth bottle of wine. Beau fist-bumped Matt.

The curtain rose, and the mood of the stage changed again to a bygone era. Men and women paraded in nineteenth-century costumes, and singers serenaded them as they danced. Chloe and Sam smiled. Men pushed women in swings covered in flowers. It was a Jane Austen-like scene that morphed into a Victorian circus act with tightrope walkers and bicycle riders, some of whom were small dogs.

The tempo of the music shifted again.

Women appeared in midcalf black dresses, the men wore nineteenth-century suits, and they all danced on roller skates. When they exited the stage, other women dressed in black bustiers and midi skirts, red ruffled underskirts, and black ankle boots pranced onto the stage doing cartwheels, back overs, and performing high kicks and splits. They swished their skirts, kicking their knees and strutting to center stage for the finale. Beau got his wish to see the famous Parisian chorus line, the Cancan. The dancers whooped and hollered, causing the audience to whoop and holler. Beau even put his fingers between his teeth and whistled. This time, even Sam and Chloe clapped along with the crowd, and to everyone's amazement, the show ended on a good note.

The dimmed lights became brighter, and all the dancers and acts received applause, even encores. The house lights came on several minutes later, and Beau and Matt waited for the girls to rise. No one said a word.

The silent treatment.

The companions exited only to be held up by a horde of people waiting to get in for the late show. Chloe and Sam stopped moving. A man bumped into Sam and stole the clutch out of her hand. "Hey, he took my purse!"

Beau tried to maneuver around the people but only managed to see the perpetrator run down the boulevard and cut left onto a side street. Underneath the neon lights of a tattoo shop, Beau spotted a man who quickly turned away, sauntering down the street away from him. "He looks familiar... Simon, the Boston guy? I've had too much wine."

Beau returned to the others. "I'm sorry, sugar, he got away. I hope you didn't have anything valuable in it."

"My credit card, the hotel keycard, some euros, tissues, a pack of acetaminophen, a pen, a pen flashlight, hand sanitizer, toilet seat covers, a tin of breath mints, and my new forty-euros Dior lipstick."

"You always pack that much stuff in a small purse?" asked Beau.

"That's what you got out of it? He took my only credit card, the keycard, what's left of my euros, and my new lipstick, in order of importance. I'm as mad as hell, and I'm not going to take it anymore! What if the creep follows us back to the hotel?"

While they were distracted, a young girl bent down on the sidewalk to tie her shoe and teased Chloe's purse out of her hand. The girl took off in the opposite direction from the first thief.

"No! Come back here. That kid stole my seventy percent off mini-Chanel clutch." The kid flew down the street and turned onto another one; no time to chase her.

"We've been set up. Come on, let's get out of here," said Beau. A block away, they stopped next to the Irish pub to talk. "We know what they were after. Did they get the memory cards, Chloe?" She shook her head and pointed to her boot. "They're getting desperate. I'll chat with Claude when we get back to the hotel. It'll be okay. Sam, we'll cancel your credit card tonight, change the keycards, and I have enough euros to share with you."

The mood was somber, so Beau changed the subject. "Well, ladies, what's the verdict? Did you like the show?"

Sam and Chloe eyed both men and then ignored them by walking as swiftly as Chloe could hobble back to the hotel in silence. Beau fist-bumped Matt and then followed behind the ladies. "They're not mad. They're glad they got to experience the Moulin Rouge," said Beau.

"Maybe, but don't count on repeating anything like that unless you want to get emasculated."

"Duly noted."

At the hotel, they found the paper burglar alarms on the floor by the doors. "Both rooms have been searched," said Beau. "Check everything while I talk to Claude."

Beau approached the front desk. "Our rooms were broken into again."

Claude motioned for him to step into his office. "Oui. I am sorry, mon ami. The detective returned with a search paper, and they also checked the cameras."

"No harm done. We're going to the embassy tomorrow, so I'll take the cameras back, and we need new keycards. Thanks."

THE EVENING HAD been exciting, to say the least. It started with a romantic dinner, during which Beau and Matt confessed their feelings and a desire to start a relationship... and then the show. The girls talked about it as they lay down on their beds.

"I can't believe that Matt pulled off the switch. Dinner with Beau was.... Okay, Chloe, give. You've been grinning for the past half hour or so."

"Have I? It must be because Matt and I worked things out. The whole 'wanting to date other people' thing in college was a setup by some girl who wanted to date him—it was all a lie. And he knows everything, the heartache, my work, and even the other men. He wants me back in his life and will meet me halfway to get another chance. So do I."

"Wow. I'm happy for you... If...that's what you want."

"It is. If it's meant to be, we'll get it right this time. We're going to take it slow. What about you and Beau?"

"He says he's serious about wanting us to be a couple. I don't want Paris to blindside either of us by jumping into anything too soon—there's too much at stake, so I've agreed to a trial run through the end of summer. We'll see."

"A trial run? I'm not sure what that means, but I'll keep my fingers crossed for you. What did you think about the show?"

"Parts of the show were a little risqué for my taste, but overall, I liked it—I'm glad I went, but I'll never tell the guys that.... Sadly, I lost my beautiful purse."

Sam slurred her words. "I feel the same way. I don't think I've ever had that much wine. I'm drunk.... We'll... tomorrow." They both fell asleep without brushing their teeth or taking off their clothes.

Chapter 16

EXHAUSTION TOOK OVER. Yesterday was jam-packed with shopping, the dinner at Le Grand Colbert, the disastrous Moulin Rouge show, and the thefts. Each rollercoaster part was a physical and emotional drain; excitement, frustration, love, lust, and the awkwardness of seeing a show with topless dancers. Then there was the wine, lots of wine.

It was going to be a long day.

It was unusual for Sam to stay in bed, so Chloe took advantage of the extra time to pamper herself in the oversized tub and to wash her hair after downing several aspirin.

Sam entered the bathroom as the hairdryer shut off. "I drank too much last night."

Chloe giggled and left aspirin and a glass of water on the counter for Sam. Chloe closed the bathroom door to give Sam privacy in the shower. There was a knock on the door.

"When you didn't come down for breakfast, I

thought I'd check on you. Are you okay?" asked Matt.

"I suppose. We overslept. We've had aspirin, and she'll need two Cokes this morning, but I'm not sure it will help. Would you mind checking my ankle? It's colorful, and I overdid it shopping." She reclined on the bed, and Matt gently touched the area.

"Yep. Colorful and still swollen. Does it hurt?"

"Yes, but not as much as the bruises under my arms. The crutch pads hurt, so I rolled up some hand towels and used safety pins to keep them in place."

"That will help. I'm sorry, I didn't think about fixing them for you."

The bathroom door cracked open. "Chloe, can you toss my clothes to me?"

Matt did the honors, "Sam, I'll pass them to you. Chloe's putting the boot back on."

Matt and Chloe talked for a few more minutes, and then she put a small purse in her backpack. Chloe yelled to Sam through the partially opened bathroom door, "I'm going down to breakfast with Matt. See you downstairs." They passed Beau coming out of the elevator. "Go on in. Sam will be out of the bathroom in a minute."

BEAU USED HIS keycard and walked in. He thought he heard Sam talking. *Rapping?* "Hey, are you coming out?" She ignored him and continued talking. He peeked around the corner and saw her eyes closed, earbuds in, rapping to something on her phone while sitting on the toilet. He smiled, reached in, and pulled an earbud out. "Hey there."

Sam looked up and screamed, "Get out!" Beau stared at her. "I'm in the bathroom, you idiot. Get out."

"It's not like I've never seen anyone pee in the bathroom."

A roll of toilet paper hit him in the chest, and he caught it before it fell. Samantha's face turned beet red, and she did her best to shut the bathroom door with her foot.

"This isn't the locker room. You can't see me like this. Go away."

Beau smirked. Another layer of Samantha peeled away. Through all her bravado and love for getting into trouble, she had girly girl tendencies— her hair nicely done, perfume, impeccable manners, and walked with a sway to her hips, loving every facet. He pulled the door handle to close it and stood by. "I'll wait here until you finish."

"I can't go while you're listening. Leave."

"I can't. I have the toilet paper, and unless you drip dry, which I think is gross for a girl, you want me to stay here." He heard a muffled string of obscenities that tickled him. Then, he listened to the water in the sink turn on to mask the sound of her peeing. Finally, the water turned off. He smiled again.

"Okay, open the door and hand me the toilet paper." Beau followed the instructions, and it was snatched from his hand as she used her foot to close the door, barely missing his fingers. The toilet flushed; the water flowed again, and then silence.

"Now what? Are you ever coming out?"

"Eventually." Minutes passed. She opened the door, assuming the haughty air of a princess, and walked past him. "That was humiliating. Don't ever do that to me again. And we will never speak of this to anyone."

He stood with his arms crossed over his chest, a smirk still in place.

"What's the first rule of Fight Club? Not to talk about Fight Club." Beau didn't flinch. "What do you want?"

"Kiss me."

"You're nuts."

"Kiss me. Your hands are clean; you've already brushed your teeth and gargled. Do it."

She leaned into him, "I hate you."

"No, you don't. Come here, darlin'." He waited for her to kiss him, then pulled her closer to make it wonderful, magical, and electrifying. They separated, panting. "You like me as I am, and you have strong feelings for me... just like I have for you. What do you say about being a couple starting now?" He slipped his hand in hers, and they looked down at the joining. When their eyes met, she slowly nodded.

Matt used the keycard before Beau and Sam moved and opened the door. Chloe was right behind him, "Come on. They're only serving breakfast for fifteen more minutes."

Beau and Sam walked out of the room, holding hands.

"Well, well, well. Paris gets more interesting by the day. Love doesn't mean never having to say you're sorry, said Matt.

"You realize that's the dumbest bad movie quote ever?"

Matt shrugged. "It seemed to fit."

BEAU, MATT, SAM, and Chloe arrived at the Musée d'Orsay for their private ten o'clock tour. "This is a stunning building. See the giant clock over the entrance?" asked Matt. "The mechanics can be seen inside the top floor, where the small Degas bronzes are located. According to this brochure, they were found in Degas' attic after he died." He continued to read aloud.

"This building was originally a train station designed to bring people to the World Exhibition of 1900. It was a modern marvel with elevators for luggage, lifts for passengers, and the first electrified tracks. The design had to fit seamlessly among the other grand buildings, like the Louvre. Eliminating vapor and soot allowed the sculpting of naves and vaults, and the stucco was painted with flora motifs. The domed glass ceiling and arched stone pillars provided the elegance and grandeur of a Roman basilica, enticing people to stay in the Hotel D'Orsay and dine in its acclaimed restaurant."

"I would have liked to have seen it back then," said Sam.

Chloe was given a wheelchair, and with their guide, Lisette, they started on the top floor and worked their way around. They went to each gift shop, producing more shopping bags, and then down to the next level. Mimi got her photo taken everywhere.

"The trains stopped running, but guests stayed in the hotel until 1973, when it was declared a protected monument and turned into a museum," said Lisette.

"I could see a statue of Wonder Woman here in this museum," said Matt, tapping his watch. Two familiar undercover policemen were casually posing underneath the clock on the ground floor.

"Now, please follow me to see the bronze Rodin—"

"Now you're talking," said Beau. "The 1956 film of Rodan was epic! Ken Kuronuma used models of prehistoric animals as monsters to terrorize the earth with characters like Godzilla, Rodan, Megalon, and the Astro Monster.

"Rodan was a colossal, irradiated, dragon-like Pteranodon that moved on camera using suitmation. If you look closely at the film, you can see wire-operated puppets in the flight sequences. Rodan was supposed to have a kind persona, whereas Godzilla was the opposite. Personally, I liked Rodan in *Godzilla vs. Mechagodzilla II*… So is the bronze statue of Rodan in flight or walking on the ground?" asked Beau.

Everyone stared at him. Matt hung his head, shaking it.

"What? Come on, which way to Rodan?" Lisette pointed in its direction, and Beau hurried along. Behind him, the snickers became full-blown laughter. When they found Beau, he had his hands on his hips, reading the placard. "This is disappointing… It's just another naked guy."

Sam rocked into his shoulder, then gently rubbed his arm up and down. "Tell you what, Vinny. When we get home, we'll have a Godzilla and Rodan movie marathon, and you can tell us all about the nuances of that genre. Okay?"

Beau smiled broadly and kissed Sam on the cheek. "Thanks, sugar, it's a date. I'll even spring for pizza, subs, and beer for the weekend." Sam's eyes widened, and his smile was big. "There are twelve films with Rodan, twenty-four hours' worth of riveting cinematography. You're going to *love* them." He wrapped his arm around her shoulder, giving it a squeeze. Sam gave him the "what have I done?" look.

An hour later, the group faced the bronze statue of Degas' *Small Dancer Aged Fourteen*. Chloe gasped with excitement.

Beau was snarky. "It's three feet high and ugly, but at least she's not naked. What's with her legs and the old net stuff?"

Chloe took over as the teacher, artist, and the confident woman made an appearance. "This is magnificent. It's my favorite bronze. This one was cast sometime between 1921 and 1931. The original was a colored wax sculpture for an exhibition in 1881. It wore a pink muslin tutu, silk top, real toe shoes, and human hair tied with a pink satin bow.

"Critics and the public were disturbed by it, saying it had a perverted, animalistic face and reminded them of a prostituting dancer. She represents a woman from the working class. In the Paris Opera House, a special room in the Foyer de la Danse allowed gentlemen to meet and proposition female dancers. This dancer may have reminded the public of that, so the sculpture was despised.

"Degas used fourteen-year-old Marie van Goethem as the model. She was the middle daughter of a working family who lived in Montmartre close to his studio. He made nude and clothed sketches of her, and her facial features were altered for the statue.

"There are twenty-eight bronze statues like this found in museums all over the world, cast after Degas died. They have different tutus and ribbons, but no hair, and the toe shoes are bronze. Degas was calling out the social injustices against dancers of the time. Since he was fascinated with them, over half of all his paintings were of dancers, and it's not surprising that his first bronze was this one.

"I like to think that he captured the young dancer's essence. She's wearing hand-me-down tights too big for her, and her ballet skirt isn't new. But look at how she raises her chin in defiance of what you may think of her because she is a dancer. Her eyes are half closed, posed with her hands clasped behind her back and her feet in fourth position, the typical relaxed dancer pose. She's listening to the music or her teacher's instruction as she visualizes herself dancing across the floor at the opera house. For me, this is an expression of hope and dreams."

"Wow, Chloe. You picked up all that by looking at this? I don't see it, but then again, it's not a bronze of Rodan." Beau shook his head and walked around the corner to see what else was there.

"Babe, that was an astute observation. You have such a good heart and think the best of people." Matt leaned down to kiss her forehead. He whispered, "Don't mind Beau, you can take the boy out of Down East—"

A voice cried out, "Miss Davis, you're here! Dad, Miss Davis is over here." Janice Miller rushed to Chloe and hugged her neck. "I can't believe it. It's so great running into you, but why are you in a wheelchair?"

Chloe started to speak as Bob Miller, Janice's father, appeared. "Chloe? Ah, Miss Davis, what a pleasant surprise seeing you here today... and in a wheelchair? You'll have to tell me all about it." He dropped to one knee, picked up her hand, and leaned in to kiss her lips. Chloe panicked and turned her face so that he brushed her cheek instead.

"Bob... Mr. Miller. You're... here?"

Matt asked Sam. "Bob? Who the hell is *Bob*?"

"Uh oh," said Sam. "Not good."

"I knew you'd be in Paris, and since school's out, I brought Janice and my niece Chelsea for the week. I had hoped you would spend time with us and see the sights."

"Uncle Bob..." Chelsea approached the group, and then she spotted Matt.

"Uh oh." Beau appeared and then moseyed to stand by Sam to watch the fireworks.

Chelsea squealed, "Matt... I'm so glad you're here." She ignored everyone else and rushed to him. She put her arms around his neck and put a lip lock on him. His eyes remained open, looking around, as he struggled to remove her arms and disengage her lips.

"Uncle Bob, this was my teaching mentor, Matt Richards, the one I told you about." She leaned in close to Matt, whispering loud enough for everyone to hear, "Now that I've graduated, it's not against the rules for us to date." She tried to snuggle up to him, but he kept her at arm's length.

"Uh... oh." Beau and Sam said simultaneously.

Bob addressed Chloe again. "You probably didn't know this, but I own Globetrotter's Travel Agency, and I knew you four won the Paris trip—I have your itinerary, and as you say, the rest is history." He held up his hand to stop the questions and comments, then looked at his watch. "Why don't we all have lunch in the museum restaurant in an hour, my treat? I'll make the reservation, giving Janice and Chelsea time to buy souvenirs." He picked up Chloe's hand, kissed it, and walked away.

"Ho...ly... shit." Sam, Chloe, Beau, and Matt said together.

Matt approached the tour guide. "Lisette, it's time to end our tour." He slipped her twenty Euros. "Thank you for all your insight and information." After she left, he faced the group. "I think we should go somewhere to talk privately."

Matt guided Chloe from the elevator to the first floor toward some wooden benches facing a group of marble statues. Away from the public, he lit into Chloe as his jealousy took over. "Don't you think he's a little old for you?"

"*That* was your student teacher? What is she like, fifteen? Don't tell me you hit on her while she was under your supervision. That's disgusting!" Chloe looked down at him as she spat out the words.

"I did no such thing. I was her supervising teacher for one semester, but never encouraged anything personal between us."

"Sure...The way she had her tongue down your throat says otherwise." Chloe crossed her arms over her chest and looked away.

"Beau knows how things went at school—he

can vouch for me. She started coming on to me, so I switched her to another teacher in the second semester and notified her college advisor of the situation. It became so bad that I requested a video camera in the classroom and hallway, and I had to make sure I was never alone with her. I would never compromise my professional standing or personal reputation like that, and I never made any advances."

"And now, she seems to have amnesia about the past semester."

"I don't know why she's so persistent, but I intend to tell her to back off because I'm not interested in her."

"Humph."

"That's the truth… Now it's your turn. How old is *Bob*? Been seeing him long?"

Chloe sat up straighter and kept her voice even. "I suspect Bob is in his late forties, divorced, and I taught his daughter this past year. She's sweet and the one to introduce us during a school open house. Bob asked me out several times, but I'm neither interested in him nor do I think it's appropriate to date a student's parent. I haven't gone out with him, and I don't intend to." Chloe's chin rose, lifting her nose higher.

"Wow. I didn't see this coming. It looks like you've both been ambushed," said Sam.

"Here's what's bothering me," said Beau, stroking his chin like he had a beard. "Bob owns the travel company that sponsored the contest. Bob is interested in Chloe, and Chloe wins the contest. Bob's niece, Chelsea, worked with Matt. Chelsea's interested in Matt, and Matt wins the contest. I smell a rat."

"*Rattus gigantus*. The most giant of rats," said Sam.

"No, Sam," said Beau. "You're confusing that with *Nezulla the Rat Monster*, a biogenetically created half-human-half rat that escaped into the sewers of Japan—"

Chloe grabbed her hair with both hands and pulled. "This can't be happening. First, I sprained my ankle on the way to Paris. I photographed bad guys fighting and a money drop. I've been followed, my camera bag swiped, threatened by monkey climbing skateboarding thugs on a mini train, nearly run over by bicycling jerks, our purses were stolen, and now you're saying that all those stupid lesson plans and toiling over the essay for a rigged contest were busy work so that Bob and his niece, Miss Nympho, could trap us in Paris?"

"I think that sums it up," said Beau.

"When you say it like that, you and Matt look pathetic," said Sam.

"The difference between a wife and a job is what? A job still sucks after ten years," said Beau. "It sucks, okay. Get it? This sucks... Never mind.

"This is how I see it. We must finish the contest requirements as planned. That way, Bob can't get us in trouble with the county school superintendent's office or make us pay for this trip." They all nodded in agreement. "Then, we need to break up the Miller family infatuation with the two of you for good."

"And how do you propose we do that?" asked Matt.

"Simple," grinned Beau. "You and Chloe get engaged. This isn't personal, Sonny. It's business."

Chloe covered her head with both hands, "Holy Rodan."

"He's right," said Sam. "Paris is a romantic place to get engaged, and Matt had planned it all along. You two wanted to keep it secret until you got home, except you told us, your best friends. Isn't that right?"

Matt looked at Sam, then at Chloe, at Beau, and then back to study Chloe.

"Uh...yes. I asked Chloe to marry me at the Wall of Love, and she said, "Yes." He looked deeply into Chloe's eyes while holding her hands. "You said 'yes,' didn't you?"

Chloe was a little starstruck, nodding with a wobble. "Yes... I said I'd marry you."

Matt cradled her face, kissed her, and then touched his forehead to hers. "I'm so glad you did."

"That's settled," said Beau. "If they ask, Chloe will get your grandmother's ring when you return home. Now, let's head to the restaurant. I foresee ordering the most expensive lunch possible, drinking pricey wine, and eating the most decadent dessert as payback to Bob Miller." He vigorously rubbed his hands together and cackled like a witch. I'm going to get you, my pretty, and your little dog, also!"

"Overkill," said Matt. Beau shrugged.

SAM THOUGHT THE restaurant must have retained its grandeur since its opening in 1900. Four-foot-wide carved crown molding framed a curved ceiling painted a soft blue with trompe l'oeil designs of cupids, lovers, and floral motifs. Three rows of large crystal chandeliers spanned its width, each placed in front of glass French doors, making the gold plaster reliefs and wood trim appear as rich as those in Versailles. She took photographs to use as the setting of a romantic interlude in one of the historical romance books she was ghostwriting.

Large floor-to-ceiling windows, no less than twenty-five feet high, filled the curved archways and along the wall that opened to a wrought iron balcony running the length of the building. She could see herself there during a literary event, listening to famous poets and authors reading their work. Cocktails and hors d'oeuvres would be passed under candlelight as a string quartet played classical music. It would also be perfect for a wedding reception.

Sam envisioned wearing a period-inspired long dress without a train or veil. Her strawberry blond hair is pulled up with curly tendrils escaping here and there. Surrounded by her best friends and family, there is a sit-down dinner and dancing after a three-tier cake is cut, and the bride and groom feed each other in a less-than-dignified manner. Laughter surrounds them, followed by good wishes for a wonderful life. When twilight fades, fireworks explode overhead, and afterward, there is a fond farewell to her and Beau as they make their getaway. *Where in the hell did that come from?*

Sam inwardly shook her head and moved toward a mismatched group of composite-top tables and funky chairs made of rigid plastics in crystalline pink, green, blue, and yellow that one might see in a café during the 1970s. *Wow*. With such an eclectic environment, she hoped that the food would also be unexpected, French cuisine with a modern twist or even trendy molecular gastronomy. Beau would hate it, but it would be something they could talk about later.

Bob stood waiting for everyone to arrive. He created a place for Chloe's wheelchair next to his seat, and Matt sat on her other side. Then, Chelsea made a beeline to sit next to Matt. Sam made room for Janice and then saved a seat for Beau. They rushed to gain their seats like playing musical chairs.

Beau stopped at the maître d's station and watched as the two undercover policemen sat against the far opposite wall. He got their attention and handed the woman forty Euros to pay for their lunches. Beau took his index finger and flicked it against his nose, referencing the movie, *The Sting*, and both men saluted him in kind. Yep, good guys.

At Bob's request, Chef George Landrieu appeared at the table to discuss today's specials, desserts, and wine pairings. Beau impressed Sam with his knowledge of Landrieu's suggested wines and approved two. The chef bowed to Beau, "Excellent choices."

Bob urged Chloe to explain why she was in a wheelchair. Everyone focused on Chloe as Chelsea's hand landed high on Matt's thigh and squeezed it. He jumped. Matt casually removed her hand, and then Beau caught Chelsea's attention, encouraging her to talk about her student teaching experience.

When the time was right, Matt laced his fingers into Chloe's. She placed them on the table and cleared her throat. "Paris is such a romantic place. You will surely congratulate us because Matt and I are engaged." Chelsea gasped, Bob looked disappointed, and Janice Miller squealed in delight as she insisted Chloe tell her about how he proposed—the details recited as they had been previously rehearsed.

Afterward, the conversation revolved around the food. The wait staff was eager to please, keeping the wine glasses filled and bringing the dessert cart for their perusal. Two hours later, when the bill came to Bob, he didn't look at it; he placed his Black American Express card on the table. Chloe, Matt, Beau, and Sam thanked him for lunch, and fortunately, the goodbyes were short and subdued.

"All's well that ends well," said Chloe when they entered the taxi.

"What a relief," said Sam.

IT WAS ONLY a ten-minute taxi ride from the Musée d'Orsay to the American Embassy. Beau burped three times.

"Excuse you," said Sam, waving her hand in front of her nose. Chloe giggled.

"Sorry, I couldn't help it. I haven't eaten that much since the "all you can eat" grand opening of The Redneck BBQ Lab in Swansboro. Jerry Stephenson smokes a hell of a brisket."

"Yeah, he does, but I particularly love his mama's sweet cornbread and banana pudding," said Matt.

Beau suddenly paled. Sam said, "I had the same roasted sirloin with chimichurri sauce and smushed herbed potatoes that you had. I thought it was tasty, but had no problems with it."

"Yeah, it was tasty." Beau groaned loudly. "The limoncello ice cream and the Bordeaux wine were yummy."

"Then what did you in?" asked Matt.

"I don't think it was the chicken pâté pastry drizzled in gravy or the soft fruit, so it had to be the cave-aged cheeses that tasted like how three-day-old athletic socks smell," said Beau. Chloe giggled and couldn't stop.

"Then why did you eat it if it was so repugnant?" asked Sam.

"Because this is Paris, and you wanted me to be adventurous about the food. It was a plate of cheese, for crying out loud. Cheese. I thought it was supposed to taste like that, but apparently, that's what wiped out the cavemen." said Beau. "Ooooh… my tummy."

Chloe continued to giggle.

"Tummy aside, I can't believe we left Bob with a six-hundred-fifty-Euros lunch bill," said Chloe. "How much is that in dollars?"

"With today's conversion rate, it's six hundred-ninety-eight dollars. Beau, your lunch alone was ninety-three dollars. Congratulations on having one of the most expensive lunches I've ever seen. It's sad, though. The four of us could have eaten at the Redneck BBQ Lab three times for dinner and had change left over to buy Dunkin' coffee for the price of your lunch."

"The sad part is that Beau will feel bloated for a while. Poor baby. He's already popped the button on his khakis and pulled out his polo shirt," said Sam. "We should clear the coal mine in the next few minutes because we don't have a canary."

Beau grimaced, and his face was flushed. He couldn't say anything snarky because she was right.

The taxi stopped, and they all got out quickly. Sam reached into her purse and pulled out a roll of Tums, an Imodium caplet, and two peppermint candies for him. "We're early, so why don't you take a walk around the parking lot and then meet us at the entrance in twenty minutes."

"Thanks, Sam." He headed downwind and walked around. The trio left behind heard a few deep burps and sounds that mimicked a car backfiring.

Chloe kept giggling. "Payback's a bitch."

COMPARED TO THE other buildings in the neighborhood, the American Embassy looked more like an ugly concrete block typical of federal buildings in D.C. rather than a French building emulating the style of all the Louises, XIV, XV, or XVI. Yet, history had been made here.

When Beau entered the front door, he told his pals, "This is the oldest American embassy. Benjamin Franklin was the first American Ambassador, with the first diplomatic mission during the Revolutionary War and then afterward when America tried to procure loans for the government. We should bow our heads and take a moment of silence in humble recognition." He looked around to see Sam tapping her foot, arms crossed over her chest, and Chloe raising her crutch, ready to swat him.

"I think he feels better," said Matt.

The receptionist showed them to the visitors'

debriefing room. Moments later, Brian Copeland, the Deputy Chief of Mission, walked in. They were introduced, and he sat down behind the desk. "When I heard why you four made the appointment, I felt it was necessary to speak with you myself. I understand you have something interesting to show me."

Chloe produced her camera and pulled up the first photos at Versailles. She told the story from then until the Musée d'Orsay. Beau talked about the narcotics detective, Jean Louis, the rooms being searched, cameras checked, purses being snatched, and being followed.

"Except for the two men fighting and then the drop-off and pick-up, we aren't sure what we're involved in. Perhaps we were in the right place at the wrong time," said Chloe. "We're leaving Paris the day after tomorrow, and we don't know what to do with the photos I have. We may be in danger. Can you help us?"

DCM Copeland picked up the phone and spoke, "Hilda, please send in Casey with a laptop and a memory card reader." After a few minutes, a man walked in. "Casey, I'd like you to download the photos from two memory cards and leave the laptop. I'll call you when I need you again."

The photos were brought up, and the memory cards were returned to Chloe. "I don't recognize anyone, but the photos of the men fighting should be turned over to the police, and I will do that for you. Hopefully, this will keep you out of trouble with the gendarmes."

"DCM Copeland, I'm an artist. I need most of these for my work," said Chloe.

"I understand. Why don't you point to the

photographs you want me to keep and delete the rest? Is that satisfactory?" Chloe nodded and began the time-consuming task. When she finished, she turned over about thirty-five photos.

"Regrettably, there's nothing else I can do except contact Detective Jean Louis' supervisor to let them know that the American Government doesn't look kindly on having its citizens harassed." He leaned forward and wiped his glasses on his tie.

"I suggest that while you are in Paris, you stay together since it is safer that way. Hopefully, there will be no more trouble before you fly home. Here is my card if you need to contact me." DCM Copeland passed out his business cards, then shook everyone's hands before escorting them to the exit.

Chloe put the business card in her wallet. "Well, that didn't go as I had hoped."

Matt opened the door for the group. "We'll continue to do as we've done, and I think we'll be okay. These goons are bad guy wannabees, and we can handle them."

"Don't worry. I am one with the Force, and it's with me," Beau grinned.

Sam patted Beau's tummy. "You're a force, alright."

Sam flagged down a taxi and hurried to get in the front seat. When the doors closed, she turned over the hotel Ibis' business card, showing the driver some words in French. The driver said, "Oui," and pulled away from the curb.

Beau's face contorted, "What did you do, Sam?"

"We're going to have another Parisian adventure." Under her breath, she added, "Poetic justice."

Chloe smiled devilishly. Claude had come through again by making an appointment for them at a funky hair salon. The guys would soon learn that the new friendship pact would include haircuts and a dye job, all in the same color.

The taxi pulled over to the hair salon, Rock Hair. Sam paid the driver, and the foursome stood on the sidewalk. Matt looked up at the retro 1980s building, which resembled a record store on the outside, and heard hard rock music coming from inside. He peered in the window and saw the hairdressers were dressed in rocker clothing with outrageously colored and styled hair. The music changed to an Elvis Presley tune, and an older lady exited with black hair and a thick white streak running from side to side and across the front. Then, two guys with dreads walked in.

"What's going on?" asked Matt.

Sam and Chloe smiled. "We have an appointment," they said together.

"Oh no. You're crazy," said Beau.

"Don't hit me with negative waves this early in the morning," said Chloe. "Hey, Oddball, this could be your moment of glory. And you're chickening out."

"Where's your sense of adventure? What's more iconic than Parisian fashion and, by extension, a haircut and color?" asked Sam. "Have faith, Crapgame. Them's gorgeous people."

"Crazy, man. Those positive waves... and we can't lose," said Matt.

"I can't believe you all know the best lines from *Kelly's Heroes*; it's humbling. Fine. I suspect this is your way of getting revenge for the Moulin Rouge, and I'm good with it. Do your worst," said Beau.

"I'm glad to hear that. *Carpe diem.* Seize the day, boys," said Sam.

Techno music blared from speakers hanging from each corner. Sam strolled to the reception desk and handed the woman the business card. Four hairstylists were waiting for them. Sam and Chloe had already chosen the bright mahogany color and asymmetrical style bobs, longer for Sam, before they even left home, knowing they wanted to have a Parisian cut as a fond memory. Sam pointed to the color swatch and then to all the members, and the hairdressers understood. Then she showed the magazine photo for her and Chloe, and asked to see the men's style books so they could choose the guys' cuts.

Three hours later, not even their mothers would have recognized the troupe members. Matt and Beau had identical styles, cut close to the scalp and going up, then longer on the top but spiked in every direction. Mimi posed with the hairdressers, and they fixed her with a human wig of Sam's hair that matched the rest of the group's hair color. Everyone took out their phones and snapped photos.

"You know, we look so good; we should go clubbing tonight," said Sam.

"I agree," said Chloe. "Let's change clothes, have dinner, and then go out."

"All the music they played makes me want to hit the Hard Rock Café. That okay?" asked Beau.

"Perfect. I'm in the mood for a killer cheese-burger," said Matt. "And Sam, they serve bottomless refills of Coke."

Sam couldn't have been happier. "Let's go back to the hotel and rest a while. Etienne recommended a club, and I plan on dancing all night."

"I'll save some room so you can rest with me," said Beau. He put his arm around her waist and kissed her. "You're not scared to do that, Sam?"

"Not in the least, but how's your tummy?"

"I plan to keep you close, not run you off, Sugar."

The friends entered the hotel in high spirits until they realized their rooms had been searched. Beau was livid. "I'll be right back," heading downstairs. By the time he got downstairs, he was much calmer.

"Claude, we went to the American Embassy today. They couldn't help us, but I think it's time you introduced us to our police friend. Could you do that? Tomorrow, here in the café at eleven o'clock. We have a soccer game early tomorrow morning at a nearby park." Claude nodded.

Beau thought, *I will give him an offer he can't refuse*. Then he called the embassy and left a message for DCM Copeland about the meeting with Jean Louis in case he wanted to be present.

Chapter 17

B EAU RETURNED TO his room to find Sam on his
bed asleep and Matt nowhere to be seen.

"Hey." Beau nudged her awake. "I know you
need a nap, but I thought we could talk a little
more." He scooted on the bed so that she faced
him. He had to touch her hair. "I like your haircut,
and the color suits you...."

"Thanks, you look pretty snazzy, too... but?"

"But I love the real Samantha even more. Tell
me you love me."

"Saying it doesn't guarantee anything. Look
what happened to Chloe and Matt. They were
together for a long time. It only took one misunderstanding, and we've been miserable for six
years."

"What Matt and Chloe went through was terrible and stupid, but I think they will work things
out. I don't want to talk about them—I'm talking
about us. I love you, Samantha Anne Williston. I
promise not to break your heart, and even though
you might still break mine, I'm willing to take the

chance." He gently turned her on her back and kissed her softly, sweetly, passionately enough that tears ran down her cheeks. "Sweetheart, don't cry. I can't bear to see you that way."

Sam smiled as she wiped away the tears. "I need to sleep now, Beau." She scooted out from under him and turned her back into his chest so he could spoon her. She closed his arms tightly around her, "I love you, too."

He was over the moon. His heart was swelling, but his head knew there were hurdles to get over. Samantha couldn't be pushed; she had to figure things out, and then she'd jump in feet first, ready to go. Patience wasn't his forte, but he remembered the race between the tortoise and the hare and had to keep plugging along. *Keep walking. I'm winning the race.*

MATT HAD CHECKED Chloe's ankle, and the swelling was down significantly, but the color was yellow and green. He propped the ankle up on pillows. "I think it's time to see if you can put pressure on it tonight, but no dancing, okay?" She nodded, but he could tell she feared getting her hopes up and injuring it more. "I'll be right there." He scooted in beside her and turned toward her. He studied her hard enough so that it became uncomfortable.

"What? Why are you looking at me that way? You don't like my hair?"

"It's perfect." He ran his fingers through her hair. "It's so much better than when it was green." He grinned. "That's not why I was looking at you. I was thinking about our fake engagement at the

Wall of Love. I know it wasn't real, but it's possible that it could be real in the future. I know you don't think I could be in love with you, but I am. Don't worry. I won't pressure you, but don't be surprised if I say it again. Why are you smiling?"

"I believe you. Let's say I'm hopeful."

"That's good enough for me." He kissed her and then held her hand as they relaxed side by side.

TWO HOURS LATER, Sam knocked before she entered her room. It felt weird, but she didn't want Chloe or Matt to be caught unaware. She was surprised they were looking at photos and talking about architecture. "Okay, guys, we need to get going. I'm in the shower first. Matt, I forgot to tell Beau not to wash his hair for twenty-four hours. Please tell him, okay?" Sam pulled out some clothes and headed for the bathroom. The shower turned on, and it was his cue to leave.

When the guys came for the girls an hour later, Sam wore a black miniskirt, a yellow scooped t-shirt, and wedge sandals. Matt looked her over, wolf-whistled, and said, "N-ice," before heading to Chloe and commenting on her beauty.

"Nice? He whistled." Beau scowled at Sam. "I saw how he looked at you, and he's like a brother. I can't imagine how other men will react to you wearing that short skirt if we go dancing. Maybe you should change."

"You're kidding, right?"

"How 'bout putting on a pair of those pants that hit above your ankle?"

Sam's jaw tensed, and her lips formed a thin line. There may have been wisps of smoke coming out of her ears. "No. I'm wearing this."

"No? Can you wear some tights under it?"

Chloe giggled. It had been a long time since someone had strongly suggested or, more specifically, told Sam what to do. This would be worth watching—like a train wreck.

"No."

"Let's go out in the hallway to discuss this." He guided her out the door. Chloe and Matt moved toward the closed door and listened intently, too speechless to comment, much less breathe. "Sam, you have gorgeous legs, and I could look at them for hours, but I don't want other men looking at them like I do. Your skirt would be perfect at the beach with me and all the other ladies wearing next to nothing, but here it could send the wrong message. Perhaps you change into something… more modest."

Sam struck her famous pose—hip jutted out, hands resting on them, and one eyebrow arched up. "Wasn't it only last night that we agreed to a trial run until the end of summer? Twenty-four hours is our limit. The trial run is over, and I'm not changing my skirt." She opened the door and slammed it in his face.

Chloe and Matt knew better than to laugh, snicker, smile, or look interested in what had happened. It was better to forget it all.

A loud thud accompanied the door shaking. Beau's fist was going to hurt for a while.

"I'm starved. Let's get a burger and a Coke," said Sam. She put on a crossbody purse and opened the door for Chloe and Matt. Beau was holding up the wall by the elevator, refusing to speak or look at anyone, both hands in his pockets.

It took only fifteen minutes to get to the Hard Rock Café from the hotel, but there was a twenty-minute wait in the lobby. They studied the menus in silence. Chloe and Matt glanced at each other. This was a new experience. Chloe had forgotten that Sam played the silent treatment card like a professional. When Sam decided on something, it was final. *Oh boy. What next?*

Chloe was concerned they would end their trial run soon under those conditions. Both Beau and Sam were wrong. Like her mother always said, "Two wrongs don't make a right." She thought maybe if she could speak to Sam in the ladies' room, she could get her to rethink things. "We may be waiting a while, so I think I will stretch my legs, test my ankle, and head to the restroom. Come with me, Sam. I may need your help."

A line formed inside the door, so it was a perfect time to talk. "I'm sorry things ended with you and Beau," said Chloe. "So why did you chicken out?"

"What do you mean, chicken out? He tried to control me by telling me what I should wear. The nerve of that guy. I certainly couldn't be with someone like that—"

"I understand he was being possessive, domineering... and protective. In small doses, those characteristics can be endearing. You said it yourself; he didn't do relationships, and I'm sure he cut girls loose when a girl was clingy. With you, it's different. He's in uncharted waters. I believe he wants to have a relationship with you, but he doesn't know how. If you decide to give him a second chance, it'll be your job to help him, like it will be his job to teach you."

"What do you mean, teach me? I've had relationships."

"Yeah. You've had several. Only one lasted a month, while most lasted a couple of weeks. So, you could also use some coaching." Sam rolled her eyes.

"Look, Sam, you know I love you and want only the best for you, so I will tell you something you already know... You are domineering, possessive, and protective, just like Beau. He always lets you take control of our group. It's different now. He wants a relationship with you, but wants to be the man in the relationship. You'll need to find some common ground and learn to compromise for both of you to thrive. Sam, don't run away from this. I get that you're scared, and so am I. You and I have a chance now for lasting love, and if you don't try to make things right, you will regret it for the rest of your life." Chloe patted her hand.

Sam had to look away. She tried to study the artwork on the walls of the small bathroom, but her vision became cloudy, and there was a tightness in her chest. Her fingers reached for her hair to twirl and found it gone. She opened her purse, pulled out a tissue, and blew her nose. Chloe made a lot of sense—she was right, but it was hard to admit it. Pride. She needed to swallow a lot of pride. It would be challenging, but if there was a way to work things out, she needed to find it so that neither she nor Beau would suffer. *Would Beau even want me back?*

WHILE SAM AND Chloe were gone, Matt moved next to Beau. He didn't have any advice, so he defaulted to menu talk. "The steak sounds good, but I want a cheeseburger and some onion rings."

"Can you believe she wouldn't change her skirt?"

"Well—"

"It wasn't an unreasonable request—Sam's beautiful. You've seen how men are attracted to her, and she doesn't think things can happen. Remember that guy in the bar? I know she can handle herself, but we're in Paris, and anything... anything could happen... She's delusional."

Matt opened his mouth to reply, but Beau kept talking.

"And then she dumps me. Can you believe it? After only one day? One efff'n day... I don't know. Maybe she's right, we don't stand a chance. I should take this as a sign and be grateful that it didn't go any further.... Yeah.... That's exactly what I will do." He slapped Matt on the back. "Thanks, buddy. Our talk really helped. Whew. I feel better already."

Matt shook his head, signaling to Chloe that he had no luck. He whispered so only she heard, "Fasten your seatbelts, we're in for a bumpy night."

She whispered, "They'll have to work things out on their own time, and we need to give them some space."

Matt's stomach growled as the hostess seated them at a four-top table in the downstairs area close to the DJ's booth. With Matt sitting beside Chloe, Beau and Samantha ended up sitting beside each other but not speaking, looking miserable.

They ordered cheeseburgers, onion rings, beer for the guys, and Coke for the girls.

Matt broke the silence. "Did you know that every Hard Rock Café has its own unique design and décor? Despite that, the food is regulated by US standards and cooking methods, and it also has bottomless Cokes, unlike other European restaurants, so Sam will love it."

"That's fascinating," said Chloe. Sam hmphed.

"I've also been told by friends who travel around the world that when they want to have a taste of home away from home, they eat at a Hard Rock Café, so this should be good," said Matt.

Beau took a long pull off his beer and flagged down a waiter, lifting the bottle as an order. He drained the rest and then worked to peel the label off, shredding paper while the music filled the silence. This was disastrous. Matt looked at Chloe and decided the two sulking children wouldn't ruin their evening, so he talked to Chloe as if they were the only ones at the table.

"Tell me about these locks you want to photograph tomorrow afternoon. They're on bridges, right?"

"Most of them are on bridges, but there were so many locks attached to the metal railings that it affected bridge integrity, adding extra weight to a dangerous level. So, the locks were cut off, and overnight, they appeared again. When the bridges were full, locks appeared on fences, the filigree work of lamp poles, and anywhere a lock could be attached."

"Was it pranking or delinquents doing it?" asked Beau.

"Not pranks. They are love locks. Although the

tradition began in Asia, it spread to Italy, England, and Russia. At first, newlyweds locked them on. They would pick a location, write their initials or names on the lock in permanent marker, attach it, and then throw the key into the river, sealing their love forever. It was so romantic. Later, couples in love followed the tradition.

"Of course, this caused lock seller kiosks to set up at the bridge entrances. On our tour tomorrow, we will walk over a bridge or two, so I can photograph the most interesting locks. That is, if they haven't been removed."

"I hope they're still there," said Sam. "The concept is interesting enough that I might want to use it in a short story or a personal essay in the newspaper. This excursion could be my research, so I'll help you."

Sam and Beau were conversing, albeit not with each other, but at least they were talking. When the DJ began playing, the friends argued about the merits of one genre of music over another, sometimes singing the lyrics. Before they left the Café, Sam and Beau were civil to each other.

"Etienne gave you a club name," said Chloe. "What kind of club is it?"

"It's called La Machine du Moulin Rouge. The cabaret is located in its old boiler room, one of Europe's largest clubs. There are two floors for live bands or DJs, a private rooftop area for drinks, and a terrace garden designed in cozy vignettes for drinks and food. It's about a twenty-minute taxi drive from here, but then we could walk back to the hotel. It's on my phone. See?" She handed it to Chloe and shared it with Matt while Beau leaned in to see.

IT WAS ONLY nine-thirty, and the club was filling. The bottom floor was the size of an airplane hangar and easily held a thousand people. There were a few tables around the perimeter, and Beau snagged one, paying an additional charge because it had a private server. Chloe had tried to put pressure on her ankle while in Hard Rock Café, but it swelled. With a pill and some water, Chloe needed to sit down while they were in the club.

"Come on, Matt, I want to dance with you," said Sam. "If I remember correctly, Beau has two left feet." She pulled Matt onto the floor.

Chloe asked Beau, "Is that true? Can't you dance? It seems like I remember you could."

"I can dance. Sam doesn't want to dance with me. I guess you heard our disagreement back at the hotel. She's right; we aren't a good fit."

"That's hogwash! Both of you were wrong. You tried to dominate her, and you backed her into a corner. She felt she had no choice but to end things because no one had ever treated her that way. You're both stubborn, pigheaded, willful..." He ducked his head, rubbing his neck. "...amazing, protective, loving people, and the best friends I could ever have.

"You've been putting the moves on her since we arrived at the Newark airport, and she finally agreed to take a chance on you. Are you going to give up now? Because if you do, you're not the Beau Jackson I know."

"It's complicated."

"She loves you. You two don't have baggage like Matt and I do, yet we want a second chance. Relationships require work. If you leave Paris and things aren't resolved, you'll never have another chance with Sam. I guarantee it. Is she worth fighting for?"

"Yeah, she's worth it. I've been in love with her since tenth grade...Ah hell. You're right, I didn't handle that well, and she overreacted, but I want to be with her, and even though she ended it, I believe she still wants to be with me. Tell me what to do."

"You need to apologize. Swallowing a little pride won't kill you. Since you took the first step to get her attention, you'll have to take this step now. Talk to her, work things out, and whatever you do, don't give her ammunition to run. I spoke to her, and she's thinking about all this, but if you hurt her, I will make you pay in ways you can't imagine."

Beau kissed her cheek, "Okay, Sugar, I'll do what you say. When did you get to be so wise?"

"I be Groot."

MATT AND SAM danced for thirty minutes before wandering back to the table. Sam was oblivious to the men who ogled her, but only looked at Beau, who gave her his killer smile. She smiled in return.

"Did you have fun out there?" asked Chloe.

"It was great, and Matt only stepped on my feet three times."

Matt blushed, "I said I didn't mean it. I'm a little rusty."

"We'll have to practice when I get off the crutches." Matt leaned down and kissed Chloe before he sat down beside her. "I had forgotten how loud it got in these clubs. It'll be next week before I can hear again."

"Maybe it's time to go back to the hotel," said Sam.

"Nonsense. Besides, I'd like to see if Beau can dance," said Chloe. He grinned, ordered more beers, and then promised to dance after *draining his lizard.* "Gross. Get out of here." That was Beau, reverting to his ninth-grade tactics to get a reaction.

Sam was about to sit down when a Middle Eastern man approached her. "Would you like to dance?" he asked. She reluctantly nodded, and they moved a few feet from the table onto the dance floor. It was a fast dance that ended in a few minutes, and he asked, "Again?"

She nodded. The crowd moved them farther onto the dance floor. Sam was enjoying herself, but then the music slowed, and the man reached for her arm.

"No, thanks. I think I'll sit this one out."

Before she could walk away, the man grabbed her and pulled her to him. Instead of dancing a respectable distance from her, he dragged her against his body and ground his hips into her.

"Whoa. Knock it off," said Sam. She pushed against his chest. He laughed. He pulled her to him again, like this was a game. This time, besides grinding his hips into her, he began feeling her up. Sam slapped his hands, pushed against him, and tried to extricate herself. "No! Stop it!"

Sam removed his hands, but he grabbed her again, determined not to release her. She tried to knee him, but it was the wrong angle to be effective. She slapped him in the face and screamed, "Fire." Spoken in English, it did no good.

Beau saw what was happening and pushed into the crowd to get to her. He grabbed one of the man's wrists and applied enough pressure to numb his hand. "Let her go."

"Find your own girl." Beau saw red. The man's eyes widened as Sam grabbed his other hand to apply pressure to the base of his pinkie nail.

"This is *my* girl." With both hands receiving immense pressure, the man screamed as he hunched over. "Consider this a divorce," said Beau.

Sam yelled at him, "No isn't just a word... It's a sentence... it doesn't need an explanation or interpretation... no, means no." Then she kicked him in the groin, and he fell in a heap, gasping and moaning. "Asshole."

Beau escorted Sam off the dance floor. She was shaking, her breath coming in short, sporadic rhythms.

"That guy shouldn't have touched you. Are you hurt?"

"My arms are bruised, but what hurts most is the rude awakening my pride and common sense suffered. I have always depended on the kindness of... friends. Thank you for coming to my rescue."

"Anytime, sweetheart. If you need me, whistle. You can whistle, can't you? Put your lips together and blow."

Sam didn't hesitate. She fisted Beau's shirt, pulled him closer, and lightly whistled. She kissed him with urgency despite the public atmosphere and Beau responded with equal enthusiasm. When they came up for air, she was shaking. Their foreheads touched, and his encircled arms didn't drop until she was ready to move. Once they got to the table, Matt and Chloe stood up and waited to leave, seeing what had transpired.

Beau possessively hugged Sam's waist as they left the club. "How about we find a hot chocolate croissant and a Coke?"

"That sounds wonderful." Sam blushed. "Beau, I'm sorry. Although it was the man's fault, you were right. I may have sent the wrong message with my appearance. I will do my best not to put myself in that position again.... Would you mind putting your arm around me?"

"It'd be my pleasure. Samantha, I need to apologize, too. In the hotel, I was possessive, overbearing, and jealous. I'll try to do better."

"This calls for a rule. Don't dance with strange men. From now on, I only want your hands on me." Beau gave her his signature smile and brought her closer.

THEY RETURNED TO the hotel while Beau still had his arm wrapped around Sam, and she was barefoot, carrying her shoes. Even though their hotel rooms had been searched again, Sam's and Chloe's purses were sitting on the bed, intact, and the contents accounted for. Sam yelled, "Dagnabbit! I canceled the only credit card that worked. I hate these guys."

"I hate them too," said Chloe, "but we'll only be here another day and a half, and we'll take care of whatever you need." Sam nodded. "Sam, I need Matt to look at my ankle. Would you mind it if he stayed with me tonight?"

"Not at all. Let me grab my things."

Beau winked at Chloe.

"Don't forget we have the soccer match tomorrow, so try to get some sleep and set your alarms for six so we can get a light breakfast. I'll pack up some fruit and drinks to carry with us," said Chloe. "See you two in the morning."

"When did you get so bossy?" asked Beau, smiling at her.

"Please. I'm a teacher. I know how to be bossy. I love you both; now go." She shoved Beau out the door and hugged Sam before she left with her toothbrush and pajamas.

Chapter 18

EVERYONE'S ALARM WENT off at six o'clock, and within a few minutes, Sam knocked on her hotel room door, still in pajamas. Matt answered, then headed next door for a quick shower and to dress for the soccer game.

"You look happy this morning," said Chloe. "You must have gotten things back on track with Beau."

"We did." Sam hugged Chloe. "We talked most of the night. We may have only dozed off a few times, but I feel wonderful. Thank you for setting me straight. I owe you."

"For all the times you were there for me? We're not even close. Besides, I'll rely on you to listen to all my complaints about Matt."

Chloe lay down on her bed with a pillow under her foot. "Matt's already wrapped my ankle, and I'm ready to go when you are, so hurry."

During breakfast, Chloe packed their snacks and listened as the others talk about strategy and tactical plays. Even though they had different strengths and favorite soccer positions, they were adaptable players. Beau thought they would play a three-on-three game, but he worried about the other team's skills. He had created offensive and defensive plays written in a notebook to take with them. "Matt, do you have any suggestions?"

"European soccer teams start recruiting and training players as young as twelve, so we don't know what we're going up against. I'll keep my ears open for anything and let you know. However, Sam is our secret weapon. They won't expect her to be so talented, so we should let her work the ball around for the first twenty minutes and set things up for you and me to score. After intermission, we set Sam up as much as possible and let her drive to the net."

"I'll do my best," said Sam, blushing. Then she offered her ideas.

Beau nodded. "Those will work. You're the most experienced and trained player. Anything else?"

"No, you have coaching experience, so I'll take my direction from you."

Beau was beaming. Sam trusted him to do this without her taking control. He placed both hands on her face and kissed her. "Thanks. I love you."

Sam was confused. Beau was the coach—he should take charge. "Um...love you, too."

"This is going to be fun," said Beau. "They won't know what hit them."

Etienne picked them up at seven-thirty. He seemed surprised that the three wore full soccer gear, including cleats. They sat in the backseat with their backpacks, and Chloe sat in the front seat with her crutches. As they pulled away, Chloe noticed a familiar undercover policeman from the Musée d'Orsay. She wiggled her fingers at him and smiled. He nodded slightly while speaking on his cell phone. Now that he had been identified, Gaston would probably make an appearance.

Etienne introduced the four friends to his two other teammates. "We will play three-on-three. Is this acceptable?" Everyone nodded. "We have time on the field for two games and an intermission, but we need a referee. We will ask around."

Sam, Beau, and Matt acknowledged the field was perfect. "It's the right size for a three-on-three game," indicated Beau. It was more than half the length of a regulation field, half the width, and only one goal box without a goalie.

Matt turned to Sam. "Beau and I haven't played this since coaching last year's soccer camp, but I understand you play it often."

Sam lifted an eyebrow. "Yeah, a few times a month. There'll be two ten-minute halves with a two-minute halftime, and it goes fast. So, the scores can get high. Before we start, I need to work in my shoes." The guys nodded.

Beau, Matt, and Sam did some stretching and ran around the field to loosen up, ensuring their shoes were adequately stretched. When they reached Chloe sitting on the bleachers, she said, "Wonder Woman." Chloe had taken the referee's photograph and allowed the crew to see. It was a disguised Gaston.

Beau snorted. "If he gets close to me, I might have to trip him hard for using us as bait."

"I wouldn't mind getting in a few trips myself," said Matt.

"He's the ref," grumbled Sam. "I'd rather leave

Paris knowing we beat these guys fair and square without getting thrown out of the game by maiming the ref, so my suggestion is to ignore him… But afterward? Who knows? Maybe Chloe will use her crutches on him." Chloe giggled.

"Chloe, be careful while we're playing. Here's my secret protection," said Sam.

"A boat whistle?"

"Hell yeah. Blow it hard if you get in trouble. The sound can be heard five nautical miles away, well, a little over six regular miles, and anyone close will have to cover their ears." Sam removed the lanyard from her backpack strap and put it over Chloe's head.

The teams met in the center for the coin toss, and Etienne's team kicked in the ball. They moved the ball well and scored a goal within a few seconds. Then Matt kicked the ball in, but the other team stole it from Beau when he collided with Sam. They made the long shot. Sam threw her hands out to the side and stared hard at Beau.

Sam kicked the ball in, and Matt managed to outmaneuver his opponent and scored. The win was short-lived as the other team pulled ahead of Beau, who was crowding out Sam, and the other team scored. Etienne kicked the ball in, and Sam overran the guy next to her to get the ball, but Beau took it, lost it, and the other guy kicked it in. Sam yelled at Beau, "Who are you playing for?" He shrugged.

Beau kicked the ball in, and Matt took it almost to the goal, but his legs got tangled up with one of the other team's players, and he fell. Sam tried to pick it up, but Beau got in her way again, and she missed the goal. The other team picked it up, and they scored.

The ref blew his whistle.

During the two-minute halftime, Sam came off the field in a huff to stand by Chloe. She pulled out a bottle of water and took a long swig. Then she gave Beau and Matt the evil eye.

"What was that out there? You guys were hovering. It's like... You were protecting me... Holy shit, you were!" Not only did Beau and Matt look sheepish, but Chloe also ducked her head. "Well, stop it." She saw Chloe's face. "Et tu, Chloe? I'll talk to you later, *girlfriend*. FYI, I play against women who eat guys like them for lunch, and I can hold my own against any of them. You're pissing me off. We're down four goals, so pass me the ball." She wiped her face on a towel, punched Beau on the arm, and left the sidelines.

"Come on, Matt," huffed Beau. "I don't like being in the doghouse for the second time in two days. Let's give her the ball."

Chloe wanted Matt and Beau to protect Sam, but deep down, she knew Sam didn't need it. Worse still, Sam knew Chloe had said something to Matt. No one could predict how these guys would play. *Oh boy. I can't let her think I don't trust her expertise. I didn't want Sam hurt. I will feel Sam's wrath, and she won't speak to me for a long time. I'll have to remind her of the last time we stopped talking to each other, in ninth grade— when she talked me into sneaking out of the house for a double date.*

Chloe smiled to herself. *We were only fourteen. It was so embarrassing to have the local police find us necking with two football players in a car parked in the high school parking lot. They took us home to angry parents. Jail might have been better.*

That first week was a killer. By the end of the first day, we had written long letters for Beau and Matt to deliver. By week two, Sam had figured out another way to talk to me—we used an old Boy Scouts' book to send messages with flags. She caught herself laughing. Of course, the guys helped. We signaled, and Matt and Beau wrote down the letters. Occasionally, they misspelled words, and the boys raced to meet in the middle of the backyard to clear up any problem. I can't believe it continued for about two weeks until our parents realized we were secretly in contact. One week shy of the month's deadline, Sam's parents had a cookout for all four of us to get together. There were lots of hugs and tears—poor Beau and Matt.

We ate and talked. We played cards and talked. Frisbee and talked. And even after the sun went down, Sam's folks brought out Coleman lanterns, bug spray, and quilts and made a fire in the firepit to make smores and talk. We hugged each other at midnight, made plans for the rest of the weekend, and headed home.

Chloe sniffed back a tear. With Sam, things usually turned out, and she needed to believe it would also work out this time. Reminiscing, she missed the end of the game. The whistle blew, and the trio returned to the bleachers smiling—they had won, seven to six. There was a twenty-minute rest period until the second game started, and during that time, another team jogged onto the field to play.

Chloe congratulated them. Sam was grinning

from ear to ear, showing she could hold her own. Perhaps Sam would forget about the conspiracy to protect her. She pulled out fruit and more water as the trio caught their breath.

Chloe tried to keep her voice low. "Don't look now, but Gaston is talking to several men. He doesn't look happy." They all snuck looks in Gaston's direction and quickly turned away. "I said, don't look."

"The short guy is Jean Louis, the narcotics detective," said Beau. "Uh oh! He got into Gaston's face and jabbed his finger into his chest. Hold on, Gaston grabbed Jean Louis by the shirt and pulled him up off the ground." Beau snickered. "Looks like Gaston just schooled him, and I think we are the reason why. I may like Gaston better now."

"Get a picture of Jean Louis and his cronies before they leave because I think I recognize the tall, skinny one," said Matt.

"Right. Here you go," said Chloe.

"Well, I'll be a dryem." Matt's Down East phrase for 'hell's bells.' "That guy was the bicyclist who took Gaston's camera at the Wall of Love. Jean Louis must be involved in all this. I wonder if Gaston knows?" asked Matt.

"If he doesn't, he will after the next game," said Beau. "I'm going to invite Gaston to our chat with Jean Louis."

"Is Jean Louis getting information about us from Claude?" asked Matt. "If he has, I'll have to hurt Claude's feelings." Sam and Chloe looked at each other and then at Matt, who had his fists opening and closing at his sides.

"After all he's done for us, with the hair salon,

the romantic dinner, and the chauffeur?" asked Sam. "Surely, he hasn't ratted us out. Beau, you said Jean Louis tried to arrest Claude's nephew, so why would he inform him about us?"

"Y'all, the chauffeur was one of Gaston's men," said Chloe.

"How do you know this?" asked Matt.

"While you all were shopping in Givenchy, a woman approached me and demanded my camera, but Victor had it to take photos of Mimi. He saw her and scared the woman off. It was how he protected me, and something that he said made me suspect he was one of Gaston's men. When I asked him, he said he was, and I asked him not to tell y'all unless it was necessary."

"Babe, you should have told us. We're in this together," griped Matt.

"I'm sorry. It happened so fast, and you were having a great time shopping." She was getting uncomfortable stares from Beau and Sam, so she talked faster. "Even if Claude told Jean Louis, Gaston has been keeping tabs on us. Today, when we left the hotel for the soccer match, one of the undercover policemen from the Musée D'Orsay was across the street, and I waved to him. He nodded and then spoke on his cell phone. Then Gaston magically showed up to ref," explained Chloe.

Beau came closer to Chloe. "No more secrets. Okay?" She nodded.

"We'll find out," said Matt. "While we rest, let's talk about the next game's strategies."

Twenty minutes flew by. Gaston resumed his role as the ref, and Sam, Beau, and Matt went to the center for the coin toss. The first half finished in a tie. The second half began, and they knew Chloe was a sitting duck. If anything were to happen, it would happen now. They had to focus on the game and Chloe's well-being.

Chloe was enthralled by the fierce play; she had taken some great action photos during the first game and had enough battery life to take a close-up video of the soccer trio working together during the second. Sam moved like a gymnast. She left the other team lagging and astonished everyone who watched. There had been no need to worry about her skills or being taken advantage of. The reverse was true. Beau and Matt set her up repeatedly to be positioned for a goal, and she scored every time. She was on fire.

Chloe put the camera beside her on the bench to clap and yell. Surprisingly, her cell phone rang. It had to be an emergency call from back home. She reached between the seats to get her backpack, rooted around until she found the phone, and answered it. "Hello…hello… hello?"

Before she could think clearly, three guys ran up to her and grabbed her backpack, camera, and Sam's backpack before scattering in different directions. Chloe blew her whistle long and loud. Sam turned in her direction, assessed the situation, and kicked a line drive into the face of the guy holding the camera. He fell onto his back.

Sam screamed at Beau and Matt, pointing to the two other guys. Matt jumped up and landed a front kick into the gut of the guy holding the backpack, while Beau tackled the third guy and punched him in the face. The assailants didn't stand a chance.

Sam's target tried to get up, moaning and holding his bleeding nose. "There's no crying in soccer," said Sam, smiling.

Gaston blew his whistle, ran over to the bleachers, and signaled for three of his men to move forward. Assailant number two tried to crawl away. "Stay down," he yelled.

"Go ahead, you can make my day," said Matt. "*C'est ma copine*, you creep."

"Am I your girlfriend?" asked Chloe.

"Damn Straight. You're my girlfriend, my sweetheart, *mon amour*," said Matt. He stepped over the assailant and kissed Chloe hard. The onlookers cheered. "I'd love to add wife to that, too."

Chloe could hardly get her breath. Her mouth opened and shut. She blushed and whispered in his ear, "Maybe, one day."

Matt was over the moon, smiling as he hugged her tightly.

Gaston spoke to the third guy, "See him," pointing to Beau, "Don't move... he's angry."

"Yeah, it's my secret cause I'm always angry," said Beau. "I have the need... the need for smacking him around some more." Gaston understood the movie reference and grinned.

Chloe got her camera and backpack as Gaston's men took the three men away. Gaston turned to speak to Beau, Matt, and Sam. "Now that those guys have been taken care of, we need to finish the last match unless you are too tired—"

"I'm ready to kick butt, come on," said Sam. She ran on the field with Beau and Matt following behind. Gaston laughed all the way back to the field.

Sam's team was ahead by three goals when the

last whistle blew. Gaston translated for the other team as Sam described how much fun playing it had been. Then, she invited them to come to North Carolina anytime for a rematch. They all shook hands. Once Etienne dropped them off at the hotel, Chloe gave him her business card and told him to check on Mimi's adventures in Paris.

THERE WAS ENOUGH time for the soccer trio to shower and return to the restaurant to confront Jean Louis. They sat in a secluded area. Within moments, Claude had brought them Cokes and sandwiches. "How was the soccer match?"

Chloe said proudly and sweetly, "We won; it was so exciting. Thank you for the sandwiches. You take good care of us, Claude."

"My pleasure." He turned to leave, and the color drained from his face. Jean Louis walked through the door. "You need to leave these nice people alone." Claude left the room and positioned himself before Chloe as Jean Louis marched inside. Claude hissed.

"I am Detective Jean Louis. You have photographs I need." Another young man, one of the skateboarders from the train, stepped forward, pounding a gloved fist in his other hand. "I will take the memory cards now."

DCM Copeland rose from a table across the room and joined the friends. His bodyguard stood close by as Gaston walked in with two of his men. Jean Louis turned ashen. The embassy representative found a chair, turned it around, and sat down facing everyone. "It's not necessary to get the memory cards, Detective Louis. Ms. Davis turned over the photographs to me, and we identified one of the men as Raul Fuentes. You may know him as the small-time ringleader of teens trained to do petty theft, pickpocketing, and such."

Jean Louis stood stiff, lips tight, his hands fisted by his sides.

"Fuentes has tried to ingratiate himself into The Spaniard's cartel—his real name is Andre Dantes. He's had some extensive plastic surgery done over the past year, and there was no photo of his new face until he was accidentally photographed.

"Since Miss Davis and her friends are teachers on holiday, there was no need for unnecessary force, so Fuentes' thieves were perfect for obtaining the memory cards for Dantes. His thieves are trained to work in packs without weapons; they rarely take dangerous jobs or hurt anyone. If they were ever caught, the charges would be misdemeanors. Therefore, your attempts to retrieve the photographs have been for nothing," said DCM Copeland.

Jean Louis lunged at him, only to have the bodyguard step in between. "She brought *you* the photographs? This is outrageous. They avoided the police at every turn. I want the camera and for them to come with me to the station for further questions.

Gaston answered while pushing Louis back. "They had every right to go to the American Embassy and to hand over the photographs. Your police tactics have been invasive, ruthless, and unnecessary."

"My tactics get results. We are on the same side, working on the case from different ends. I suppose you've also seen the photographs and know what the Spaniard looks like?" asked Jean Louis.

"Not yet. The photographs will need to be verified by our superiors, but Fuentes was officially identified. So, in this case, your involvement is no longer required."

"We shall see about that." Jean Louis stormed out of the room, followed by his sidekick.

Beau, Matt, Sam, and Chloe were outraged. They threw out questions and accusations and yelled loud enough that Claude, concerned with their welfare, appeared at the door. DCM Copeland raised his hand to silence them.

"Why wasn't Jean Louis arrested?" asked Matt. "His companion was one of Fuentes's men who assaulted us on the train—Chloe took his photograph. Jean Louis must be working for Fuentes."

"Yes, we know about his association, but we can't prove that he had anything to do with the attacks. Even the cyclist caught at the Wall of Love claims he and his buddies were working on their own to rob you." The yelling began again, and Gaston whistled to stop the noise.

"I assure you that we will catch him in the act and verify the connection to Fuentes, however long it takes," said Gaston. "We are looking for Fuentes now, and once The Spaniard's photos are circulated, we hope to lock him away for a very long time."

DCM Copeland rose from his seat and faced

the Down East four. "You can be proud of how you handled this situation. The United States and French governments thank you for being model citizens and helping to apprehend these criminals. Despite all your problems, I hope you have enjoyed most of your stay here and that your trip home is uneventful." He first reached over to shake Chloe's hand and the others before leaving. "Should you need me again, I am at your service."

Gaston stayed behind. "I am impressed with your fast thinking and devotion to each other. I'm also glad you four are honest people instead of criminals—you would be formidable foes." He laughed, walked to the doorway, and then turned. "I think you're safe now. Don't worry about Jean Louis. I'll take care of him…. By the way, you three play soccer very well. I was quite impressed with Sam's skills."

Beau, Matt, Sam, and Chloe sat at the table, speechless but mostly relieved. It was finally over. They could relax and try to enjoy their last day and night in Paris.

"I need a nap," said Sam.

"Me too," said the others in unison.

Beau pulled Sam up, and they walked hand in hand to the elevator. "We'll see you guys later," said Sam. "Jeannette will come for us at two o'clock for our last tour. Don't be late."

Matt helped Chloe up, and they headed for her room to rest. It was the perfect way to end their ordeal with Jean Louis and gear up for their last tour of Paris.

Chapter 19

J EANNETTE BAKER APPEARED at the hotel for the final tour of Paris' national historical monuments: the Arc de Triomphe, the area of the Bastille, the Hospital de Invalides, and the Louver. The white van arrived, and the driver, this time, was not Gaston but Detective Pierre Durand.

"We can't get a break, can we?" asked Beau.

Chloe carefully entered the van. "Are we still in danger, Pierre?"

"I don't think so, but I will look after you until you board your plane tomorrow. Think of me as Papa Pierre." He looked at Chloe in the rear-view mirror and winked. Matt rolled his eyes and mumbled something that sounded like "…tired of guys flirting."

Jeannette asked Pierre to take his time driving around each site and then one more time around in case there were questions. They stopped only long enough to take photos and return to the van. Since Chloe requested to visit the bridges holding the love locks, the rest of the group's sightseeing time in Paris was spent doing that.

"This is the most beautiful bridge in Paris," said Jeannette. "It is noted for the laurel swags hanging between the pediments, with the copper reliefs and bronze sculptures. You may stroll along the bridge on the side pedestrian walkways or drive over it using the middle lanes. Underneath the bridge and along the banks of the Seine are walking areas with cafés and places to relax. It is common to see married couples pose in their wedding attire on or around the bridge, and at night, it is very romantic to take a carriage ride."

Minutes later, they drove over the oldest bridge, the Pont Neuf, crossed the Seine and the Île de Cité, past Notre Dame, to the next bridge. "The last stop on our tour is the Pont des Arts, facing the Louvre. This pedestrian bridge used to have metal sides covered in love locks, but they are no longer here."

"Oh no. I was so looking forward to photographing some. Are there any other places that have love locks?" asked Chloe.

Pierre looked in his rear-view mirror at Chloe's face and then to Jeannette. She nodded back at him. "Before I answer that, does anyone want to walk over the bridge?"

There was a unanimous "No."

"Then, Pierre is going to drive us to a secret location. While we drive there, let me explain about the locks. Over many years, tens of thousands of locks were attached to bridges, making them unsafe, not to mention that all the metal keys were lying on the bottom of the Seine. When the locks were removed, they appeared at other places, like the wall at the base of Sacré Coeur, but I didn't have time to mention them with all our excitement that day.

"When the Pont des Arts bridge sides were removed, some citizens wanted to do something—to memorialize the love demonstrated by putting a lock on it." She cleared her throat. "Some people," she hesitated, "eh hem, acquired the parts and stored them until something can be done to preserve them."

"Pierre, you old romantic dog, you," said Beau, grinning. "Jeannette, were you part of the conspiracy to keep love alive?"

"I will neither confirm nor deny any such accusation," said Jeannette, smiling. "However, we might know where love locks are in Paris. Not many, but the city will remove them if there are complaints. I'm assuming you all will not issue any such complaint?"

They all said, "No."

"Then we're off to the Trocadero Gardens. The open space has beautiful gardens and magnificent fountains. You can even see the Eiffel Tower, the Palais de Chaillot, and the Seine River from there. The buildings house various galleries, but we won't have time to visit. Pierre will walk us over to where the locks are, and we will stay in Trocadero for about an hour."

"The fountains are amazing," said Sam. "Are those water cannons? Can I fire one?"

"Twenty water cannons fire over its basin each night, framing the Eiffel Tower's light show. And no," said Jeannette. "I'm surprised Beau didn't ask."

"She beat me to it," Beau grinned.

When the group ventured out, so did Mimi.

Pierre walked them to short wrought iron fencing delineating the sculptured shrubbery closest to the buildings. "Here are the love locks. They are also on the other side of the fountain," said Pierre, pointing to the other area.

Chloe pulled out Mimi and handed her to Pierre. He helped pose her in the right places. "When we get home, Pierre, I will send you some photographs. You've been a good sport to help with this." Chloe leaned in and kissed his cheek. Sam did likewise, and then, surprisingly, Jeannette did too, although she was blushing. He laughed for only a moment and became the straight-faced undercover policeman again.

Pierre pulled his hat lower and adjusted his sunglasses as he followed Sam and Chloe. Chloe had her SLR camera and took photos of the locks with the Parisienne sites in the background, and occasionally of the people strolling along Trocadero. Matt posed for her as she directed, pretending to put on a lock and then pretending to be a tourist for her other commercial shots. Pierre's snorts brought laughter to everyone.

"I don't understand what women see in Matt. He's ordinary if you take away the tall, dark, and geeky stuff," said Beau. Matt gave him the finger.

"Laugh it up, fuzzyball," said Matt. "You wish you were half as photogenic."

"Bahaha…"

"Beau, it's your turn. Bring Sam."

Beau, shut up.

Sam pulled him along and posed for some photographs until Beau became uncomfortable and walked away. Chloe didn't tell him that she had photographed him and Sam together at other times and would keep shooting them secretly. Sam would love the photo album Chloe intended to make for her, and so would Beau, eventually.

PIERRE INTERCEPTED BEAU. He reached into his jacket pocket and pulled out two brass locks with their keys dangling. "Give one to Matt." Then Jeannette produced two markers.

Beau handed Matt a lock and a marker, leaving him and Chloe alone. He turned to Sam and held out his hand. She laced her fingers with his, and they moved further toward the buildings.

"Sam, this may seem premature, but it's perfect timing for me. I think we should add our lock as a commitment to each other, and the beginning of our relationship, because... every real story is never-ending. One day, I hope our story will be added to your book."

"Have you always been like this with your other women?"

"No. Hell no... Frankly, I've never had to pursue a woman this hard."

"Right, they fell in your lap with a look or a wink. I get it now; only the chase attracted you to me, right?"

"Sam... You're goading me. Grrr... With you, nothing is easy... and yet nothing seems hard. I'll admit, the chase has been fun, and I'm positive you will keep me on my toes for the rest of my life, but I've only ever loved you."

The sun couldn't have shone brighter. "You're

also saying there will be no other women, ever in the future?"

"That's exactly what I'm saying. You're *the only* woman for me. You're perfect for me."

She wrapped her arms around his neck and moved into him; his arms encircled her to pull her closer. "I never knew you were such a romantic."

"Only with you, Samantha. Only for you."

She lightly kissed his lips. "Let's put that lock on, "My only precious."

MATT HELD UP the lock in one hand and a ring with two keys in the other. "Chloe, we should put a lock on the fence."

"Why? These locks were put here because couples were in love. They wanted to show the world they were dedicating their lives to each other. Aren't you jumping the gun again?"

"Think of this as a promise lock." He held her hands and moved in close. "I will promise to take things slow," He kissed her cheek. "To honor what we have now," He kissed the corner of her mouth and lingered, letting her feel his breath. Her eyes were closed, and she inhaled. "To give you time." He kissed her lips gently and again with his tongue, caressing her lips. Her eyes remained closed, and his breath lingered on her cheek as he moved toward her ear. "To give you space and protect your independence." He kissed her earlobe. "I promise to talk to you and not jump to conclusions." He kissed her below her earlobe, and she sucked in a breath. He smiled. "I will be honest with you, and I'll be your friend, no matter what." He kissed the place where her neck and shoulder met, a place that gave her the shivers and melted her insides. His lips moved back up her neck to her ear and whispered. "I promise to love you with all my heart for as long as I live."

"You always knew how to make my insides turn to jelly... Please don't make promises if you can't keep them. You'll break my heart for good, and I'll never recover—"

"Beau and Sam promised me that if I hurt you, they would dump my lifeless body into the Seine as fish food...I would deserve no less."

They locked eyes. She studied him intently without saying anything. Matt's frown spoke volumes: "If... you can't promise anything... I will accept that and still attach the lock to affirm my promises to you."

She touched his cheek. Despite the past and because of the present, she loved this man. "This is what I can promise—to be honest and share things with you. I *want* to be your girlfriend, but I'm scared of losing myself in a relationship with you, so please be patient. Whatever happens, I also promise to be your friend."

He nodded and handed her a key.

"If...I mean, *when* the time comes for us to make our relationship permanent, we should return here and exchange this promise lock for one that's lasting. What do you think?"

"I can't fault your optimism, so yes." She turned to studying the surroundings with the Eiffel Tower in the background. "This place is perfect. It looks to the east where a new day begins, and this is the day we can begin our life together... Let's put our lock here."

He wrote Matt and Chloe on the lock, and they

hooked it to a link in the fence. He kissed her, turned the key, locking it in place, and then tossed the key into the fountain's basin. Chloe placed the other key in her zippered backpack pocket before returning to find Beau and Sam.

Pierre and Jeannette were waiting by the van. They touched their foreheads and spoke softly. Her hands were in his, and he lightly rubbed her fingers.

Beau snickered. "Here's a marker for when you buy your lock." He handed it to Pierre. Sam smacked the back of his head. "What? They're toast, and you know it."

Pierre and Jeannette grinned as they entered the van; the rest followed. At the hotel, Jeannette received hugs from everyone. "I can't believe we all survived your Paris adventure. Please keep in touch and make sure I get wedding invitations, okay?" Beau, Sam, Chloe, and Matt grinned and nodded, blushing.

Pierre said, "I will see you tomorrow morning. Is there one last thing you want to do before I take you to the airport?"

"Since our flight doesn't leave until three o'clock, we're going to sleep in tomorrow, but we also need to go to the VAT counter before the flight," said Matt.

"I'd like to head down to the park by the Eiffel Tower to take more photographs," said Chloe.

"Then I will pick you up at ten o'clock. Please check out of the hotel and leave your suitcases with Claude. We'll pick them up on the way to the airport."

"Sam, we need extra suitcases unless you want to put your VAT items with mine," said Beau.

"The souvenir shop next door has some. Come on."

"We're coming with you," said Chloe. "I need one, and Matt needs two." Matt shrugged.

SAM AND BEAU decided they could share a large suitcase for their VAT items. She brought her items to his room with all the paperwork and watched him carefully pack his things—he was meticulous. "Are you always this fastidious?"

"I guess so. I like things clean, organized, and tidy."

"You didn't use to be that way."

"I suppose not, but in college, my roommate was a nut about keeping our room spotless, and he stayed on my back about it. Now I wouldn't have it any other way," said Beau.

"I tend to be OCD about that too, especially when I've got a deadline or I'm trying to work something out in my head. Cleaning is therapeutic, like running." He grunted and continued packing, half listening to Sam speak.

Sam jumped when her phone rang. She and Beau looked at each other, knowing everyone knew where she was. An emergency? She answered it, but her editor spoke before giving her a chance to say hello. "Sam, I have great news. Carris Jones was so pleased with your writing that she wants you to ghostwrite her next book. I told her I'd let her know next week. However," pausing for dramatic effect, "I'd like you to write your own book. Both ideas you pitched are great.

"This is a big decision, Sam. I'm sure Ms. Jones would be thrilled for you to continue ghostwriting, yet this would be a wonderful opportunity to establish your name in the literary world. Think about this and get back to me when you get home from Paris."

"Thanks, Gloria, for your encouragement and support. I will think about it and call when I get home." Sam found loose hair near her ear and twisted it as she put her phone away.

"What is it? Is there something wrong?" asked Beau.

"No… nothing's wrong… I need to think for a while." She crossed the room and exited. Beau shrugged and finished packing. When he finished, he headed to Sam's room, knocked, identified himself, and then used his keycard to enter. Chloe was helping Matt get his clothes situated in his suitcases.

"Mind if I put my shoes in here?" she asked.

"Go ahead." Matt pointed to a good spot. "There's more space if you want to add anything else."

"I knew you'd have to sit on your suitcase to get it closed," teased Beau. Matt gave him the finger. "Where's Sam? Did she need a Coke? She said she needed to think."

"Really?" asked Chloe. "I wondered why she changed into shorts and running shoes. She didn't say anything, but if she said she needed to think, she went for a run."

"By herself? In Paris? I don't believe it," sputtered Beau. "Where do you think she'll go?"

"I don't know. You're scaring me. Is it dangerous?"

"Did she take her phone with her?" asked Matt.

Chloe checked Sam's purse. "It's not in here. I'll call her.... It went to voicemail... Sam, where are you? I—I thought you'd bring me a Diet Coke. Call me, please."

"Does she always run the same areas or find new places to run?" asked Beau.

"She only goes to places she knows or with someone when she runs somewhere new."

"Then it's either Montmartre or down the boulevard around Moulin Rouge," said Matt.

"I'm going to change. If you hear from her, Chloe, get details," said Beau.

"I'm coming too," said Matt. "Do we split up or go together?"

"We split up. You're faster, so take the route up Montmartre. If you find her, call me, and bring her back to the hotel.... Then I'm going to kill her," said Beau.

THE HOTEL DOOR opened. Sam found Chloe trying to pace the floor on crutches and teetered on her good foot to see who came in. Sam was soaking wet. "Hey. I'm going to hop in the shower. I also need a Coke and a nap," said Sam.

"Where have you been? Why didn't you tell me you were going for a run?"

"I spoke to you while you were packing, and you saw me put on my running shoes."

"Why didn't you return my calls? I was so worried. The boys are out looking for you now, and you've scared ten years off Beau's life—"

"I'm sorry I worried you, but my editor called—she offered me two great opportunities, and I needed to think. Call the guys and let them know I'm back. Thanks," said Sam as she shut the bathroom door.

When Sam finished blow-drying her hair, the guys pushed into the room. "Where is she?" demanded Beau.

"In here," said Sam.

"Uh… I'll keep Matt company while he cleans up—"

"But I want to hear what she has to say and where she went," Matt said, a little testy.

"Later. We'll find out later," said Chloe, urging Matt out the door.

"If I had known you wanted to go for a run, you could have gone with me," said Sam.

"Are you crazy? Going for a run by yourself in Paris? Anything could have happened to you." Beau grabbed her arms and found himself on the floor before he could shake her. Her self-defense reactions startled him.

"I told you, I can handle myself. I didn't think my running would have caused such a panic, but you were busy, and I needed to think." She extended her hand to help him up. On the way, he changed her momentum and flipped her over onto the bed with him on top.

"You don't listen, do you? It's dangerous to be out by yourself with those bad guys still out there. I've been worried sick. Matt's been worried. So has Chloe. Did you even check your phone? We've been calling for the last hour to reach you."

Sam's countenance changed from being sorry to being obstinate and defiant. Instantly.

"You're not my boss, so don't try to jerk me around." She pushed at him, raised one eyebrow, and crossed her arms.

He stood up. "Jerk, *you* around? You've been leading me around by the nose forever. I've been watching out for you since you developed breasts in ninth grade, and after a water balloon fight when your t-shirt got wet, they were the only things I could focus on. And baby, your ta tas were spectacular."

Sam's mouth formed an O and then into a mischievous grin.

"After returning from football camp going into the tenth grade, I found out scumbags had been spending time together at your house, taking you and Chloe out to eat and to the movies. By the time school started, I had it bad for you."

"You never said anything to me. Why not?" said Sam.

"We were best friends, the four of us were always together, and I couldn't ruin that."

"Back up. You were always dating different girls. Chloe and I were the only ones in high school who didn't get in the back of your Mustang."

"Merely substitution for you."

"Really. All the action and all the fun, with remorse? Hardly."

"In college, you saved my GPA and my football scholarship. Yeah, I dated a lot and even had a few girlfriends, but when I saw you, it all came back… I was in love with you then, and I still love you…. I've loved you forever but knew you didn't feel the same way. I couldn't tell you… I have a big ego, and I had an image to keep up."

"*Had* a big ego? You still do, but we were both

stupid. I suppose it's time to confess… I've loved you since high school, but you never looked at me like that. I guess we both hid it well. Chloe cried with me back then. In college, it was even worse. So, I made lots of excuses not to see you. I dated often and had a few boyfriends, but they weren't you."

Beau pulled her up and wrapped his arms around her waist. "Sugar, it was tough on me in college, too. I had nightmares when you brought home that frat guy who pinned you. Then Matt told me about your fight with him and the breakup. I was so relieved that I got drunk and wrecked my car."

"Really? That was eons ago." Sam's arms wrapped around his neck.

"Now, it's going to be different. First, you're going to stop giving me heart attacks. Then, we're going to stop acting ridiculously and get engaged. The only thing we haven't done is the physical stuff, and we'll take care of that before we get married."

"Are you nuts? You're trying to manipulate things again—"

"Simply maneuvering things so that you will see the logic. We know everything about each other, and we could consider Paris our dating time and as a prelude to marriage."

"Dating time, here? No. I need time and lots of romance. Besides, who says I'll marry you? I don't know if we can stand living together, much less get married?"

"When you realize you want to spend the rest of your life with someone, it should start as soon as possible. Blame it on Paris! It's the city of love—"

"The city of light."

"Whatever. I'm proposing now, so we'll be engaged before we return home. Deal?" Beau looked ridiculous, holding his hand out for her to shake.

"You're proposing to me with a deal and a handshake? *I don't think so.* If you're serious, then take me somewhere special and propose properly. Then, we'll see about the rest."

"I can do that right now." He pulled her down the hall, into the elevator, and through the lobby foyer where Matt and Chloe ate ice cream. Beau grinned as he threw Sam over his shoulder. "Matt, Chloe, see you later." He walked down the street to Montmartre Cemetery. Chloe took a few photos of them on her phone.

"You're sweaty and stinky, and I just showered," complained Sam.

"Too bad, serves you right," Beau said. Sam was giggling and squirming at the same time. Beau swatted her on the butt. "Are you going to say yes?"

"Not if you ask me on a grave."

"How about a park bench in front of a fountain surrounded by lots of graves? It would be something for your book."

"Matt and Chloe get the Wall of Love, and we get a cemetery." She was laughing hard now. "Somehow, it's perfect for us." Beau found the right spot moments after entering the gates. He placed Sam on the bench and then knelt on one knee.

"Are you going to say 'yes'?"

"You haven't asked me yet, and even if I say 'yes,' we can't be officially engaged without a ring."

"Who says I don't have a ring?" He pulled out a small black velvet pouch from a hidden pocket inside his waistband and removed an eighteen-karat yellow gold band formed with iconic Paris sites joined together. He had been carrying it around since the first day in Paris. "Call this a temporary engagement ring, and we'll get something more appropriate back home." He placed it on her left ring finger. "In front of all these future zombie witnesses, Samantha Anne Williston, will you marry me?"

"Yes." She threw her arms around his neck, ready to seal their deal.

A clock chimed in the distance, and iron gates squeaked. They didn't even have time to kiss. "Come on, let's get out of here, or we'll be spending the night." They joined hands and ran as fast as they could through the exit as the attendant closed the gate. They climbed the stairs and ran across the street to the hotel to show Matt and Chloe the engagement ring.

"Let's go down to the corner café for dinner and celebrate," said Matt. "My treat."

BEAU AND SAM had every reason to feel like they were flying on cloud nine. It was miraculous that the two had accepted what they felt and admitted it. "Can you imagine the gossip on Harkers Island when they find out we've always been in love and were planning on getting married?" asked Beau. "Our family? They're going to faint. Our colleagues or friends? They'll want to know how much we had to drink and if it was a prank."

Beau still couldn't believe she said "yes." All the stars and planets had positioned themselves in perfect alignment for this to happen, and with Sam, they would have a lifetime of fussing, fighting, making up, and working hard to stay together. The challenge was issued, accepted, and relished. Their life together would be unpredictable and exciting, complementing their personalities to a tee. They would love every minute. They strolled hand in hand to the café ahead of Matt and Chloe, wanting a few moments to themselves. By the time Matt and Chloe arrived, they had already shared a beer on tap and had menus waiting.

"Sam, Matt ran through Montmartre, and I headed past the Hop on Bus, but we didn't see you. Where did you go running?" asked Beau.

"I went to the cemetery and ran through the entire place—it was quiet, and no one was around."

"We didn't think you would go there. What was so important to run off to think?"

Sam grinned. "My editor offered me an option to ghostwrite another book for Carris Jones or to write my novels. Ghostwriting could be more of a sure thing since I'd get other offers, whereas writing my books would be risky, with school and all."

"Congratulations are in order. Well done, Sam," said Matt.

"I'm so proud of you," said Chloe. "This is

wonderful news."

"What did you decide?" asked Beau.

"I wanted to talk to you first before I decided." Sam blushed.

"With me, why?"

"You understand me, and I wanted your advice. Now that we're engaged, it seems relevant to talk about our life goals and how this career choice will affect us."

"Sam, that's the most unselfish thing I've ever heard… Thank you for including me." He kissed her cheek. "When do you need to tell your editor?"

"When I get back home."

"Then we have time to talk." Beau's eyes glistened, and his smile told her everything. They were a couple, a team, and in this together. Finally.

Matt ordered a bottle of wine. Beau looked at the label. "This looks vaguely familiar."

"It should. This was the wine my family used to drink. It was Grand-mere's favorite, and we had it at dinner on the weekends. You've tried some."

"Only got a sip because your dad knew my parents would disapprove. Naturally, it incentivized me to learn about different wines and collect the ones I like."

"I hate to admit it, but your palate is more sophisticated than mine—I'm not willing to splurge on expensive wines when there are comparable ones that are less expensive," said Matt.

"You mean, you're cheap," said Beau.

"Hardly," said Matt. "You took the classes. You should pick the wine so that I can drink it."

"Sounds logical," said Chloe.

Sam agreed. "Then, Beau should be our sommelier from now on."

"It would be my pleasure."

Matt filled Beau's glass and encouraged the others to try the wine. They toasted to new beginnings and chatted about their Paris adventures and the soccer match they played. Appetizers came, they finished the bottle, and Matt signaled for another one brought by a Middle Eastern waiter with a heavy accent. Everyone got steaks, pom frites, green beans, salads, and crusty bread. The waiter spoke to the guys only. "Can I get you anything else?"

Beau shook his head, and Matt said, "Another bottle of wine, four chocolate eclairs, and coffee."

By the time the friends left the café, four and a half hours later, they had consumed six bottles of wine, mediocre meals, dessert, and lattes. It was a good thing the hotel was across the street—the street appeared lopsided. It was close to midnight before they fell into their beds, but they promised to see each other by ten o'clock for a late breakfast.

Chapter 20

S AM BARELY MADE it to a chair in the restaurant. "Mou-f numb. Ton gue... th-ick."

Beau staggered in wearing disposable eye doctor shades under sunglasses. "Who... has... aspirin?"

"My lips are swollen, and my tongue is itchy. How much did we drink?" asked Chloe.

"It wasn't the quantity... it was the embalming fluid." Beau grimaced, sitting down.

"How's everyone this morning?" Matt appeared at their table, all smiles and chirpy.

"What's... wrong with you, man?" Beau whipped around to chastise Matt, but the motion hurt so severely that he cradled his head in his hands. "You drank more than I did...Where's... your headache?"

"I was raised on French wine. I don't get drunk or have a hangover on it. Maybe it's my strong constitution and all the vitamins I take."

Beau's voice was low and raspy. "I... hate... you... I... really... hate you."

"Look what I brought," Matt said in a sing-song voice, holding up two bottles of vitamin B complex and Tylenol, shaking them like maracas. Everyone covered their ears. "Two pots of coffee, croissants, and fruit are coming. This should take care of you so that we can meet Pierre."

Beau's voice was still low and raspy. "I... love you... man."

"Has anyone seen Mimi?" Chloe's voice was almost too soft to hear. "I remember taking her to the café, but haven't seen her this morning. She's going with us today."

"Found... Mimi... crushed... in bra," said Sam, slurring her words. "Mimi... drunk-weird photos. Did I do upside-down mar-ga-rita?"

"Yes, but I kept you from putting it on Mimi's Facebook page," said Matt.

"Th...anks—"

"Or sending the one of you dancing on the bar top. Beau pulled you down before you took off your top."

"You... g-ood friend," said Sam, lowering her head to the table. Chloe tried to giggle, but it ended up as tiny squeaks.

Matt assumed his teacher mode. "Our luggage must go to Claude, and we have to check out by the time Pierre comes. I will bring them down if you want." Slowly, hands magically lifted with room cards in them. "Alrighty then." Matt texted Pierre that the group was ill and for him to come an hour later. When Pierre asked why, he replied, "Too much wine."

Pierre surprised everyone by bringing Jeannette with him. "I had the day off, and I wanted to spend it with you all now that things have been cleared up," she said. Pierre was grinning from ear to ear, holding her hand as they walked into the lobby.

"You look like the love bug bit you," said Beau.

Pierre turned to Jeannette. "Love bug? *Qu'est-ce que c'est?*"

Jeannette translated, "Le bug de l'amour."

Pierre blushed. "*C'est possible.*"

Chloe, Sam, and Beau hid behind sunglasses and hats pulled down low. Sam showed Jeannette the engagement ring, getting a gingerly hug. Jeannette clapped Beau on the back, "Congratulations."

"I need a barf bag." Sam pulled one from her purse and stuck it in Beau's back pocket.

Claude kindly provided a picnic basket for the van containing two large blankets, a coffee thermos, and several Cokes. Everyone piled into the van except Beau and Jeannette.

"You're still packing for bear. Do you know something we don't?" he asked.

"A lady can't be too careful… Okay, between you and me, my instincts tell me this thing with Jean Louis isn't over. If I can help, I want to."

"Thanks. You're getting a wedding invitation. Bring Pierre with you."

THE VAN PULLED onto a side street close to the river under the shadow of the Eiffel Tower. They found a picnic table for Chloe to sit on while Jeannette,

Pierre, and Matt unloaded the food, and Beau spread a blanket on the ground for him and Sam to stretch out. Chloe straightened her leg longways across the bench and leaned against Matt. After a lunch of baguettes with ham, cheese, and fruit, the group had time to stroll to the water's edge for photographs.

"Stay together, please," said Pierre. "I do not want to fish you out of the Seine; it's high today and moving fast."

Chloe presented Mimi to the group dressed in black pants, a black and white striped top, a red scarf around her neck, and a black beret. Between Pierre and Jeannette, Mimi posed in various locations and on the selfie stick. The others laughed at Chloe as she spoke to her, "Little girl, you've had some great adventures. I can't wait to work on your book when I get home."

They moved back to the lunch area. Mimi returned to the front zippered pocket outside of the backpack, and then she and Matt watched as Pierre and Jeannette took turns throwing a Frisbee. Jeannette threw the disk badly enough that Pierre ran a distance to retrieve it. She covered her mouth, laughing at her mistake. "I'm sorry, Pierre. I'm so bad at this."

The Frisbee landed on the top of a tall shrub, so she ran after Pierre to help. He lifted Jeannette on his shoulders to retrieve it. Everyone clapped and whistled as Jeannette held up the Frisbee like a trophy and Pierre danced around.

Chloe photographed the play, then placed her camera in her backpack so she could clap. Without warning, a young man ran to the table, grabbed her backpack, and jumped on a skateboard. She screamed.

Sam grabbed Chloe's crutch and used it like a hockey stick to flip the guy's feet from underneath him. "Take that, you moron." When he fell, she landed an atomic drop with her elbow to his stomach. Another young guy ran up, grabbed the backpack, and hit Sam in the face as he jumped on his skateboard. Sam saw stars and lay in a heap over her unconscious victim.

Chloe yelled, "Matt, clothesline."

Matt clotheslined the thief with his left arm, flipping him down on his stomach a second after the thief threw the backpack to a third guy. He yelled, "Beau, flea flicker." Matt held both wrists, put a knee into the assailant's back, and pressed down. "Ask yourself one question: Am I lucky? Well, are ya punk?"

The guy tried to wiggle out, but Matt demonstrated a classic choke hold, and the guy was out in a flash, but something snapped on Matt's left side. "Aww, shit." Using his right arm, he shifted the thief's arms under him and sat down. He saw stars, recoiled in incredible pain, and was forced to readjust his body to cradle his left wrist before passing out.

Beau rammed the third skateboarder hard enough that the skateboard popped up and hurled downward across Beau's left eyebrow, across his eye, and over his cheekbone. The guy rolled over and tried to make a run for it, but Beau tackled him from behind above the knees, flipped him over, and rammed a fist into his face. Lights out. "Hasta la vista punko."

"Beau, Sam's hurt!" Chloe yelled as she hobbled over to Matt. "Please open your eyes, Matt. Where does it hurt, darlin'?"

He moaned but didn't open his eyes. "I think I dislocated my shoulder."

"Don't move. I'll get help."

"No, stay with me."

"Anything you say."

His eyes fluttered open. "Anything? Then I say, marry me."

"You're crazy…you're delirious." She knew she could never say no to him as he looked at her in pain. "Okay… yes, I will marry you. Now let me get help."

"Not yet. Kiss me like you mean it."

"My pleasure."

Beau punched his assailant again, dropping the backpack and running to Sam. He knelt and scooped her up into his lap. "Samantha. Sugar. Sweetheart, talk to me." She tried to open her eyes, but only one opened. She winced. He lightly touched her cheek, and she winced again.

"Did we get them?" she asked. Beau grinned.

"We did, but you'll have a shiner, and your nose may be broken. I'm so sorry, Sam."

"Well, it's not like I haven't had a black eye before, and you once said my nose was a little too perfect. I'll live, but it hurts, Beau."

He kissed her forehead and then gently touched her lips. "I know, sweetheart, we'll find some ice and Tylenol."

Three bad guys were down, and the backpack was on the ground. Jean Louis strolled in, picked up the backpack, and turned to walk away. Jeannette intercepted him and sprayed him in the face with hairspray, "Say hello to my little amigo." He screamed, dropping the backpack. Pierre grabbed him and then cuffed him with zip ties.

This time, a hidden Gaston videoed the event with his cell phone.

"Uh oh, we have company. Can you stand up, Sam? I'll get you to a seat," said Beau.

Suddenly, police surrounded the area. The assailants were zip-tied and placed in a police van that quickly drove off. The man and woman who had been keeping them under surveillance since the cemetery positioned themselves around Matt and Chloe. At the same time, the two undercover policemen from the Musée d'Orsay moved in to guard Beau and Sam.

Gaston remained in the shadows with several police officers positioned at various locations. He saw a man casually walk away from the commotion—Raul Fuentes. He directed two officers to apprehend Fuentes, moving him quickly to another police vehicle.

Matt, Beau, Sam, and Chloe were corralled at the picnic table more roughly than was needed. Jeannette and Pierre moved in closer. "We can't be under arrest. *They* are the bad guys," said Sam, talking to the policemen. "You saw what they did, and we protected ourselves."

Chloe yelled, "*Mes amis ont besoin de* medical attention."

Everyone talked at once.

"*Silence!*" It was the man that Chloe photographed at the trash can drop.

"Who are you, and what do you want with us?" asked Chloe.

"That will be answered at police headquarters. Detective Durand, take care of them."

Pierre nodded and then loaded the troupe into his van. Jeannette held their backpacks and rode in the front seat. "I am taking you to the nearest clinic. You are not under arrest, but I must take you to police headquarters so you can give your statements. Unofficially, I suggest you call your embassy contact to meet you there."

The four looked at each other. If they weren't under arrest, why did they need DCM Copeland? Chloe called the number on the business card and asked DCM Copeland to meet them at police headquarters. She also explained they had been used again in a sting operation and were now heading to a hospital. She handed her phone to Jeannette to explain further.

Chloe sighed heavily. It was all her fault that her best friends and Matt had gotten hurt. They needed to concentrate on their injuries for now, but somehow, she had to make things right.

Sam's nose was broken. She was given a shot of painkillers and pain pills for later. Beau held her hand with the one not wrapped in a thick ace bandage—his hand was severely bruised, luckily not broken, considering all the guys he had decked this week.

Sam yelped when the doctor set her nose. She saw stars, and her eyes rolled to the back of her head. About thirty minutes later, when her good eye opened, she was lying on her back, Beau still holding her hand.

"Please don't cry." Sam gently wiped Beau's tears away.

"I can't bear to see you hurt, my love."

"Then kiss me and make it better."

"Whatever you say, baby."

They sat together in the treatment room, waiting to be released, and wondered what had happened to Matt. Seconds later, Matt screamed, and then silence; his dislocated shoulder needed to be reset. It was put back in place, but Matt passed out. They gave him a shot of painkillers and a bottle of pills. While he was out, they cleaned his bloody knee and patched that up too.

The only one left unscathed was Chloe, aside from her sprained ankle. Pierre and Jeannette stayed with them until they were ready to leave. Late in the afternoon, the painkillers had made them chatty.

Matt was giddy and goofy. "Chloe said she'd marry me. Didn't you, Chloe?"

"You remember that?"

"Of course. I asked you to marry me when I hurt my shoulder, and you said 'yes.' We're engaged. I can't believe you said 'yes,' but I'm so happy."

"Is that right, Chloe?" asked Sam. "That's wonderful. Beau, Chloe, and Matt are engaged, just like us, engaged. Isn't that wonderful, Beau? I think that's wonderful, Chloe. Did he give you a ring? Beau gave me a ring. It's a beautiful ring, but he'll give me a proper engagement ring when we get home. Isn't that right, Beau?"

"Yes, babe. Congratulations, Matt… and Chloe… but I don't know what you see in the guy." Sam swatted his arm. "What? Okay, he's a good guy and my best friend."

"Are you happy, Chloe?" asked Matt. "I'm happy, Chloe. I love you." He tried to kiss her, missed her face, and kissed her ear.

"I love you, too, Matt. Yes, I'm happy. Now, why don't you rest for a while? You don't get drunk on wine, but this stuff has knocked you for a loop."

"Any…thing you want… Sugar." He placed his head on her shoulder and began snoring.

Sam continued to speak rapidly, "Y'all know we can't put this in our school journal. No one would believe it. It's all too fantastical. It's like a novel. That's it. I'll make this into a novel. There are bad guys that get punched out, and Beau saves the day. We have a big soccer match, and I save the day. And we go shopping, and Chloe saves the day. And Matt, well, Matt does stuff, too, and he saves the day. I could call it *Taking Paris by Storm*. What do you think?" The others nodded and then started laughing.

"It'll be a best-seller," said Chloe.

Beau kissed Sam's cheek. "I want to pick who will play me in the movie adaptation… What? I can dream, can't I?"

Chapter 21

SEVERAL POLICEMEN ESCORTED the Down East friends into a large meeting room guarded by five additional policemen. A man dressed in a coat and tie, standing behind a podium, motioned for the group to take a seat.

Chloe exclaimed, "You're the man I photographed taking those red boxes out of the trash can. Who are you, and why have you brought us here? We've done nothing wrong."

"I am Deputy Chief Inspector of Narcotics, Jacques Clouseau." Silence. He silently counted to ten.

Sam and Beau looked at each other before bursting out in laughter. Chloe and Matt also laughed, but they tried hard to stifle it. Several policemen turned their heads, and others left the room. Apparently, it was a huge joke in the department, but not to the inspector. He had no sense of humor. DCI Clouseau raised his voice. "My parents thought it was funny, too. I... do... not!"

He spoke broken English with heavily accented French. "Mademoiselle Davis, we tried to protect you and your friends *en votre vacances*, but I need the memory cards from your camera and *tous vos téléphones portables, s'il vous plaît.*"

She produced all the phones and handed them to him. "The cameras are in my backpack. Copy the photos you need, but I want all the phones, cameras, and memory cards back intact."

"*D'accord.*"

Gaston's phone video was played for the group while they were asked numerous questions. Chloe, Matt, Beau, and Sam were there for hours, telling their story again and again. Matt slurred his words in mixed French and English, making it hard for him to understand, while Sam spoke fast in her Down East brogue. Ultimately, the policemen needed Chloe and Beau to translate.

"You have the photographs. It's all there," whined Chloe.

Beau stood. "This is ridiculous. We've told you everything, and the policemen have corroborated our stories. We're tired, and we hurt."

The metal door slammed into the wall. DCM Copeland stomped in. "So, this is where you take American citizens trying to help your investigations and interrogate them like common criminals. Even worse, you have deliberately kept them from me! I intend to take this matter up with your government. Now leave us."

Beau stopped pacing to face DCM Copeland. Sam and Chloe looked over from where they were sitting, leaning against each other as Chloe's foot was iced and propped up. Matt was lying on a large table in front of the podium, his eyes were closed, and he was snoring.

"I will return in thirty minutes," snapped Clouseau.

"Jesus, Mary, and Joseph, what happened to you four?" DCM Copeland pulled up a chair. Beau filled him in. "I'm thankful you weren't hurt more seriously. I imagine the other guys look much worse. Without sounding condescending, I'm proud of you all. Things should wrap up here shortly. They have Raul Fuentes, some of his men, and Jean Louis. All because of you. Remember, you have done nothing wrong, so don't let DCI Clouseau intimidate you."

There was a knock on the door, and Simon Brown from Boston walked in.

Sam perked up, "Simon? Why are you here?" Beau positioned himself between her and Simon, holding Sam's shoulder possessively. Even bruised and bandaged, Beau the warrior was ready to fight again.

"Hello, Sam. I heard you and your friends got hurt. I'm sorry about that. Uncle Claude tried to keep an eye on you for me—"

"Uncle Claude? You're the nephew that Jean Louis tried to bust for drugs?" asked Beau.

"Yeah. I was on holiday, in the wrong place at the right time." He flashed his FBI badge. "Officially, I'm Special Agent Simon Brown with the Boston bureau. When I first met Jean Louis, I knew that something was off. So, I did some digging and heard rumors linking him to The Spaniard."

Simon picked up Sam's backpack. "If you don't mind, I left something in here." He opened the front zip pocket, pulled out a Burt's Bees lip balm tube, and held it up.

"That's not mine. I thought it was yours, Chloe."

Chloe shook her head no.

"It took some time, but my associates located the Caribbean plastic surgeons that altered his face, and I bribed one of the nurses to take his photograph after every portion of the procedure." He twisted the bottom and pulled it away, exposing the end of a thumb drive.

"The Spaniard's photos are stored on this. He's still ugly, but now we can put him away. I'm sorry, Sam, but I needed your help, or rather, your backpack, to hide it. Jean Louis knows the photos exist. He has people everywhere, so if I got searched, it would look like I was only visiting and not carrying evidence. As soon as you said where you would be staying, I asked Uncle Claude to watch out for you until I could get Detective Gaston to protect you."

"So, you were there at Sacré Coeur?" asked Chloe.

"Yeah. I've tried to stay hidden from you this week, but at Sacré Coeur, I saw some of Fuentes' men gathering, so I notified Gaston, and he came up with the mini train escape and then the trap at the Wall of Love. Of course, I had no idea that the four of you were so capable of protecting each other."

"Did I see you when the girls' purses were swiped at the Moulin Rouge?" asked Beau.

"Yes. Jean Louis left the hotel and made a phone call for Fuentes' teens to stake out the Moulin Rouge. Their purses were stolen to get Chloe's memory cards. I hung out in case there was a problem. Gaston and his men guarded Chloe while Pierre kept an eye on Sam and her backpack. We tried to keep you safe between Gaston's and Pierre's efforts, but you almost didn't need us, especially while playing soccer. By the way, Sam, you are a phenomenal player."

Sam blushed, and Beau growled.

"Anyway, I need to pass this on to Clouseau. Thank you for all your help, and I hope, despite the problems, that you had a memorable adventure in Paris. Have a safe trip home." He turned and walked out the door.

"The nerve of that guy! And to think I thought Claude was looking out for us because we were nice people," whimpered Sam. "I'm ready to go home. Tell me we're going home, Beau."

"We're going home soon, babe. Now, rest."

INSPECTOR CLOUSEAU RETURNED long after Simon left. Chloe was livid. She jumped up, hobbled forward, and got in his face. "All this torment and look at the time—we've missed our flight!"

"Oui, *malheureusement, c'est vrai.* Sadly, it's true. Merci, *pour votre coopération. Votre bagages,* luggage waits at Charles De Gaul *aeroport,* Norwegian, *vol* 5-2-7-8, à New York."

"New York?" yelled Chloe. "You booked us on a flight to New York? Beau, wake Sam and Matt."

Chloe spoke to the police officer again, assuming her authoritative teacher persona. She was determined to use French and English so everyone could understand. Matt plastered a half-grin on his face, watching her.

"*Non! Nous voulons un vol*, we want a flight... *avec repas et boissons*, meals and drinks. Ah, *classe affaires*, Business class... *avec...* leather reclining seats. We also need our VAT items checked." Chloe paused long enough to see the Inspector's eyes grow wide, and his face turned red.

"And we missed our connecting flight home. In New York, *Disposer de deux chambres, a la* Marriott Hotel on Broadway... *avec billets d'avion*, plane tickets from New York... *en quatre jours à partir de maintenant*, four days from now, *s'il vous plait*. Otherwise, I will lodge a formal complaint with the French government through DCM Copeland on how we have been detained and mistreated."

DCM Copeland smirked as he crossed his arms over his chest. Clouseau had met his match. Chloe lifted her chin in defiance. There was a lot of chatter in rapid-fire French, and the inspector left the room in a huff. Matt sported a goofy grin. "You go, girl."

Thirty minutes later the inspector returned. "*D'accord, tout est arrange*, everything has been arranged. *Merci pour votre coopération. Temps d'aller. Prochaines vacances, Londres, s'il vous plait.*"

Clouseau left the room quickly, not wanting to bargain further with Chloe.

"He said, next vacation, please choose London," said Matt, grimacing in pain. "Let's go."

DCM Copeland shook Chloe's hand. "You understand the art of negotiation well. Bravo. I will stay with you all until you leave for the airport."

By the time the friends were released, another hour had passed, and the pain medications had worn off. Pierre gingerly took the companions in a comfortable SUV to the airport. The vehicle was flanked by another SUV in front, carrying the male and female undercover cemetery police who had changed into uniforms, and another SUV behind, carrying the two male undercover policemen from the Musée D'Orsay. Jeannette was waiting at the corner to be picked up and hurried to sit in the front seat.

Matt shifted in his seat. Sam leaned into Beau. Chloe asked Sam and Matt, "Do you need pain meds?"

"No," they chorused.

"I have Tylenol and water," Jeannette passed some over.

"Thanks," they chorused again.

"Chloe, you picked up a lot of French," said Sam, wincing.

"Matt reads to me in French… and he… talks in his sleep." She blushed.

Matt brought her close with his good arm wrapped around her and moaned, "I do?" She nodded, and it was his turn to blush. He kissed Chloe's cheek. "You took charge of the situation when none of us could help. It was amazing to watch you. You're so sexy when you take charge."

"I like being in charge." She whispered in his ear, "I think while we're at the Marriott, you're going to find out how sexy being in charge can be." Matt turned red and was so turned on— another side of Chloe he was eager to see.

Beau was too busy kissing Sam to hear the conversation.

"Well, Sam. You got your wish—we had a once-in-a-lifetime adventure, and now we're on our way to New York for another one," said Beau.

"It was a great adventure, and the four of us are still a force to be reckoned with. I'll never forget spending it with you. And now we're finally together."

"*We'll always have Paris.*"

"You've been waiting this entire trip, to quote Rick from *Casablanca*. Haven't you?" His smile was so big that Sam had to kiss him.

"Look out, New York. I hope you can handle us."

NEE-EU NEE-EU. THE siren wailed across the concourse. Startled travelers wheeling their luggage jumped aside as two large golf carts raced through the Charles de Gaulle airport. Alternating blue lights flashed a continual warning for the drivers speeding through Terminal 2E, determined to get their charges to a waiting plane.

Norwegian Airlines 5278 from Paris to New York conveniently had mechanical problems that delayed its departure. When it was ready to leave, airport authorities held it on the tarmac for an additional hour, awaiting the arrival of four priority passengers escorted under heavy guard.

At Gate K35, two French uniformed policemen presented four tickets and passports to the customer service agent, then requested assistance to help four injured American travelers find their seats on the plane. Behind the Americans, two other gendarmes stood with their arms crossed.

The Down East travelers faced their escorts. Detective Pierre Durand smiled broadly, "Paris will not be as exciting without you. It has been my pleasure, our pleasure." He reached for Jeannette's hand as she smiled. "Bon voyage."

"Please keep in touch," said Jeannette. "Perhaps the next time we meet, it will be for a wedding." Her eyes twinkled, and the detective squeezed her hand. Sam and Chloe hugged and kissed them on the cheek, then Beau and Matt shook hands.

Chloe pulled out her phone, and the crumpled paper doll dressed in black pants, a black and white striped top, a torn red scarf around her neck, and a black beret pushed over her eyes. The six of them huddled together for a selfie with Mimi. Chloe handed the paper doll to Jeannette. "Perhaps you could use an assistant tour guide. I'd love to see where Mimi goes."

"Or when she gets into trouble," said Sam.

Goodbyes were repeated as the four friends hobbled down the gangway. Behind them, blocking the doorway, were four Gendarmes under orders to prevent the group's reentry into the airport. Samantha and Chloe turned and blew a kiss, receiving friendly waves in return.

Sam, Beau, Chloe, and Matt settled into the last four business-class seats in the middle section after Chloe's crutches were stowed in a closet by the first-class area. The others placed their backpacks under their seats and opened their pillows, blankets, and eye masks. The hatch was secured, and the plane immediately pulled into the first-place position for takeoff.

Chloe had time to look at the others and reflect on their marvelous adventure. Sam's appearance reminded her of their elementary school days when they played rough on the playground. She wore a ripped t-shirt that read, "Paris, City of Light." The word 'Light' was crossed out by a black magic marker and replaced with 'Love.' Her left cheek was swollen, sporting a black eye and white surgical tape across her broken nose. Her hair was a tangled mess of bright mahogany. Chloe smiled.

Sam held hands with Beau, who wore grass-stained khaki pants and a blood-stained T-shirt that read, "Oink if you like Eastern North Carolina Barbecue." He had a black eye, his eyebrow was covered with two butterfly bandages, his left cheek bruised, and one hand was heavily bandaged.

I'm so glad they found each other.

Chloe glanced at her sweet Matt. Hers. Bloody jeans were ripped at the knees, exposing large bandages and a heavily grass-stained shirt. His left arm was held tightly to his chest in a sling. Their heads were touching, and both wore smiles. *Everything was as it should be.*

Once in the air, a flight attendant came around, bringing hot towels, bottles of water, snacks, and four sleeping masks for the new arrivals. Since it had been many hours since they'd had any pain medication, Samantha passed out sleeping pills.

"There's no place like Down East," Beau said.

The gang repeated the sentiment, "There's no place like Down East." They swallowed their pill and shared the water.

Beau leaned into Samantha and kissed her goodnight. "Love you, sweetheart."

"Love you too, babe."

Matt kissed Chloe. "Next stop, New York City, and another weekend of adventures, thanks to you. After a long rest, we should hit Tiffany's and get properly engaged. What do you think?"

"That would be perfect, Justin." He blushed and whispered, "Goodnight."

Their extra-wide leather seats moved into a reclining position with extended footrests, and sleep quickly overcame Matt, Sam, and Beau. Before Chloe could pull her mask down, through sleepy eyes, she thought she had caught a glimpse of a man who looked vaguely like Simon. *Nah, it couldn't be.*

Blame It On Real Life

Blame It On Paris was inspired by actual events. In 2019, my next-door neighbor, Marsha, and I took what was supposed to be a quick four-day trip to Paris. Thanks to an airline mechanic's strike, it became seven days. Like the many faux pas and misadventures, I wrote about in my humor book, *It Only Happens To Me*, this Paris trip took on a similar vibe with snafus and glitches. Except for soccer games and criminal conspiracies, we experienced nearly everything Chloe, Matt, Samantha, and Beau did.

At the time, I needed a knee replacement and often walked with a cane or used a wheelchair. My doctor prescribed a sleep aid for the plane, and we took it in Newark before being delayed for hours due to mechanical failures. Like the Walking Dead, we boarded another plane that didn't serve meals or drinks unless preordered—we didn't preorder but ate snacks from our backpacks. As a result, we also missed the hotel shuttle and had to get a taxi.

My credit card and money problems caused frantic calls to the banks from the back seat, and Marsha unknowingly dropped her passport in the taxi. The next day at Versailles, she called the embassy for an appointment—miraculously, the taxi driver returned it that afternoon.

We stayed in the Ibis Hotel, bordering Montmartre Cemetery. Thankfully, it wasn't Halloween, and no zombies appeared. We located an ATM, but I could withdraw only 300 Euros and had only one working credit card. Marsha and I missed the Hop On Bus for the night tour of Paris and had to grab a taxi. Nearly missing the tour bus, it stopped at a stoplight, and we ran to it and got on just in time to see the Eiffel Tower sparkling underneath fireworks.

During our visit, we rode the funicular up to Sacré Coeur, bypassing the 300 stairs, and then toured the curvy streets to Pigalle on a mini train—designed for mini people.

We passed couture shops on our way to the Louvre, but their massive sales were several months away. Since Marsha was a teacher and I was a former teacher, we had no money, unlike the Down East four. However, I spotted colorful poodles and witnessed the money drop, but thankfully, an undercover policeman didn't track us.

We entered the Louvre via escalator but couldn't leave that way. Chloe, Matt, Samantha, and Beau exited through the shopping center, but I felt trapped. So, we used the handicapped open elevator to the street level, but this wasn't in the book.

After the Louvre, we visited Notre Dame, and three weeks later, it caught fire—I had nothing to do with it. Nearby is the department store Zara. Marsha went wild and needed to buy another suitcase.

The idea of Mimi came from Flat Stanley, an elementary school paper doll project. When I lived in Okinawa, people would mail us Flat Stanley to carry around Japan, snapping photos and sending stories. So, of course, Mimi had to be included.

The nightclub scene where Samantha is accosted didn't happen to me in Paris, but in Amsterdam in 1975, while traveling with my brother and sister. I yelled, my brother rescued me, and the man left with a broken nose. The scene was added so that Beau could solidify their relationship.

Love locks are found across Europe and Asia, but not on Paris bridges. However, they can be found in other locations. And if you go to Paris, go to the Wall of Love. You can't place a lock there, but you can trace the red dots to form a heart.

The Eiffel Tower is massive, windy, and terrifyingly high—ideal for launching Mimi, but illogical, so I just imagined it could happen. Then Marsha insisted on counting her steps from the first viewpoint upward and back. I laughed as Beau experienced it.

Our evening cruise on the Seine was magical—Paris lit up in all its romantic glory. Naturally, Samantha imagined herself at the helm, Beau felt it was an actual date, while Chloe and Matt finally cleared the air so that they could start over.

On the way home, airline strikes stranded us an extra three days. With my depleted medications, Marsha's persistence with airline customer service earned us an upgrade to business class and meals.

I hit another snag at customs: my passport lacked an entry stamp. I suppose, being in a wheelchair, speaking broken French with a Southern drawl, and having no criminal record, they realized it wasn't my fault and stamped my passport. There was no need for policemen to barricade the gangplank, prohibiting my reentry into France, like the Down East friends were.

However, we missed our connecting flight in NYC and had to spend the night. Naturally, Chloe, Matt, Samantha, and Beau also had a layover there and a chance for another adventurous weekend. Perhaps their trip will become *Blame It On the Big Apple*. Who knows?

In my world, every day is an adventure. The Paris trip was memorable enough (or cursed) to inspire a story with Down East characters, a mysterious thumb drive, clueless villains, and estranged friends finding their way back to each other.

Here's to more travels and adventures that might appear in another book. Next month, I'm off to southern Spain, solo this time—passport in hand, active credit cards, lots of Euros, and the American embassy on speed dial.

Helen Aitken is a former science educator and award-winning writer who lives in coastal North Carolina. Freelancing since 2006, she spent nine years as the "Safety First" columnist for *Lakeland Boating* magazine and is a lifetime member of the National Society of Newspaper Columnists.

She's the author of the humor book *It Only Happens To Me...* (available on Amazon) and her debut novel, *Blame It On Paris*, was inspired by real-life misadventures during a 2019 trip to Paris. Helen caught the travel bug early: her first flight, at thirteen, was to Rome, and she's since visited thirty-two countries (some repeatedly) and lived for five years in Okinawa, Japan, as a USMC spouse.

While in Japan, her husband, Scott, served as a commanding officer and gave Helen strict orders to stay off the "blotter"—the military police activity log—and avoid causing any international incidents. She will neither confirm nor deny how well she followed those instructions.

Despite having a "black thumb" in the garden, Helen is a Fourth Degree Master of Ohara Ikebana, Japanese flower arranging, and has exhibited in Japan, Washington, D.C., and North Carolina. She's also taught countless workshops and demonstrations—none of which involved setting anything on fire.

Helen loves the beach, classic wooden boats, sweet tea, chicken salad, and her husband and son, Scott and Will—but not necessarily in that order. These days, she divides her time between writing, spoiling a very entitled cat, getting into mischief, and occasionally putting out kitchen fires.

Website:
www.helenaitkenbooks.com

Email:
helen.aitkenbooks@gmail.com

www.ingramcontent.com/pod-product-compliance
Lightning Source LLC
Chambersburg PA
CBHW032335310726
48973CB00007B/1726